Kevin Smith was born in London and grew up in Northern Ireland. He has worked in print, broadcast and newswire journalism and was a foreign correspondent in Eastern Europe for a number of years. He lives in Dublin with his wife and two children. *Jammy Dodger* is his first novel.

JAMMY DODGER

Kevin Smith

SANDSTONEPRESS
HIGHLAND | SCOTLAND

First published in Great Britain by
Sandstone Press Ltd
PO Box 5725
One High Street
Dingwall
Ross-shire
IV15 9WJ
Scotland.

www.sandstonepress.com

© Kevin Smith 2012
Editor: Moira Forsyth

The publisher acknowledges subsidy from
Creative Scotland towards publication of this volume.

ISBN: 978-1-908737-08-3
ISBN e: 978-1-908737-09-0

Cover design by Graham Thew, Dublin.
Typeset by Iolaire Typesetting, Newtonmore.
Printed and bound by OZGraf, Poland.

For Eve, for everything

Brain, character, soul – only as one sees more of life does one understand how distinct is each.

– *The Lost World*, Sir Arthur Conan Doyle

PROLOGUE

All that is left of the castle now are three stumps of wall, like broken teeth, sticking up on the edge of the crag. Down below, the North Atlantic worries at the base of the peninsula and in the distance, when the weather is clear, you can make out the coast of Scotland beyond the dark crescent of Rathlin Island. A couple of hours' walk round the headland and you come to the vast geometric puzzle that is the Giant's Causeway. None of this is particularly relevant, by the way, it's just that the signpost for this place, Dunseverick, caught my eye as I was driving back to to the city and, without thinking, I turned off the road into this little car park to take a look.

You see, I've never actually been here until now, even though the name features strongly in an unfortunate episode from my past that unfolded sixty miles away in Belfast and that gnaws at me to this day. It was, I'm afraid, a shameful affair, a farrago of deception, betrayal, embezzlement, and even outright fraud. Furthermore, others were led astray. I'm going to put my hands up right away and take my share of responsibility for what happened – no doubt I should have known better – but in my defence I believe there was an extenuating

1

circumstance. And it is this: I was in love. To be exact, I was in love with Poetry. I'm aware of how odd that sounds, so let me explain.

Long ago in Belfast everything was *nice*. The sun shone out of a powder-blue sky most days and when it didn't there were warm, fuggy cafes to sit and drink tea in, attended by lovely old ladies in black and white uniforms. In the sunshine the terraces of red-brick astonished the eye and the long avenues foamed with cherry blossom. When it rained, the blaze of darkness from the roofs of Bangor Blue slate led all the way to the hill at the top of every street. That bank of mountain, reaching round the city to the mouth of Belfast Lough, seemed to shelter us, like a comforting arm around a shoulder.

In the mornings, yeast aromas from the bread factory drifted across the River Lagan and through the Botanic Gardens, sweetening the air on Botanic Avenue where, at that time – the year is 1988 – I both lived and worked. Late afternoons smelled of a mixture of frying meat and turf smoke which, as night fell and the lamps came on, began to be overlaid with vapours of perfume and alcohol: mystery and promise. It was in these slipstreams that my friends and I journeyed into the outer reaches. We had lots of well-lighted places in which to down pints and play snooker, and to meet well-fed young Ulster ladies with fine-grained skin and glossy hair, who we would take back to parties in our appallingly unkempt flats. There were love affairs and inevitably, I admit, some broken hearts. But there were no mortgages. And

2

no children to suck away the money (what there was of it). And we were young. We were bullet-proof.

Long ago in Belfast everything and everyone was nice. As if bound together in recognition of the precarious nature of existence, shopkeepers, bus drivers, barmen, cabbies . . . everyone was nice to everyone else. In everyday speech, the world was diminutised and made more manageable, friendlier, by the prefacing of everything with 'wee', as in: 'Just hold on a wee minute', or 'Would you get me a wee Big Mac?', and 'Yes, Mr Johnson, it *was* a wee stroke, but we've also found a wee tumour'. The food we gave each other was nice too – wholesome broth and homemade wheaten bread, and the national dish: comforting mashed potatoes flecked with emerald-green scallions and whipped through with reckless weights of butter.

The climax of all this *bonhomie* occurred each summer when thousands of men draped in iridescent colours paraded through the streets to celebrate the glorious victories of an ancient king on his snow-white charger and all the people came out of their houses to cheer and wave flags, and everyone was happy.

Actually . . . Hang on. Let's go back. That last bit's not quite right. Not *everyone* was happy. In fact – well, let's face it, about half the people *weren't* happy. And that was the problem: not everything was nice, and not *everyone* was nice. Some people, indeed, were downright unpleasant, as we shall see.

My name is Arthur Conville, Artie to my friends, and in the dog end of the 1980s, freshly-hatched from university, I believed in Poetry. I had faith in the power and importance of Poetry. I breathed it and was consumed by it. I recited it and discussed it. I mulled over the meaning of certain lines, sometimes for weeks on end. At night I dreamed in iambic pentameters. From Milton and Spenser to Keats, Shelley, Wordsworth, Coleridge, (the odd helping of Tennyson for roughage); the Americans, Whitman, Berryman, Dickinson, Frost, (Lowell if you were feeling robust), through the Modernists, Eliot, Auden, Stevens, Moore (let's not forget Yeats) to contemporary British, Larkin, Hughes, MacNeice, (Dylan) Thomas, and Northern Ireland's own gallery of live pyrotechnicians: Poetry, I was sure, could change things. Naïve you say? Perhaps. But the poetic world of sensitivity and beauty and eternal truths was far nicer than the one on the evening news – a bomb-lit domain of chaos and violence and dangerous, tattooed men incapable of second thoughts.

Besides, poetry paid my bills.

You see, a dividend (if that's not too callous) of Northern Ireland's 'Troubles' was a torrent of cash from the British exchequer aimed at 'normalising' life in the province, and a fat tributary of that *largesse* was directed towards 'the Arts'. 'The Arts', where people like me were waiting with open bank accounts. I was proud to preside (along with my co-editor Oliver Sweeney) over a small magazine called *Lyre*. It was subtitled 'A Supplement for the Imagination' (is that pretentious enough for you?), and it specialised in, yes, you've guessed it, poetry.

4

Generous quarterly grants from the government meant we had an office of sorts to lounge in and enough money to pay our rent and cover sundries such as lunch and twice-weekly drinking sessions (thrice-weekly if we cut corners on the stationery). Did it sting that we, once the cultural revolutionaries of our generation, were kept by the state, that our's was a life lived in captivity? Not a bit. We sang in our chains like the sea. Times were good. Top quality angst and misery flowed from many pens and all we had to do was sieve and print. Northern Irish poetry was hot. *Lyre* thrived. Oliver and I were interviewed with tedious regularity by every foreign news crew and magazine passing through in search of *conflict chic*, including an appearance, at one heady juncture, in a *Vanity Fair* centre spread, with poor old Oliver made up like a homosexual vampire and me (I'm not proud of this) moodily astride a beanbag in black polo-neck and leg warmers.

And then, just when we had become really cosy in our subsidised nest, we encountered a problem: the poetry ran out. There was no more poetry. Or rather there was no more poetry of the *right type*. There was a shortage, specifically, of 'Troubles poetry'. The heavyweights who had caused all the hullaballoo in the first place had fought their way through blizzards of praise to higher, greener pastures and these days would just about deign to be published in the *London Review of Books* or *The New Yorker*. They hadn't even an old shopping list left for us. Meanwhile, the handful of 'promising newcomers' we had been milking, sorry, nurturing, seemed to have developed some kind of literary stage-fright (okay, the one who had the nervous breakdown had an excuse), and more worrying, the second division of established 'war' poets we relied on for the critical mass of each issue, had quite simply dried up. In short, the cupboard was bare.

So, what happens when you run out of poetry?

Let's find out.

PART ONE

'It's the prince of biscuits really, isn't it? The custard cream.'

Oliver Sweeney, aesthete, gourmand, bon viveur, had assumed his mid-morning tea-break position – sprawled in his chair, feet on the desk, mug in fist. The trouser legs of his Oxfam suit, an incongruous pinstripe, had ridden up, revealing odd socks and several inches of white, hairless shank. Frustrated all morning by his overgrown wheat-coloured mop flopping into his eyes, he had gathered it into a top-knot using an elastic band and now looked slightly surreal, like a gigantic baby or a failed sumo wrestler forced to work in advertising.

For a moment I considered ignoring him. I was tired, having been woken early by the actor in the flat above me doing his voice exercises. I reached across the ancient, formica-topped office table we shared and extracted a biscuit.

'Isn't that the Garibaldi?' I said.

'No, no, no.' He glared at me. 'You're getting mixed up with the, er . . . with Machiavelli. No, none of your foreign muck here . . .'

He paused while his inky fingers stabbed again at the packaging.

'No, there's no doubt, the custard cream has it all: fine texture, nice filling, not too sweet, holds together in a tight spot, but at the same time not afraid to show its feminine side.'

He leant his head back and dropped the tea-logged oblong of stodge into his greedy mouth. I noticed the soles of his Nature Treks were badly worn on the outside edges.

'Sounds more like my uncle Toby,' I said. 'By the way, what's your position on the Jacobs' Mikado?'

'Ah, now.' Oliver set down his mug and clasped his hands together under his fleshy chin, making a steeple of his index fingers. 'Essentially a satirist. Walks the line between biscuit and sex toy.'

'Yes, I've always considered it a bit of a tease myself.'

I was warming to the topic.

'Give me the firm handshake of a chocolate digestive any day.'

'Or the iron fist of the gingernut.'

We ate and sipped in meditative silence. We were in no hurry. Large expanses of our working day often passed in this way.

'I have to say,' Oliver continued. 'I'm quite partial to a Hobnob, although they can be a bit hairy without a cup of tea.'

'Aren't they just digestives with bits of rope mixed in?'

'Well they have a certain rustic charm . . . I'm not sure about *rope*.'

'No no, Gypsy Creams have rustic charm – you can see it in the adverts – Hobnobs are just agricultural . . . like being taken roughly by a farmhand with eyebrows on his cheeks. They should put a bit of chocolate on them.'

'Actually, I believe they *have* brought out a chocolate version . . . Hang on . . . Jesus!' Oliver swung his legs down from the desk with a double thud, splashing hot liquid over his trousers.

'Man-over-board . . . Where's my spoon?' He began fishing disintegrated biscuit from the bottom of his mug and I briefly wondered, not for the first time that week, where my life was headed.

'More chai?' I said, rising and moving towards the cupboard containing a fridge and a sink that we referred to as 'the kitchen'.

'Go on then. Plenty of milk.' Oliver thrust his tannin-streaked beaker at me.

'Now where was I? Oh yes . . . you know two items whose credentials I view with suspicion? The Jaffa Cake and the Wagon Wheel, and here's why . . .'

I managed to tune him out, and while I waited for the teabags to infuse I gazed down from the window into Botanic Avenue. Even though our office was at the top of a tall Victorian building the street always seemed an inordinate distance below. *All that air* . . . I imagined jumping off the sill, the downward pluck of gravity, the upward rush of blood, the violence of impact. I wondered whether I'd survive. Unlikely. (Though it's not the fall, they say, it's the sudden stop at the bottom.) Looking up, my eye was led across the rooftops of Cromwell Road and Wolseley Street to the warren of redbrick terraces harbouring chintzy bed & breakfasts and nests of slumbering students. Further up, to the right, was the glowering granite presence of the theology college, softened by the tropical promise just beyond of the Botanic Gardens; turn left and cross the railway bridge and the nexus of Shaftesbury Square offered conduits to six different worlds, including the delights of 'Loyalist Sandy Row'.

It was a mellow summer's morning with a slight haze to the light and the boulevard was busy: the whistling postman, the breadman unloading trays of loaves, Mrs Adamson from the stationery shop returning from the café swinging an extra doughnut in a paper bag. Office workers, traffic wardens, Chinese cooks, tramps . . . *I had not thought death had undone so many.* Not really the weather for Eliot. No brown fog. Still, what was the next bit? *Sighs, short and infrequent, were exhaled | And each man fixed his eyes before his feet. | Flowed up the hill and down King William Street* . . . Unreal city indeed. *I will show you fear in a handful of dust.* What a great line. Fantastic line. *What are the roots that clutch, what branches grow| Out of this stony rubbish?* Another good one. *In the mountains, there you feel free.* Not bad. *Good night, ladies, good night, sweet ladies, good night, good night.* Or was that Lou Reed? From the *Transformer* album?

As I stared down at the wretched creatures of the lower air my reverie was broken by the realisation that I was being stared back at. Leaning against the wall outside the newsagent's was a short, thick-set man in his early to mid-thirties with black hair that was cropped at the sides but long and curly at the back, and the kind of moustache that in Belfast suggested tattoos couldn't be far away. He was wearing dark trousers and a Harrington jacket. He had a tabloid open in his hands but his attention was fixed very intently on me, or at least on the window I was framed by, because I couldn't be sure, with the sunlight reflecting off the pane, whether I was in fact visible. Either way, it unnerved me and I turned back to the room.

'. . . Okay, I'll make an exception for the Choco Leibniz,' Oliver was saying. 'I mean that's German engineering at its best – the way they embed that, well what is essentially a rectangular Rich Tea, in that slab of chocolate . . . Hats off. That Leibniz was a smart cookie – no pun – designing treats as well as being a philosophical genius.'

I peered round the corner of 'the kitchen' but couldn't tell from his expression whether he was serious or not. This was, after all, a man who had signed up to a degree in Classical Civilisation in the hope of toga parties.

I dropped the teabags into the sink, trying not to focus on the debris already in there.

'Hey, you did a bit of philosophy, what was Leibniz on about anyway?' he asked as I handed him his cup.

'I think he believed the world is as good as God could make it.'

'Oh. Really? In that case, God help us.'

There wasn't much happening in the office so we knocked off towards lunchtime and headed for The

Betjeman Arms, a Victorian spit-and-sawdust pub popular with the artistic demimonde. While Oliver bellied up to the bar to order pints and food, I staked out a booth under one of the ornate stained-glass windows. As I slid along the cool leather I realised with a frisson of dismay that Mick the Artist was already installed, coiled in a corner reading a newspaper, a glass of brown lemonade in front of him and a smouldering roll-up between his thin lips.

'Alright?' he enquired, appraising me with shiny, feral eyes while drawing heavily on his cylinder of Old Shag.

'Not too bad. Yourself?'

Mick the Artist was the unspoken, unelected leader of the city's painting fraternity, a formidably combative forty-year-old who was constantly goading the others about their duties and rights – like a union boss. Sooner or later everyone who knew him would find themselves squirming in the merciless grip of his dialectic. He had never been known to laugh. (I could never quite grasp the concept of a dour artist, given they got to play with colours and paintbrushes every day.)

'Ah y'know, chippin' away as usual.'

'Yes, well, what else can you do?' I observed, glancing around and finding the snug a little too . . . well, snug.

Mick the Artist, whose fibrous body supported extensive piercings, stroked the silver ring in his left nostril.

'When's your next issue due?' he demanded.

'Oh, shortly, we're just waiting on a couple of – '

'Johnny Devine says you haven't paid him for the artwork he gave you last time . . .'

'Did he? I mean, does he? That's strange, I'm pretty sure cheques – '

'You know you're going to have to put your rates up. You know that, don't you? We've all got to . . .'

He stopped.

'What the – ?' He was staring at my co-editor who had arrived with our drinks and had, I now noted, forgotten about his Pebbles Flintstone top-knot.

'That big barman there was giving me a really weird – ah Mick, how's the form?' said Oliver, setting two Rembrandtian pints on the table.

'Yeah . . . Sweeney. Yeah, I was just saying to Conville, we've all got to make a living – you guys are going to have to pump up the money a wee bit.'

Oliver jabbed a finger of acknowledgement in Mick's direction.

'You're absolutely right. We were just discussing exactly the same thing this morning,' he said. 'We've already asked the Arts Council for extra funding.'

He stared encouragingly at me. It was the first I'd heard of it.

'Really?' Mick was taken aback.

'Yep. To pay you guys for your work. Mag wouldn't be the same without the pictures.'

(Personally, I would have had no truck whatsoever with the artists, but one of the conditions of our funding was that we find space for their onanistic daubings. This meant that not only did we have to suffer relentless challenges to our 'poncey bourgeois' ideas about art but we also had to put up with their self-consciously unhinged behaviour. What was that remark of Paul Valery's? *Everything changes but the avant-garde?*)

The Artist's metal-heavy nostrils were attempting to flare with excitement.

'Well that's . . . that's fucken brilliant,' he concluded. He ground out his rollie, then appeared to have a thought. 'Hang on a second, are you sure The Hawk will actually sign off on this?'

At mention of The Hawk, an icy sensation shivered through the booth and Oliver's right eye flickered briefly, like a faulty fluorescent lamp.

'The Hawk,' Oliver said, taking a ravenous swig of stout, 'is right behind us and he loves you guys down at the Collective.'

'He does?'

'Oh yeah. Thinks you're . . . dedicated and cutting edge.'

'Sweeney,' said Mick, his eyes contracting to the size of ball-bearings. 'Are you taking the piss?'

'No, I swear. He's keen as mustard. The cash is as good as in the bank.'

The waitress bustled in with our bangers-and-champ, which Mick regarded with a look of distaste. He didn't strike me as someone who liked food.

'Well anyway, I'll be heading on here and leaving you two to your grub,' he said, getting to his feet. 'But a wee tip for you – Marty Pollocks has been doing some great stuff. He has a series of close-ups of penises – ' For a clenched nanosecond we all avoided looking down at the plates. '. . . in really wild acrylic colours. Bit Mapple-

14

thorpe, bit Warhol, very strong. Would look fantastic in the next magazine . . . Right?' He gave us a fisty salute and disappeared into the throng.

'Yeah right,' I said, having fully exhaled.

'In a pig's arse, friend,' said Oliver.

We took up our eating irons and addressed the carbohydrate clouds in front of us.

'What was that bollocks about extra moulah for the artwork? The Hawk hates the artists.'

Oliver, traditionalist that he was, had made a well in the centre of his mashed potatoes and was scraping the second foil wrapper's-worth of butter into it.

'Listen, you just gotta tell these people what they want to hear and they leave you alone. First rule of business.'

'Yeah but Mick – '

The Artist's close-cropped bony head reappeared, shockingly proximate, above the door of the snug.

'Forgot to say, there's a happening at Johnny Devine's on Friday night. You should probably be there.'

Oliver and I exchanged glances.

'Alright?'

'Sorry Mick, what is it that's . . . happening?' said Oliver.

'A happening. You know.'

'Sorry, a . . .?'

'A happening. You know what a happening is.'

'You mean like . . . a party?' asked Oliver.

'No, not a party, a happening.'

'I'm not sure . . .' Oliver began.

'Come on lads!' Mick's pupils, I noticed, were getting

small again. 'A happening. You know? A *happening*?'

We were maintaining eye contact but it was becoming more difficult.

'Jesus, you're not *that* young! A happening. It's a . . .' Mick's face was deepening in colour.

'Is it a *kind* of party?'

'No, it's not a fucken *kind* of party!'

What was he talking about?

'FOR FUCKSAKE!' he shouted. 'A HAPPENING! A FUCKEN . . . *HAPPENING*!'

This was scary. What was wrong with Mick?

'A FUCKEN HAPPENING! A *HAPPENING*! ARE YESE THICK?' he shrieked.

A tiny comet of spittle streaked from the corner of his mouth and landed in Oliver's lunch.

'Mick, Mick, Mick,' I said, rising to my feet and holding up my hands. 'Take it easy. We just need to clarify: will we see you at Johnny Devine's on Friday night?'

He was panting.

We waited.

'Yes,' he said.

His head swivelled and was gone again.

I looked at Oliver. 'What in the name of fuck was *that* about?'

'I've no idea. What's his problem? He makes me very uneasy.'

'Not sure, I think he's just a bit – pass the ketchup would you – intense.'

'*Intense*? His balls are going to go off like popcorn any day now.'

'Like *popcorn*?'

'Forget it.'

The old pub was in full lunchtime swing now, a sense of well-being rising through the soft hubbub of voices and the clinking of silverware on ancient china. Doors opened and closed, admitting the wah-wah of traffic and the ululations of the newspaper boys. The place smelled, as it had done for a century and a half, of treacley hops, gravy-steam and tobacco. The filigreed ceiling was stained the colour of a chain-smoker's fingers. Every few seconds another pint of black or gold would arrive with a clunk, foaming, on the granite counter-top and another hand would reach out for it . . .

The booth door was ajar and I could see the lifers at the far end of the room, arrayed on their stools like prisoners of a morality play, their faces already heavy with alcohol, their movements sclerotic.

'*The weeks go by like birds,*' I murmured.

'What?' said Oliver, unwrapping another lozenge of butter.

'*And the years, the years | Fly past anti-clockwise | Like clock hands in a bar mirror.*'

'What?'

'Oh nothing.'

*

The poet E.E. Cummings once said running a literary magazine was like pushing your head through a straw. Having been involved in more than my fair share over the years I have to disagree: it's nowhere near as easy as that. My first, *Dystopia Now!*, folded after three issues, largely because people seemed to assume it was a journal for sufferers of chronic indigestion. More successful (in that it lasted for four editions) was *Uranus*, but again, I think the name may have been transmitting confusing signals to the astronomy crowd.

Titles are crucial. You've got to get it right, and get it right from the off, because once that beast is released into the wild it can never be recalled. I'm thinking now of the appearance of the first (and only) issue of *Epididymis*, which one of our ill-fated editorial committee at that time had mis-remembered with *absolute certainty* as the name of one of the Greek muses. Words can be treacherous. (As, of course, can memory.)

We were very pleased, then, when we came up with *Lyre*. It was classy and classical and unambiguous, and felicitously alluded to a famous work by Shelley, one of our favourite poets (*Make me thy lyre, even as the forest is* . . .) Scholars would also know that the instrument itself was invented by Hermes, who was the messenger of the gods and the god of literature in his own right – which made us feel clever. We also liked to think that we, as editors, were following a line all the way from the harp pluckers of Ancient Greece in providing a harmonious space for the poetic impulse. But that's by the bye.

So, once you've got the name right, you then have to formulate a coherent editorial policy and this is trickier than it sounds. I mean, what do you say when you set out your stall in the first issue? 'We will only print stuff that is *good*? Kind of obvious. And yet, that is somehow what you have to tell them, the standing army of would-be poets. Not that it will make any difference in the long-run to the quality of the submissions. (You could always try something like: 'Please note, if your stuff isn't quite up to scratch, may we suggest you send it to – *insert name of rival magazine*.')

Okay, you have your title and your policy; you also have to decide on a format. Let's play it straight: A5 size, an oldstyle font such as Garamond for the poems and a sans serif for the titles, let's say Arial. Now you need some stuff to put inside – and this is where the trouble begins. Once you fire the starting pistol you will not believe the avalanche of psychic waste that will explode through your letterbox. Who knew there were so many tortured souls pouring their hearts out in back bedrooms and garrets in all the cities of the night? Who knew there was so much backlogged *angst*? So much pent-up ambergris? So much pain? Not me. I was shocked by the outpourings triggered by my first couple of ventures. The manuscripts, with their accompanying letters (by turns pleading and belligerent), came in waves, week after week, and for a while I really did try to keep up. I relived the feverish torments of adolescence and lost love, nodded in slack-jawed recognition at the brutal injustice of society, wept empathetic tears over mankind's inability to live in peace. I endured bad spelling, horrifying syntax, nightmarish typography. I had insights that no young man should have. I became a human superconductor in a *weltschmerz* machine.

(Here's another quick tip for the novice editor: discard immediately any submission that begins with '*As a fan of the good old-fashioned kind of verse . . .*', includes works entitled *Ode to My Cock* or *Period Pains*, or is accompanied by a photograph of the sender in a state of undress.)

Needless to say, it had to stop. It was them or me. I had lost the capacity to risk damaging these fragile egos by sending their stuff back *and* the will to read anything that wasn't obviously good within the first four lines. Consequently, manila envelopes (some of them very heavy) began to pile up in my spare bedroom. As the gaps between the magazine's appearances lengthened, they spilled out of the bedroom into the living room and from there into the hallway. Their presence, their sheer *bulk* became oppressive. I was racked by guilt. At first I tried sticking a couple of them under my arm each morning and leaving them on the bus but it became apparent that that would take years, especially as upright citizens kept running after me and handing them back. I also briefly tinkered with an arson plan but in the end I just went out and found another flat. And I never looked back.

Of course, after a while you master your qualms: you realise you have a responsibility to the reading public. To literature. To art. You are a custodian of all that is true and real, a nurturer of intellects, a shaper of sensibilities, a midwife, a parent, a judge. *A piper at the gates of dawn.* There will be casualties: tears, broken hearts, livers the size of space hoppers. Some will have to accept that there is just no room for them, standing or otherwise, in the pantheon. There are no extenuating circumstances you see, just *the thing itself*.

There will always be some (rejected versifiers mainly) who demand to know by what or on whose authority you act. *Surely it's a matter of taste*, they cry. *Who polices the police?* And so on and so forth, and that is to some extent true. But here's the real beauty of it, the killer line when the whip comes down and the bolt is shot and the fat lady has exited stage left – when all the bitching and whining and carping and theorising is done: THE EDITOR'S DECISION IS FINAL.

God, it feels good.

*

Occasionally I would call for Oliver in the morning at his flat in the student-infested Holy Land (so-called because of the street names: Jerusalem Street, Palestine Street, Damascus Street, and so on). It was a ten minute walk in the opposite direction to the office but there was a good patisserie on the way and if I could get him moving early it meant we had more chance of getting some work done before the first tea-break.

Later that week I rang the bell for a third time and at last heard the sound of a second-floor sash window being hoisted upwards. Oliver's head appeared over the sill, puffy and full of sleep. He focused on me and withdrew. A minute later a cluster of keys landed with a complicated jangle at my feet and I let myself into the pungent hallway.

As I picked my way through the usual student-house snowdrifts of flyers and junk mail a young woman emerged from the ground-floor flat. She was naked. Her body – not slim, not plump – was luminously white. She held her hand up as a shield against the sunshine streaming through the fanlight and when she saw me gasped (I had a sharp intake myself) and jumped back over the threshold, shutting the door behind her. I stood there for a few moments, listening, then, blinking rapidly to savour the eidetic imprint of her nudity, I proceeded up the stairs. What was that line of Milton's? *In naked beauty more adorned | More lovely than Pandora . . .*

Oliver greeted me in a quilted satin dressing gown I'd never seen before, bright amber in colour with crimson oriental-style embroidery. It had a large upturned collar and a slight flare above the knees. Even by Oliver's haphazard sartorial standards this took some beating. He looked like a gigantic Christmas cracker.

'I didn't know you were gay,' I said, handing him his keys.

He yawned elaborately and clawed at his groin.

'What time is it?'

'Nine-thirty. Are you ready?'

'Does it look like I'm ready?' He shuffled towards the bathroom.

I surveyed the wreckage of his living room. Had he been *burgled*? There was an odd smell.

'No. It looks like you had a good opening night at the Old Vic and celebrated with rent boys and Angel Dust.'

'Didn't catch that,' he called. 'I'm having a quick shower.'

I headed into the kitchen. The smell was stronger now – sickly, sharp. I filled the kettle at the sink, which was overloaded, needless to say, with soiled crockery. Crumpled Chinese takeaway cartons lay across the work-top; a pizza box complete with gnawed crusts had been discarded on the cooker. No obvious culprits. Then, as I turned to rummage in a cupboard for the coffee jar I saw them: about a hundred empty milk cartons in a jumbled heap beside the bin. At some point there had been an attempt to stack them but they had cascaded. The remnants of their contents were all over the floor. Sour milk! That was the stench. I opened the fridge. It was full of milk.

'Oliver,' I said, when he had completed his *toilette*. 'What's the story with all the cow juice? Are you bathing in it?'

He was ensconced in the armchair opposite me, trying to unknot the laces of a pair of caramel brogues. At his feet, which I was avoiding looking at and, indeed, across most of the floorspace, were his possessions – books, records, videos, clothes, used tissues – abandoned where they fell.

'Oh the milk, yeah, I'm trying to win an all-expenses-paid round-the-world trip.'

'Right. And . . .?'

'Well, you need tokens from twelve milk cartons to enter.'

He was concentrating hard on the shoes now, avoiding eye contact.

'And . . .?'

'And I intend to enter many times in order to maximise my chances. You also have to come up with some slogan about the Sunnyland Farm Bunny – ' He waved a hand in the air. 'But I'll crack that.'

He was hiding something. I already knew what it was.

'Am I right to conclude you're using *Lyre* money?'

'No, no, no. Well, kind of . . .'

The bastard.

'I'll pay it back though, don't you worry. And it'll be good for me to see the world – broaden my horizons and so on. It feels like I've been in this place forever. It's too small. And nothing ever happens.'

'*Gods make their own importance,*' I reminded him. 'By the way, I just encountered a buck-naked female in your lobby.'

'What? *When?*' I had his goggle-eyed attention now alright.

'On the way in. Woman who lives below you. I've no idea what she was doing but it was a very pleasant start to the day.'

'You lucky – What was it like?'

'You mean what does a naked lady look like?'

'Yes. I mean no. Was she . . . nice?'

'Very. Who is she?'

'Dunno, she only moved in a week ago. I think she's final year accountancy.'

'Ah well. Never mind.'

'You're such a snob. Bugger it! These laces are knackered.'

The smell of rancid milk was beginning to make me feel ill so I went outside to wait while Oliver scoured the crime scene of his flat for functioning footwear. A moment later the door opened and the startled nymph from earlier appeared, concealed in a crisp linen shirt and jeans, her dark hair untethered. She started up the street then stopped, turned and looked at me. She retraced her steps.

'Look, this is really embarrassing,' she said in a low voice. 'Was that you earlier on?'

'You mean . . . in the hallway?'

'Yes.'

'Yes.'

'I'm really sorry, I thought you were the postman.'

'Pardon?'

'I didn't think there was anyone there, I was just coming out to get my post.'

'Oh, I see. Well, you know, these things happen. I didn't . . . I wasn't . . .'

She was watching me very intently. Cool blue inquisitive eyes. (Or they might have been green, it was hard to tell.) Now it felt as though I was the one that had been caught in the buff. How did that happen? I turned and stared at the door, willing Oliver to arrive and cauterise the situation. No show.

'Anyway, no harm done,' she said. 'Worse things happen at sea.'

'Indeed.'

She lingered. I didn't know what to say.

'Well, cheerio then,' she said.

'Yeah, see you.' That didn't sound right.

I watched her walk away.

'Hold on, what's your name?' I called.

She turned again.

'Rosemary McCann. What's yours?'

'Artie Conville. Pleased to meet you,' I said, moving towards her and extending a hand, which she took and held lightly as though judging its weight.

I ransacked the air for something to say.

'And are you, in fact, the Star of the County Down?'

'I beg your pardon?'

'*Young Rosie McCann, from the banks of the Bann*?'

'I'm sorry?'

'It's a song. Same name as you. She's the gem in Ireland's crown. It's famous.'

She shook her head. 'I don't think so.'

'Never mind.'

She grinned. Nice teeth.

'I have to go now,' she said.

We arrived at the office just in time for the morning tea-break. While Oliver busied himself in 'the kitchen' I had a shuffle through the pending file of material for the forth-coming issue. Whichever way you sliced it, this was thin fare: a borderline prose poem on love across the barri-cades, a sonnet sequence detailing Catholic persecution, and a haiku entitled *Protestant Guilt*.

'Bad news,' said Oliver, poking his head out of 'the kitchen'.

'You're not wrong,' I replied. 'This is woeful.'

'No, I mean there's no milk.'

I gave him my most ironic stare.

'You've gotta be fucken kidding me.'

'Relax, it's no problem. I'll just scamper out and get some. Now, where's the petty cash?'

'As if you didn't know,' I muttered.

'What?'

'Nothing.'

I listened to his heavy footsteps (cerise Dr Marten boots) fade on the staircase and then strolled to the window and opened it. A smell like ice-cream vans drifted up from the street, and from somewhere else a scent of cut grass (*Brief is the breath | Mown stalks exhale . . .*). Early summer was the best time. Down below I could see Oliver – highly visible in his khaki and orange Hawaiian shirt – crossing the road diagonally, headed for the mini-mart. Sandwich boards on the pavement outside the newsagent's proclaimed the day's headlines: Six Soldiers Killed in Lisburn Bombing, (*Long, long the death . . .*), Provos Claim Fun-Run Slaughter, (. . . *Lost lanes of Queen Anne's lace | And that high-builded cloud . . .*), Ten Civilians Injured In No Warning Blast, (. . . *Moving at summer's pace.*)

'Moving at summer's pace.' I said it aloud. Sublime. . . . *In the white hours | Of young-leafed June | With chestnut flowers, | With hedges snow-like strewn . . .* My grandfather – long since gone out of the world of light – once told me he had measured his life by the number of summers he (likely) had remaining. 'When you're young you've got so much time,' he would say, rolling one of the cigarettes he would continue to smoke into his eighties. 'And then, as you get older it disappears like water down a plughole.' *Whether or not we use it, it goes . . .* He had fought in the second battle at Ypres and walked away from the impact of a heavy artillery shell ('They were known as Jack Johnsons after the heavyweight champion') that killed nine of his company, including his best friend. 'You never take anything for granted again after that,' he told me. When he arrived home after de-mob he married my grandmother within a month and cradled his first child in his arms within a year.

For the most part a cheerful man, he became morbidly preoccupied by his war experiences later in life. He started reading everything he could find about the struggle on the Western Front and set about trying to track down survivors. A man from County Cork who had also been at Ypres answered his advertisement in the *Irish Times* and they began a correspondence, but after the second or third letter, the Cork man died. For several years then, around the time when the later of his ten children, including my father, were teenagers, he became a morose insomniac, prone to periods of crippling depression. The war poets brought him some comfort. He was particularly fond of reciting those famous lines of Rupert Brooke's: *We have found safety with all things undying, | The winds, and morning, tears of men and mirth, | The deep night, and birds singing, and clouds flying, | And sleep, and freedom, and the autumnal earth.* And when he did, water would leak out of the sides of his eyes and, being a kid, I'd be embarrassed and not know where to look.

I found myself thinking about my earlier encounter with Rosie McCann. She certainly was eye-catching, with a forthright aspect to her that I found attractive. But what on earth was with that smartarse song reference? What was I thinking? On the other hand it was hard to believe she had never heard of it. With that name. And she did have nut-brown hair. And it was definitely natural –

'Buggering fig rolls!' yelled Oliver from the doorway.

My delicious solitude had ended.

'Problem?'

'That's all they had. Bloody stock-taking or some excuse. I fucken hate fig rolls . . .'

'So, did you buy some?'

'No, I had to get Kit Kats,' he said sulkily. The bag he was carrying appeared weighty.

'What's in the bag?'

'Milk.'

I grabbed a stack of envelopes from the floor and returned to the desk. Sounds of effort drifted from 'the kitchen'.

'You know, Oliver,' I said. 'We really need to get cracking. There's virtually nothing to go in the next issue – '

I ripped open the first submission ('*Dear Sir, As a fan of the good old-fashioned kind of verse . . .*') and flung it over my right shoulder.

'. . . And the clock's ticking. The last thing we need

now is undue attention from the boys up on the hill. I hear budgets are under horrible pressure.'

I opened another. The fridge door slammed. I could hear the kettle nearing climax. I examined a polaroid of a topless middle-aged woman holding a cat and smiling enigmatically into the camera. On the wall behind her was a painting of a bare-breasted woman holding a cat. I tossed it and its accompanying sheaf over my left shoulder.

Oliver emerged with the tea.

'Yeah, I know,' he said. 'It's been on my mind. I've even had a couple of dreams about The Hawk. In one of them he was sitting on my chest, smoking cigarettes – not saying anything, just . . . smoking . . . and looking at me . . . Everything was dark except his face. It was really creepy,' He shivered. 'In another he was trying to push my mother out of a window.'

He disappeared into 'the kitchen' again.

'Speaking of creepy,' he called. 'There's a guy I keep seeing downstairs, in the street. He's been hanging around for a couple of weeks now. Real mean-looking hombre.'

He returned and settled himself opposite me.

'Yeah?' I said, slitting another envelope. 'What's he look like?'

'Bad hair, moustache, Harrington jacket. Five'll get you ten he has a tattoo of a spider's web somewhere.'

'Yeah . . . really?' I was only half listening. There was something about the letter I had just extracted that was demanding the bulk of my attention.

It was hand-written – left-leaning black cursive – on crackling, yellowish paper.

'*So yous think your smart do you?*' It began. '*Well I don't. In fact I think your dog shite.*' (This was more abusive than usual.) '*Compleat dog shite. Yous would'nt know good riting if it bit yous on the arse so yous would'nt. Yous are wankers. Yous think your so high and mitey passing jugement, on evrybody else. Well let me tell yous something. Your not. And yous will reep what yous soe. Beleive me. Evry dog has it's day.*'

I read it several times just to make sure I was understanding it correctly and passed it across the table.

'Looks like we have a dissatisfied customer,' I said.

Oliver studied it carefully, taking an occasional slurp of tea. He pursed his lips.

'Mmm, it's not signed . . . and I could be wrong . . .' He snapped a finger of Kit Kat. '. . . but I think that's Seamus Heaney's handwriting.'

He flicked it to one side. I noticed he had a pint-glass of milk on his desk.

'Am I right in thinking you're having tea with a milk chaser?' I asked. 'Or is it the other way round?'

'Actually, it's a milkshake. I got vanilla syrup at the shop. You want one?'

I declined.

'You know, this is quite worrying,' I said.

'What is?'

'What we have here is a genuine threatening letter. We should probably show it to the cops.'

'Nonsense. It's just some weedy little poet whose stuff we slagged off. Forget about it.'

We lapsed into silence to dispatch our Kit Kats. Oliver had another milkshake.

Despite what he said, I was finding it difficult to forget what I had just read. I'd had countless insulting missives from spurned 'geniuses' in my time but this one was different. Raw. Point blank. Distressingly badly spelled.

'Right, back to work,' I said, clapping my hands together in a motivational fashion. 'We're going to have to do a round of begging letters – all the big names. Let's make a list.'

We fed a sheet of paper into the trusty Remington and typed out the names of ten well-known poets, then dug out the all-important black book and retrieved addresses for six of them. The rest we'd write to care of the publishers.

'It's nearly lunchtime,' observed Oliver. 'I suggest we do a bit of – ' He performed bunny ears in the air with two fingers of each hand. ' – "signing" now, and compose the letters this afternoon. Petty cash is getting very low.'

One of the more dubious money-making schemes Oliver had come up with involved inscribing bogus autographs on the flyleaves of books and selling them to second-hand book merchants. To begin with it was mainly unwanted review copies of poetry collections that were doctored but we soon moved on to medium-rank novels and the odd memoir (I remember a hardback copy of *The Moon's a Balloon* signed by the old Pink Panther himself fetching thirty quid). We deliberately kept it low-key – no James Joyces, no Shakespeares. It was, Oliver argued, a victimless crime: 'What they don't know doesn't hurt them. Everybody's happy.' We liked to think we became quite expert with a variety of writing implements at matching signatures to styles and epochs, favouring elaborate swoops and swirls for the Victorians, for example, and sober, stubby script for the Modernists.

The trick was not to saturate the market and, of course, to keep Oliver on track. I caught him on one occasion inscribing a 1934 edition of *The Mayor of Casterbridge* with '*All the best, Tom Hardy*'. What made it worse, somehow, was that he was using a biro.

*

On Friday night, in the spirit of cultural solidarity, I shuffled along to a book launch in the university common room. These were invariably ghastly affairs but there was free booze and, besides, I had nothing else to do. Of course, it was supposed to be the night of 'the happening' but that had been postponed indefinitely due to Johnny Devine's arrest for indecent exposure (some kind of protest against the 'fascism' of clothes) on the steps of City Hall. I wasn't looking forward to the photos in Saturday's papers.

So, there I was approaching the ornate neo-Gothic façade of my alma mater, both cheered and depressed by its familiar red brick and mullioned windows. I wasn't really in the mood for a literary event with its attendant 'paranoic bores' but I'd earlier run into the publisher's PR officer and been assured the work was in no way about Sylvia Plath. 'Not at all,' she gushed, 'It's a wide-ranging jaunt through all kinds of things – it's fun, fresh, engaged . . . *definitive.*' It wasn't that I had anything against Plath, it just seemed every other scholarly work in the past five years had been about her. I'd seen her sad face, and that even sadder ponytail, so often I felt sometimes like we were related.

A table had been set up just inside the entrance to the common room and optimistically loaded with about a thousand copies of the book, *Erato's Labia: Sextra-Textual Aesthetics and the Margins of the Poetic,* a 500-page monolith that had cost Dr Marianne Trench ten years of her life. Unfortunately for her, the decade in question had been one of white-knuckle acceleration in the development of critical theory and this had necessitated many, many return trips to the drawing board. Eventually, her fear of new, and potentially contradictory, additions to the debate meant she couldn't see a copy of the *TLS* without having difficulty breathing. This cumulative neurosis had left her with a permanent look of bloodshot dread, like the Ancient Mariner staring into a hurricane.

Trench, a slim fifty-year-old with cropped salt-and-pepper hair and dangley earrings, sat now – mute, spent, wrapped in a tweed shawl – behind the display stand, accepting best wishes and scribbling (literally) on the flyleaves of books thrust at her by her colleagues. A tweed-clad counter-feminist of similar years, also with short grey hair, leant over the table, her earrings a good inch longer than Trench's: 'Of course you do realise

Marianne that the semioticians are going to have a field day with your chapter on performative erotics . . .' The author began rocking to and fro, whispering to herself.

I examined the work in question. The picture on the front was a close-up of a white, multifoliate flower with the blunt head of a bee entering the frame bottom right. I flipped it over: '*In this compelling exegesis, Dr Marianne Trench lays bare the hypodiegetic paradox at the heart of l'ecriture feminine and asks whether it is appropriate, in an era of sundried sexual dysfunction and balsamic mimesis, to apply phallocognitive criteria to the 20th century's most cliterogenic hegemonies.*'

I read it again, this time moving my lips . . . Nope. Professor Cecil DeVille – known to students as 'the Sea Devil' – was standing nearby, also reading with a furrowed brow. An Anglo-Saxon specialist, he was famous for having painstakingly transformed his office into a simulacrum of his oak-panelled rooms at Oxford College Cambridge or wherever it was he had been, and for plying first-years with cheap sherry while he recounted tales of his glory days playing darts with J. R. R. Tolkien and arm-wrestling C.S. Lewis. I greeted him and we exchanged pleasantries.

'Listen,' I ventured. 'Have you had a go at this?' I held up the book.

'Of course. Excellent piece of scholarship.'

'Can you enlighten me as to what it's about?'

'It's, um . . . it's about the paradox at the core of er, *l'ecriture feminine* . . .'

I watched him closely, nodding encouragement.

'And, you know, whether we should be using phallo . . . whatsits, to um, investigate gynecological er . . .'

'Go on.'

'Well, that's about it.'

He shuffled away, fiddling with the tideline of white hair that frilled his bald dome, already back in the age of wanderers and seafarers.

I scanned the length and breadth of the low-ceilinged, badly-lit room: a big turnout of academics and writers, a contingent of students, a couple of artists, some theatre types, and a scattering of civilians. I headed for the bar where ready-poured drinks had been set out in rows, and downed a glass of Lithuanian Merlot in a single gulp. Speed and quantity, that was the secret to these events. I paused for a moment to make sure it was going to stay downed, then helped myself to another.

'Artie, how's it hanging?'

It was Dylan Delaney, one of the province's up and coming poets, a melancholy young man with vaguely Latin good looks and a fearsome reputation for womanising. We'd published much of his juvenilia in *Lyre*. His real name was Keith.

'Oh you know, slightly to the left. What about you – how's the poetry going?'

He selected a goblet of Nigerian Chardonnay.

'Oh, so so. Having trouble, to be honest, since the first collection, getting traction – '

He took a large gulp of wine, looked startled and swallowed with difficulty several times before continuing.

'. . . on new material. It's very frustrating.'

'Pity,' I said. And I meant it.

'I know. What about you? I haven't seen the magazine in a while.'

'Fine, fine. Slight delay with this issue but we're getting there. Just got to keep the Arts Council sweet, keep the cash flowing, you know how it is.'

'I hear you. Speaking of which, isn't The Hawk due to pop in tonight?'

There was one of those sudden, momentary outages in the conversation grid. We both looked around. Everyone else in the room was doing the same. I was having difficulty with the concept of The Hawk 'popping in', used as I was to picturing him swooping down out of a darkened sky.

'I've no idea. We usually deal with his deputy, Stanford Winks.'

'Oh he's here alright. I saw him earlier deep in conversation with that theatre guy Quigley. Talk about camp.'

'Indeed.'

'Not that there's anything wrong with that,' he added.

'Of course not.'

There was a silence. We both took a pull of wine.

'So, have you read Trench's book,' I enquired. 'I haven't had a chance myself.'

'Kind of. It's not exactly a crotch-gripping read . . .' He scratched at his designer stubble. '. . . It's mainly about Sylvia Plath.'

'I fucken *knew* it!'

'Anyway, I'd better go and lay some groundwork.' He drained his glass and picked up two more. 'As the Chinese say: *dig the well before you're thirsty.* Catch you later.'

He slid away in the direction of a group of under-graduettes who were chatting innocently near the snacks table. I could almost hear the theme from *Jaws*.

Further down the room, in the armchair section, the silverbacks were in their customary drinking forma-tion, their leader, an out-of-focus Ernest Hemingway, holding court. Near them, in trademark Resistance-style beret and cloak, was the Irish-language poet Grainne McCumhaill. She had backed one of the librarians against a pillar and was stabbing her repeatedly in the chest with an emphatic index finger. I made a mental note to steer clear.

There was a sudden whiff of expensive leather and Boyd Monroe, my former tutor, swept up on my blind side.

'How's the wine? Is it amusing?' he asked, slapping my shoulder.

'Oh, it's hilarious. Just don't get any in your mouth.'

He sipped, swilled, did hamster cheeks and a couple of fake retches.

'Mmm, I'm getting . . . molasses, burnt hair . . . a hint of tramps' underpants. Yes, I do believe they've broken out the good stuff. By the way, have you seen the state of Trenchie?'

We settled in for a session of mockery and cynicism. Monroe, tall, languid, prematurely grey – a man for whom soft corduroy had been invented – had briefly, as a young buck, been the toast of academe for an elegant treatise on the poems of Louis Aragon but had long since given up on conventional measurements of success and dedicated himself to a life of indolent hedonism. Robert Frost's epigram, '*College is a refuge from hasty judgment*' – a handy ice-breaker for postgraduates – had eventually hardened into his credo.

Beside us at the bar, Professor DeVille was sparring with Professor Cornelius O'Toole, a diminutive medievalist from Limerick. O'Toole had come north for a weekend in the late 1950s, ostensibly to buy a copy of *Lucky Jim* (which was banned in the Irish Republic), and never found his way home. They were supposed to be entertaining a visiting poet, one of the Martian crowd, who was blinking suspiciously at them through large steel-rimmed spectacles.

'That reminds me of the story Dougie Dunn tells about arriving at Hull, do you know it?' DeVille was saying in his best Oxbridge drawl.

'Yes, old Phil Larkin,' he continued. 'Who was quite senior by then, calls him into his office. *There's too much poetry in this department, Douglas*, he says, *and I'm relying on you* – wait, wait, this is good – *I'm relying on you to STAMP IT OUT!*'

DeVille and O'Toole broke into uproarious high-pitched laughter.

The poet nodded humourlessly. He was wearing a strangely-textured, cream waistcoat that appeared to be made of tripe.

'Yes, I had heard that one as a matter of fact. From Dougie himself.'

'Tell me, is this your first visit to the land of saints and scholars,' O'Toole enquired.

Before the Martian could reply Monroe broke in: '*Scholars and saints my eye, the land of ambush, / Purblind manifestoes, never-ending complaints . . .*'

They stared at him. Monroe beamed back.

'Good evening Boyd,' said DeVille icily. 'Still working part-time for the Irish tourist board I see.'

We persevered with the red, which had stopped stinging and become sweeter after the fifth glass. The evening had already passed the half-way stage and gone through a perceptible step change in noise volume, collective animation and traffic speed. Faces loomed in and out at the bar. More drinks were poured. More words filled the air. Faster. More.

Monroe had settled fully into the quotation mode that alcohol seemed to activate in him – a facility that even I found wearing after a while.

'I think I'm starting to *feel the drunkenness of things being various*,' he remarked, as Grainne McCumhaill came to a swaying halt in front of us. Her beret was askance and the red wine stains curving up from either side of her mouth were reminiscent of Batman's arch-enemy The Joker.

'What are you two laughing at?' she demanded.

No answer.

'I've been watching you,' The finger was cocked. 'And you're up to some kind of . . . *badness*.'

'Grainne, I assure you, there's no badness here, only love, peace and understanding,' Monroe said. 'How's the poetry going?'

'I don't believe a word of it – you're a pair of . . .' She caught sight of the librarian heading for the door and took off in pursuit.

The Merlot and the tobacco fumes were starting to get to me so I excused myself and slipped out for a Marlboro. It was warm outside and the air was musky with the scents of blossom and cooling vegetation. Overhead, the odd star was just visible above the yellowish aura of the campus lights. I ignited the cigarette and it too was sweet, and dry, and somehow empowering. It tasted good. I goldfished out a row of blue-tinged smoke rings and watched them disintegrate into the ambient darkness: chaos theory made visible. From beyond the cloisters came the sounds of the city at night: whoops of desire, sirens, cars, rhythmic bass, the grunts and cries of the higher primates at play . . . It was nice here. I felt safe. The wine, inferior though it was, had done its job on my bloodstream and frontal lobe. This wasn't such a bad life. Okay, so there was pretension, and pretentious people, and incomprehensible prose, and migraine-inducing poetry, and smart-arse theories, and false bonhomie, and paranoia and spite and all those other human failings that become evident in a tight space, but there was also vitality and creativity: a need to examine, to explore, to know. *Attunedness*. To the sonic boom of being here. An awareness that *world is crazier and more of it than we think*. That all this is *incorrigibly plural*. Besides, what was the alternative? As the man said, *the unexamined life is not worth living.* That's a bitch of a responsibility to bear on your own.

I blew a solar flare of smoke towards the moon, which was new and as slender as a fingernail paring. I was just thinking about rejoining the fray when, out of the corner of my eye, I noticed a small movement and, as I turned my head, I saw it: a fox, slinking between the shrubbery and the wall of the building. Leading with its nose, the animal sniffed its way delicately to the edge of the lawn where it stopped, one front paw poised in mid-step, to listen. Even in the shadow I could make out the almost toy-like sharpness of its muzzle and the creaminess of its breast. I tried not to breathe. Commitment made, the creature launched forward into a single-minded, staccato trot across the grass. *An urban fox!* I caught myself grinning inanely. Then, halfway across it sensed my presence, halting as suddenly and completely as a freeze-framed film, and I was given the full-beam brilliance of its amber-green eyes. A moment later it was in the bushes on the other side. Gone.

I could hear, now, the throb of music starting up in the students' union – Disco Night – Hot Chocolate's belief in miracles drifting across the quadrangle . . . Did I believe in miracles? I flicked the cigarette-end high into the air where it seemed to hover at its apogee before falling to earth in a burst of fiery flakes.

Look around you, I know of nothing else.

When I returned to the bar Monroe had just been joined by Tristan Quigley, the Lagan Theatre's resident director.

Beside him was a young man dressed entirely in black, smoking a Sobranie Black Russian.

'God, is everybody here drunk or what?' Quigley exclaimed, plucking imaginary fluff from the lapels of his immaculate cream jacket. 'We're a bunch of degenerates!'

'There's nothing like free booze to bring out the greed in people,' I observed.

'*When night | Darkens the streets, then wander forth the sons | Of Belial, flown with insolence and wine,*' Monroe said.

Quigley flapped his hands and rolled his preternaturally blue eyes to the ceiling.

'Don't tell me, don't tell me . . . I know this . . . *Paradise Lost!* Am I right?'

'You are, sir.'

'God, aren't we cultured!' he crowed.

'*Culture is always something that was, | Something pedants can measure,*' Monroe intoned. '*Skull of bard, thigh of chief, | Depth of dried-up river. | Shall we be thus for ever? | Shall we be thus for ever?*'

'Right, okay, you have me there,' said Quigley, crestfallen. 'Here, have you met Barney? Barney is Stanford Winks' partner.'

We shook hands with the cartoonishly handsome Barney.

'Look, there's Stannie over there! Stan-nie . . .' Quigley called.

On the other side of the room, the bespectacled Winks, dressed as though for the golf club in gold-buttoned blazer and grey slacks, waved back bleakly, the lower half of his face periodically eclipsed by the angry bobbing of a beret-clad head.

'Barney's an actor. A very good actor,' Quigley announced.

'We're all actors,' Barney said, expelling a geyser of smoke.

'He's right, you know.' Monroe, bang on cue. '*All the world's a stage | And all the men and women merely players . . . | And one man in his time plays many parts.*'

'Jesus, Boyd, have you been revising all day or something?' Quigley said. It wasn't clear whether his irritation was real or not.

'Tell me, Tristan, what's up next at the Lagan?' I asked in an attempt to distract.

'Oh, don't talk to me!' he cried. 'It's an almighty bollocks. Those old . . . *scrotes* on the board want to put on some boring old crowd-pleaser but I've told them – and I've told them loud and clear – it's something new or I *walk*. I am *fucked* if I'm doing *Where's The Vicar's Trousers?* AGAIN! They just cannot seem to grasp that I am about the transformation of metaphor into stage reality! That theatrical conceptualisation is my raison d'etre!'

'Fuck them,' said Barney.

'Oh I *will* fuck them Barney, don't you worry,' Quigley muttered and, again, it wasn't quite . . . clear.

Attention shifted to my left, where DeVille and O'Toole, having been ditched by the Martian, had been joined by an exceedingly drunk civilian deflected from his homeward path by the buzz of conversation in a well-lighted space. He was of indeterminate middle age but dressed in the frosty-wash-denim garb of a younger generation. He sported a full dark beard, wore his hair tied back in a ponytail and reeked of kebab. I'd noticed him when he first came in, how he was walking as though his feet didn't quite reach the ground. The professors were willing him not to be there and had switched into scholarly vernacular in an attempt to drive him away.

'In that case one would need to access Continental, ah, thinking,' DeVille groped. 'Phenomenology, hermeneutics and so on – not particularly helpful in this analysis.'

'Christ, you said it mate, my hermeneutics are killing me,' groaned Frosty-Wash, leaning one hand on the bar for support.

'But when you posit such a situation, are you doing so in a Kantian or a Marxian sense?' bluffed O'Toole.

'Oh Kant, of course.'

'Who you calling . . . *Kant*?' growled Frosty-Wash, attempting to focus.

DeVille took a deep breath.

'I see what you're getting at Cornelius and I agree with it up to a point, but these are, don't forget, essentially postmodern modalities . . .'

'I'm not so sure,' said O'Toole, wiping the sheen off his bald pate.

'Well, let's face it, none of us are Saussure,' cracked DeVille. Both men guffawed.

'Foucault . . .' O'Toole began.

'Foucault yourself . . .' yelped Frosty-Wash, who was

gripping the bar with both hands now and making ominous Funky Chicken movements with his neck.

'I don't like the look of that,' said Monroe, catching my eye.

'Stanford, darling, there you are!' Quigley shrilled.

Winks had been delivered to us via the peristaltic motion of the crowd.

He shook hands with each of us in turn, including Barney. He was noticeably sober.

'Stanford, you look miserable as sin,' said Quigley. 'Who pissed on your chips? You just tell me and I'll deal with them.'

'Wind your neck down, Tristan, no one, as you put it, pissed on my chips. It's just been a long day and I want to get home and have Barney here work on my back.'

'Ooh, you dirty skitter,' Quigley squealed.

'He means a massage,' said Barney, holding up muscular, manicured hands.

Winks turned to me.

'How are things Artie? Everything under control?'

'Steady as she goes, captain,' I replied, raising my glass.

'Good, good, glad to hear it.' He continued to stare at me. 'Um, by the way, I'll be dropping round to you on Monday, to the office – we need to look at the *Lyre* accounts and to discuss a couple of, er, matters.'

'Anything specific?'

'No, no. Just stuff.' He pointed at the ceiling. 'From on high.'

'The Hawk?'

Winks glanced round fearfully.

'What? Where? Is he here?'

'There was a rumour he might be,' I said.

'*The awful shadow of some unseen Power | Floats though unseen among us,*' Monroe chipped in. He followed up with a horror film laugh.

'You're not as funny as you think you are, Boyd,' said Quigley. 'In fact you're – '

At that moment Frosty-Wash, having vainly tried to refresh himself with the Vietnamese Shiraz, lost the tug-of-war he'd been having with his vestibular system and full-scale chaos broke out at the bar. Panicked drinkers stumbling back in waves from the epicentre were treading on the feet of those behind them, the resultant shrieks of pain mingling with screams of terror. In later accounts, some would claim the situation had been exacerbated by Frosty-Wash, disoriented but still active (in the volcanic sense), attempting to flee his own handiwork. Escape was further hindered by the prone – and not insubstantial – figure of the Sea Devil, who had gone down heavily in the initial melee. My own lasting impression from the cavalcade of broken images that night was of a frieze of anguished faces painted in the style of Edvard Munch. That, and the Martian poet tearfully contemplating the encrusted mosaic that had been applied at high velocity to his tripe waistcoat.

Outside, we regrouped, swapping cigarettes and stories like refugees from some terrible occurrence which, in a way, we were.

'Early yet,' chirped Monroe after a while, rubbing his hands together. 'What about a jar at the Arts Club?'

'Not for me, Boyd,' I said. 'I'm gonna call it a day and grab some sleep.'

'Artie, Artie . . .' His voice was thick with rebuke. '*What hath night to do with sleep?*'

'No, seriously. I need some decent shut-eye.'

'Artie, you're a young man, have some respect for that fact.'

'Boyd, I'm going home and that's final.'

On the way to the Arts Club we commandeered the poet Dylan Delaney and his companion, the leader of the undergraduettes. Afterwards we ended up back at Delaney's flat where we settled down to an unmarked bottle of firewater from his latest travels in Bohemia. Later, Monroe began reciting *The Faerie Queene* and I closed my eyes momentarily, the better to enjoy it.

★

I awoke to the sound of a woman having a baby. There was music in the background and she was being chivvied along by her birth partner, Van Morrison, who was also, from time to time, counterpointing the shouts and groans prompted by some of her more violent contractions. I was bolt upright in an armchair. A silver thread of drool, as though spun by a large spider, connected my chin to my shirt. The sunlight, which was streaming through filmy orange curtains behind me, was illuminating, on the collapsed sofa-bed opposite, the fully-dressed figure of Boyd Monroe, one arm across his chest, the other outflung, like an opera singer in mid-aria. Glasses, ashtrays, cassette cases and books crowded the carpet where one shoeless foot hung down. A fishing-line of saliva glistened on his jowl. The music and the child-birth noises, I now ascertained, were coming from the bedroom and, as a more realistic explanation for them dawned, I identified the album as *Astral Weeks*.

There was no coffee or bread in the poet's kitchen so I closed the door softly behind me and tiptoed into the street. It was another fine June morning with just a hint of cool, and the residents of Stranmillis village, perched proudly on its hill overlooking the Gardens, were just rising to greet the sun – no doubt with freshly-perked, sweet java and hot, yeasty loaves, straight from the oven. A faint breeze riffled through the trees. Birds were singing . . . I felt like shit. Bloody Monroe.

I burst into the first bakery I could find.

'Oh, Holy God, would you look at the state of that! Have you a wee hangover son?'

The little old lady in her crisp apron was so full of concern I had to resist the urge to cry.

'I'm fine.' Bloody Monroe.

'What'll you have? A wee sausage bap? A wee bacon & egg soda? Or maybe just a wee doughnut?'

'Um . . . not sure.'

I surveyed the cholesterol bombs and lard grenades behind the glass. I wanted all of them.

'What about a wee eclair? Or a wee tray bake? Those wee vanilla slices are lovely, so they are.'

I was starting to sweat.

'Where were you, at a wee party?'

'No. Yes. No. Kind of. Stayed up too late.'

'Oh that'll be it alright. I have to say, you're looking a wee bit peaky. Eileen – ' she called over her shoulder and a moment later another, slightly older, old lady in an apron appeared from a doorway.

'Eileen, look at this wee lad – doesn't he look a wee bit peaky?'

Eileen agreed that I did indeed look peaky.

'Has he had a wee feed of bad drink?'

'I think he has. And he stayed up too late.'

'And now he feels rotten.'

'He does. He feels rotten. Look at his wee eyes.'

'I know. All pink. Like a wee rat's.'

'And his hair. Look at his hair, it's mad.'

'And his wee purple teeth.'

I again fought the urge to cry.

'Give me five sausage rolls!' I shouted.

Bloody Monroe.

A few minutes later, finding it difficult to chew and walk at the same time, I sat down on a bench in the grounds of the university. The cool breath issuing from its stone-flagged interior was soothing. My heart was trying out a distressing new reggae-style rhythm and my face was sticky with a sheen of food and alcohol sweat. Why couldn't I have just said no and gone home last night? I'd be refreshed and reading the newspaper over a nice cup of coffee by now. I drew another sausage roll from the paper bag: greasy pap of pastry enclosing molten pink slurry. Don't think about it. Good and peppery though. Essential. Never understood why white pepper fell from grace. Great in mashed potatoes too. Didn't Christopher Columbus stumble upon the New World while in pursuit of peppercorns? Nearby, a gardener was trimming the edges of the lawn with a long-handled clipper, humming to himself. *Spanish Ladies?* In front of the main building a couple of tourists were photographing each other. A man and a woman in their mid sixties. Americans, by the look of them: pastel windcheaters, battenberg trousers, peanut butter shoes. Man approaching.

'Hi there!'

Sunglasses. Fishing hat. Scrabble tile teeth.

'Hello.'

'We were wondering – say, are you okay, you look a little . . .'

'Fine thanks.'

'We were wondering if you could direct us to the mail depot.' He pronounced it dee-poe.

'I'm sorry?'

'The dee-poe? The big mail dee-poe?'

I had to think about it. His wife followed him over and stood smiling at me.

'Ah, the post office. Yes, there's . . . well, the big one is in Tomb Street. It's a bit of a walk though . . .'

'That's okay, we got time.'

I gave the best directions I could in the circumstances. His wife took a photograph of me.

'That's very kind of you, we appreciate it. And let me

say, you have a very beautiful country here, you should be very proud.'

I had to think about this too.

'Thanks,' I said.

As I watched them disappear along University Road I polished off the last sausage roll and began to feel slightly better. In my mind I assumed an aerial view and imagined them moving through the city. I wondered what they'd make of its all too human scale compared with where they'd come from, its mish-mash of grandeur and desolation. Did they have any idea where they were? (It fleetingly occurred to me that they might be looking for the GPO in Dublin.) I panned out a little, so I was at the height of a bird or a helicopter, say, and then ascended a little further until I could discern the shape of the land mass.

On the points of the compass, a line drawn directly north would pass through the bank, church and newspaper quarter, over Cave Hill and eventually traverse the Antrim coast road into the North Channel on a latitude, roughly, with Moscow in one direction and Edmonton, Alberta in the other. Taken south, it would plunge through County Down, over the Mourne mountains, and pop out into the Irish Sea, parallel with Port Erin on the Isle of Man, and Morecambe on the Lancashire coast beyond. West would slice across the Falls Road, under the shadow of Black Mountain and end up in the moiling waters of Lough Neagh, a basin formed, as legend would have it, by the giant Finn MacCool scooping out a missile to lob at his Scottish enemy. East takes us past the parliament building of Stormont Castle, along the top of Strangford Lough, through the upper arm of the Ards Peninsula and once more into the waves –

I was brought back to earth by a sudden flurry of wingbeats and the arrival on the lawn in front of me of a pigeon, joined almost immediately by two others. This villainous-looking trio (one of them had a scabby head, another a calcified foot) proceeded to strut around in a near-parody of nonchalance, all the while edging closer to where I was sitting. I glanced down. Pastry crumbs. That's what they were after. I shook the remaining flakes from the bag and the breeze stepped in and deposited them on the pathway nearby. The birds, emboldened by the safer distance, deigned to try a few. I resumed my bird's-eye daydream . . .

To the northeast, Belfast port communes with the lough that gave birth to the city. Here's the source of our current metropolis: a wet quickening on a sandbank beside confluences of fresh and salt water, the Farset River joining the Lagan and meeting an inwash of the Irish Sea. A ford. A toehold. A place to trade. The ships weigh anchor: sweet Ulster beef and butter go out; fine liquors from Bordeaux and Cadiz come in, sugar and tea from the Indies, tobacco from the Americas. This *river-straddling, hill-rimmed town* begins to swell, with Scots and English, with westerners from Donegal, with fleeing Huguenots bringing knowledge of weaving. The industries grow: brewing, cigarettes, rope-making, ship building, heavy machinery. And linen, with the Farset powering the water mills and supplying rinse for the heavy acres of cloth on the bleach greens. The merchants raise their solid, handsome homes, and bring craftsmen in from Italy to tile the floors and carve pineapples on the newel posts.

The buildings – the Grand Opera House (which the Americans should be passing shortly), the Linenhall Library, the Customs House, the Palm House, this majestic university – tell you all you need to know, really, that this place hit its high water mark in the surge and clamour of the nineteenth century and everything since has been a falling away. The ghosts are everywhere; in the deserted wharves and map-rooms, the drawing offices and vaults. If you listen you can hear them whistling in the marketplaces and along the towpaths; you can smell their pipe tobacco in the evening air outside the churches. The laughter of the mill-girls echoes in the entries . . . Falling away? Eating itself, more like: bombs and incendiaries taking bites out of it; gap after gap refilled, built up again. So much scar tissue.

When I arrived at Oliver's he was busy in his kitchen. On the milk-napped table, amongst half a dozen Sunnyland Farm cartons and most of his *batterie de cuisine*, was a copy of *Mrs Beeton's Book of Household Management* open at Creams, Whips and Custard Puddings. There was a strong smell of scalded lactose in the air and a sense of something fermenting somewhere. Something malevolent.

'I've got a gallon of ice cream in the freezer, two junkets in the fridge, and a bucket of Angel Delight on the windowsill,' he announced. 'And a rice pudding about to come out of the oven.'

I told him about Winks' impending visit.

'Oh shag it.'

I hit the shower while Oliver rooted out the file marked 'Accounts', which he'd brought home to work on six months ago and flung in the bottom of his wardrobe.

It wasn't pretty. We were looking at a dozen tea-stained pages of indecipherable symbols and random numbers. I stood up and started to pace the room. The sausage rolls were wearing off.

'What the fuck are we going to do? Winksie'll shit a brick if we hand this to him.'

Oliver, who was still wearing his bikini-ed breasts apron, suddenly sat up straight and clapped his hands together.

'I know!'

I stared at him, more in surprise than expectation.

'Let's have some rice pudding, while it's hot. It'll make us feel better.'

We ate in silence. Apart from a ghostly, and un-explained, undertow of garlic, it wasn't actually too bad (how can you mess up rice pudding?) and as I spooned it down, the conglutination of sugar, milk, and starch began have a warm, unifying effect on my shattered system.

There was music coming from somewhere, a heavy, tamping beat, a see-sawing drone of accordion – Paul Simon singing *Boy in the Bubble*. It was drifting up through the floorboards. I listened for a while, sifting through my small mental cache of Rosie McCann images. And then it struck me.

'Holy shit!'

Oliver spat out a mouthful of pudding.

'Oliver, didn't you say Rosie – the woman who lives below – was final year accountancy?'

'Yes, she is but . . .' His face lit up. 'Bingo!'

'It's worth a try.'

Strangely, Rosie wasn't falling over herself to help. It took ten minutes of intense, spaniel-eyed begging before she caved in and admitted me to her flat.

'I'm playing squash in an hour,' she warned as I slunk past.

While not the tidiest female living space I'd ever seen, it was a paradigm of cleanliness and order compared to the midden above. It contained the usual girlie stuff: scarf-bedraped lamps, striped 'throws' from Habitat, bowls of sinus-searing pot-pourri, a collection of gauzy panties drying on a radiator. On the wall above the television there was a poster of Terence Trent D'Arby smirking from behind his bead curtain of hair.

'Nice place,' I commented, but there was something underlying the masking scent of dried frangipani and cloves that . . . What was it?

Rosie noticed me sniffing.

'I know. A sour . . . sickly kind of smell? It's driving me mad. I've searched everywhere but I can't work out where it's coming from.'

We both stood there interrogating the air like meercats.

Overhead I could hear the Milky Bar Kid clumping around singing to himself (the clarity of the accoustics was startling and it occurred to me that before too long Rosie would come to dread the night).

'Right, show me what you've got,' she said, hopping onto the sofa and folding her legs under her.

She was wearing black tracksuit bottoms and a white aertex tennis shirt. Her hair was tied back and her face free of make-up. Her eyes were greener than I remembered from earlier in the week, and she seemed shorter.

After a few minutes of staring incredulously at our ream of hieroglyphics, she stopped to massage her temples.

'I'm pretty sure I'm going to regret asking this but do you have a record of income?'

'Er . . .'

'Do you have a record of your outgoings?'

'Well, you see . . .'

'Have you saved your VAT receipts?'

'Um . . .'

'I'm going to need a coffee. Black. No sugar.'

Upstairs, Oliver was singing along to *Yellow Brick Road* in a tortured falsetto. ('*I'm just a horny old toad . . .*')

Half an hour later, Rosie summoned me over from the window seat where I'd been engrossed in a copy of *Elle* magazine.

'Listen carefully,' she said, tapping the arm of the sofa with a biro. 'This is what you must do . . .'

She started to speak. She was looking at me very intently, her mouth moving very quickly and precisely.

Flashes of small, even white teeth. Lips moistened by tongue-tip approximately every thirty words. I nodded to show I was taking in what she was saying and then realised I wasn't. What *was* she saying?

'. . . added to the balance sheet. You got that? Then subtract the square root of the hypotenuse . . . and index link ten percent of your risk profile to your Bollinger curve. Have a Hang Seng haircut, narrow your spread to twelve basis points and seasonally adjust your liquidity. After that it's just a question of killer bees and fallen angels. Okay?'

I nodded a few more times. Her eyes were mesmerising.

'I'm sorry, could you repeat that?' I said. 'I'll take notes this time.'

Overhead, Oliver emitted a long, shrill, Wookiee-like belch that reverberated through the light fittings.

Rosie leant back and regarded the ceiling while I folded up a sheet of paper and gently extracted the pen from her fingers. She began again. I tried to avoid looking at her. Tried to concentrate on the words.

I wrote: 'Income on one side, outgoings on the other.' No problem. 'VAT receipts. Subtract.' Got it. This was good . . . She really did have fine skin tone, though. Very healthy. A slight flush just below each cheek bone. Thick eyelashes. And how soft and white her throat was. Pulse and flow. I caught myself remembering the dazzle of her nakedness . . . Dammit! Not again. What was she saying?

'. . . on a Japanese Candlestick Chart. That's important. If they use the Macaroni Defence you're going to get a Keynesian kickback . . . at the very least a dead cat bounce and if that happens . . . zero percent kruggerands . . . hedge wrapper . . . Joseph Effect. That's it. Do you think you'll manage that?'

'What? Oh yeah, no problem. That's great. You're a star.'

'I know. Of the County Down.'

'That's right. *The maid with the nut-brown hair.* I can't believe you've never heard that song.'

'Actually I have.'

'What? I thought you . . .'

'Of course I have. I just get tired of people pointing it out every time they hear my name.'

'Sorry.'

'That's alright.'

She smiled.

I smiled.

'Listen,' I said. 'Obviously we can't pay you for helping us out here but what would you say to me buying you a drink some time?'

She blushed instantly, laughed, then looked away.

'That's very nice of you and I'd like to but, um . . .'

'Yes?'

'I have a boyfriend.'

Spoiler.

Back upstairs, I found Oliver absorbing a half-gallon of strawberry milkshake.

'Well? Are we sorted?' he squeaked, wiping away a pink moustache.

I nodded.

'Yep, Rosie's saved our bacon,' I said.

'Are you sure? This could really mess things up.'

'Don't worry. We've a bit of work to do but we'll blitz on it tomorrow.'

'You're confident?'

'Absolutely. Then we just need to make sure we're at the office early on Monday in time for Winksie.'

'Brilliant!' He drained his glass. 'This calls for a celebration. Let's have a milkshake.'

We moved to the kitchen, where the stack of Sunnyland Farm cartons had been rebuilt and now formed a head-height wall between the fridge and the window.

Oliver assembled his syrup bottles and took up his whisk.

'Oliver, do you mind if I make a suggestion?'

'Not at all.'

'I'm just going to run this up the flagpole as it were . . .'

'Fire away. Chocolate or strawberry?'

'Chocolate. Wouldn't it make more sense to cut the competition coupons *out* of the cartons?'

'Yeah, definitely.'

'Right, so . . .?'

'Well I would but I haven't got any scissors. Mick the Artist ran off with them that night he was going to kill Marty Pollocks. Remember? After the last *Lyre* party?'

I cast my mind back. The artists had been particularly volatile that night.

'Fair enough.'

I sniffed.

'You do wash them out, though, don't you? I saw some in the bathroom. And the ones at the office are getting a bit whiffy . . .'

He handed me my drink and raised his own.

'Slainte.'

'Cheers.'

It was horribly sweet. This couldn't be good for Oliver, I thought, and looking at him now I noticed he had gained weight. His face was slabby and had a dense, pearlescent pallor to it that surpassed the bleaching effect of the light from the window. Some lines of Heaney's – from *The Milk Factory* – popped, unbidden, into my head: *There we go, soft-eyed calves of the dew / Astonished and assumed into fluorescence*. Was Oliver turning into a veal calf?

I asked him if he had any plans for the night.

'You better believe it. Iris is coming round.'

He smirked and began involuntarily licking his lips like a cat anticipating . . . well, cream. Oliver had been seeing Iris for nearly a year and their mutual lust – instantaneous and irrestistible – showed no signs of flagging. In fact, according to him, it was still as urgent as the first time. They had met in Crazy Prices, where they contrived a flirtation over the last packet of mint Viscounts and, three hours later, after a flurry of drinks in the Parador Hotel, found themselves naked, slicked in sweat and sharing a cigarette on Oliver's fragrant futon. (Yes, it was a mystery to me too.) There was just one drawback: Iris was the middle-aged wife of Samuel Niblock, a high-ranking and notoriously uptight policeman.

'You know Sammy'll have you killed – or at the very least gelded – if he ever finds out?' I said.

'He won't find out. He'd better not.'

'And it'll be even worse when he twigs you're a Catholic.'

'He won't. Anyway, I'm not a Catholic.'

'What?'

'I'm not a Catholic, I'm a Buddhist.'

'Since when?'

'About a year ago.'

I let that one slide. As far as I was aware, Buddha took a pretty dim view of alcohol abuse, junk food addiction *and* sexual gluttony.

'Do you know much about this guy?' I asked.

'Not really. Just bits and pieces Iris has told me.'

'Such as?'

'Well, his nickname in the force is The Mongoose. You know why?'

'He looks like one?'

'No. Well, a bit apparently, but that's not it.'

'Because he likes raw eggs?'

'Okay that's enough. No, it's because he goes after villains the way a mongoose goes after snakes. He has no fear. He's impervious to their venom.'

'And you're doing the Cucumber Rumba with his wife. Are you mad?'

'What can I tell you Artie, I'm ruled by my heart.'

'Yeah, or something further south,' I muttered.

'What?'

'Nothing.'

Before I left, Oliver insisted I eat a cup of half-set panna cotta and a basinful of butterscotch Angel Delight.

It was the wrong thing to do.

'You know, you could probably use an early night,' he observed. 'You look a wee bit peaky.'

★

Nothing concentrates the mind quite as sharply as the arrival in the room of a man with a gun. If it's never happened to you – and you should count yourself lucky – the sensation is akin to what they say drowning is like. As you glimpse that precision-engineered black hole, every-thing you've ever experienced is sucked in an instant through your memory and compressed into a pinhead-sized ball of light that dances just above the bridge of your nose. With the logic of a dream everything suddenly makes sense: you didn't know it, but everything in your life has been leading up to this adrenaline-drenched moment.

This particular man had a moustache and wore a black Harrington jacket, and the gun in his right hand was a Browning nine-millimetre semi-automatic, part of an arms cache that went missing from a County Armagh police barracks in 1985.

But, let's backtrack briefly.

By the time Oliver arrived at the office on Sunday night (clutching a carton of curried chips and a flagon of banana milkshake) I had already pulled together a va-guely plausible set of *Lyre* accounts. Rosemary's tutorial had somehow paid off. All that was left to do was sort through our expense receipts and make them correspond to the numbers I had typed out. This proved more difficult than you'd think: for a start, there were two or three million of them, bursting like confetti from a dozen overstuffed envelopes; secondly, half of them related to biscuits and milk. The remainder were for unauthorised lunches, bogus equipment, stationery and, most testing of all, 'miscellaneous' – a category of mys-teries that included a chilling invoice from The Honeypot Salon for 'intimate waxing'. (It wasn't mine.)

At midnight, we both lost the will to live.

At 9:03 a.m., Stanford Winks rapped crisply at the door.

I woke with a start, still sitting at the desk, looked at my watch and then across at Oliver who stared back at me with one open eye, tattered receipts stuck to his face where he had lain in them.

'Get the kettle on,' I hissed.

While Oliver stumbled to 'the kitchen', I managed to sweep the evidence into a plastic bag and – 'Coming – ' stash it in a drawer.

Clawing my hair into shape I greeted the man from the Arts Council, who was dapper in a chocolate corduroy suit and pink floral tie.

'Apologies for my lateness, Artie, the West Link was jammed. Always is when it rains,' he said, propping his umbrella against the wall and pulling out a tissue to polish his large round spectacles. 'My God, it doesn't get any tidier in here does it? Don't you ever clean up? Where's Mr Sweeney?'

'Here I am . . .' Oliver poked his head out of 'the kitchen'. 'How are you this morning Stanford?'

'Very well, thank you. Bit wet.'

'Cup of tea?'

'That would be lovely.' Winks sniffed the air, his eyes narrowing. 'On second thoughts, make it a coffee. No milk.'

We settled down for a chat. After a brief treatise on soft furnishings from our visitor, who was redecorating his house, we turned to business. He wanted to know when the next issue of *Lyre* would appear (he wasn't alone). He also led us to understand ('Don't get me wrong, we love the mag') that 'some people' had noted a deterioration of quality, a lack of focus, in the previous two editions. Could this be rectified? People were hungry for local flavour, very keen that emphasis be given to the issues and concerns of the day. 'After all, we live in a very special part of the world with problems that are peculiar to us and we have a responsibility to recognise and confront those issues,' he said, as though reading from a teleprompter. Oliver and I nodded and looked grave.

Despite the pleasant tone, Winks was agitated and after just two Crinkle Crunch Creams he was popping the catches on his briefcase and asking for our accounts.

'I'm sorry to be uptight about this, but there's real pressure coming down to make sure taxpayers are getting bang for their buck. A certain person back at HQ, *you know who*, seems to think some recipients – not you boys, obviously – are . . . how should we put it, having a laugh. And unfortunately, that means we're all under the microscope – ' He dropped his voice to a stage whisper. '. . . Just *entre nous* he has me half demented.'

I handed him the sheaf of figures I had conjured from the void the previous evening.

'Thanks Artie, I'll pass them on to finance. All in order?'

'Oh yes.'

'Wait a minute, where are the receipts? No good without the receipts.'

'Actually, they're – '

It was at this – I hesitate to say fortuitous – moment that the man with the gun arrived.

The door burst open, propelled by a size twelve boot, and he was across the threshold, breathing heavily, gun arm outstretched, assessing the room's danger potential. It was, it has to be said, low: Walter the Softy on one side, Oliver and I like rejects from a *Waiting for Godot* audition on the other. All motion ceased. There was no sound except for the drumming of raindrops on the skylight.

Keeping his eyes on us he crept sideways, then wheeled, *Miami Vice*-style, into the doorway of 'the kitchen'. He sniffed a couple of times and withdrew. Having satisfied himself that everyone was accounted for, he approached the desk, whipped a chair around and straddled it bad-cop-style, resting his arms on its back. (I'd always thought people only did that in fiction.)

No one spoke.

He pointed the pistol at Oliver.

'Which one are you?'

Oliver's face was the colour of lemon posset.

'Listen, it wasn't me, it – '

'Shut up. Sweeney or Conville?'

'Sweeney, but I swear I never touched her – '

'Shut the fuck up. That makes you Conville, right?'

'That's right.'

He smiled, showing smoke-lacquered teeth. I noticed he had L-O-V-E tattooed in Indian ink – homemade job – across the knuckles of his right hand, H-E-A-T across the left. *Heat?*

Oliver was highly agitated.

'If you'll just let me explain, this whole thing was an innocent – '

'HEY! FAT BOY! I DON'T KNOW WHAT THE FUCK YOU'RE TALKING ABOUT BUT IF YOU DON'T FUCKEN STOP YOU'RE GOING TO GET A SECOND ARSEHOLE.'

Oliver stopped.

The man with the gun contemplated Winks for a moment but detected no possible threat and moved on.

'Now there's a few things I want to know from you two tossers: firstly, who the fuck d'you think y'are . . .' He squinted down the barrel of the gun. 'And secondly, WHAT GIVES YOU THE RIGHT TO SHITE ON ME LIKE YOU'RE GOD ALMIGHTY?'

'Pardon?'

'SHUT UP.'

He helped himself to a biscuit.

'Fuck me, these are rotten. Have you no fig rolls?'

'We – '

'Shut up, Oliver,' I said. ' Listen, Mr . . . um, sorry I don't know your name . . .'

He took his time chewing a mouthful of biscuit, swallowed and ran his tongue round his gums.

'They call me Mad Dog.'

Winks whimpered.

'Mr Mad . . . Dog. If you'll just tell us how we can help you, maybe we can – '

'No, no, no, no, no. No . . .' He shook his head and looked to the heavens. 'No, no, it's WAAYY too fucken late for that. Way too late. You had your chance. And you fucken blew it.'

He rubbed biscuit crumbs from his moustache, then ruffled his hair, checking its dampness level. The style was what cultural historians would later term 'the Weeping Willow Mullet': flat on top, with long sideburns and a semi-perm effect at the rear. 'And yese call yourselves editors.'

'I'm sorry,' I said. 'I'm not sure what – '

'SHUT UP! What do editors do?'

'What?'

'WHAT DO EDITORS DO?'

'Edit?'

'They edit. And what does that mean? I'll tell you what it means. It means they find new writing by new writers and they publish it. Isn't that right?'

'Yes, but – '

'You couldn't see what was in front of you, could you? You could NOT see what you held in your hand. Why? Because it was different, it was real. It was from *real life*. It wasn't smartypants, it wasn't fancy, it wasn't – ' His features twisted horribly – '*nice.*'

He glared at each of us in turn.

'Mad Dog didn't go to a posh school. He didn't go to bigknob university. And that means he couldn't be in your nice wee fucken magazine, for your nice wee friends to put on their nice wee fucken coffee tables in their NICE WEE FUCKEN HOUSES . . .'

He was perspiring and a jagged blueish vein had surfaced in the crescent of tiredness beneath his left eye. (It occurred to me on some abstract level that he might have a point, and a quick, hot jolt of ill-defined shame swept through me.)

'And yese didn't even have the COMMON DE-CENCY TO REPLY. To put one wee FUCKEN LET-TER in the FUCKEN POST!'

He stood up (Winks cowered), set his gun on the desk and removed his jacket. A white cap-sleeved T-shirt revealed extravagant tattoo work, notably a three-headed hellhound on his right forearm, the ace of spades with a grinning skull at its centre on his left. In gothic script beneath the playing card was *Do'nt forget the joker.* Sound advice. Assorted other creations adorned his heavily-muscled upper arms. (Despite the abject terror I still found myself puzzling over the H-E-A-T on his knuckles. Could it be a phonetic spelling of the Belfast pronunciation of hate?)

'So you see,' he said, sitting down again. 'In my world, it's very important that people are nice and polite to each other. It helps keep everybody calm. So, when people are rude, what generally happens is that they get a wee lesson . . .'

'Now hold on – ' Oliver tried again.

'SHUT THE FUCK UP I AM FUCKEN WARN-ING YOU I AM GOING TO FUCKEN SHOOT SOMEONE!'

A new vein sprang to life in his temple, as though a countdown timer had been triggered. There was froth on his moustache. He continued.

'. . . A wee lesson in manners which, in your case, will mean stairs could be a wee problem for yese, if you know what I mean. In fact, yese might want to think about taking an office on the ground floor. I think you'll find that will suit yese better.'

He didn't smile. There was a hint of the whiskey drinker's broken glitter in his eyes.

'Mr Mad Dog,' I began.

'HEY . . . Just Mad Dog, you fucken tube.'

'Mad Dog, if you'll just listen to me for a minute?'

He paused. Focused his attention on me. Readjusted his grip on the gun.

I took a deep breath.

'We've had some technical problems here – I won't bore you with the details – but it's resulted in a massive backlog. As you can see – ' I waved at the drumlins of paper around us. 'We've had a lot of submissions. But the fact is, we had just got to your work and, funny enough, it was due for discussion at today's editorial meeting.'

He leaned forward, his chin jutting.

'Do you really think,' he said. 'Mad Dog's head buttons up the back?'

'I beg your pardon?'

'One more fucken lie out of you son and you'll have trouble taking a piss let alone getting up the stairs.'

'No, I'm serious. We were very impressed – just on a first reading.'

'YOU ARE ON VERY THIN ICE SONNY JIM. DO NOT BULLSHIT ME OR I SWEAR TO GOD I WILL FUCK YOU UP!'

I had the drowning sensation again. *I can't go on.* How much of this could I get away with? What did it matter? There was no turning back. *I'll go on.*

'No bullshit. Your stuff was top of our agenda and you were the first in line for a copyright check.' *A copyright check?* This was risky stuff.

'I'm not going to ask you this again,' He spoke very deliberately. 'Are you telling me the truth?'

'Yes I am. But let me just refresh my memory. Oliver, would you fetch Mr – I mean Mad Dog's . . . material? I think you had it last.'

Oliver, to his eternal credit, took this one squarely on the chin. He rose from his chair like an elderly man recovering from a haemorrhoid procedure and shuffled to the far corner of the room where he began scrabbling at the largest mound of envelopes.

The rest of us were temporarily hypnotised by the sound of rain on glass.

'Artie, maybe you could give me a hand here?' Oliver queried a few minutes later, his voice reedy, plaintive, as though he were calling across a roaring hillside. 'The In-pile has got mixed up with the Out-pile again.'

I looked at our captor. He swore and waved me away with his gun.

I got to work on an adjacent stack, opening the envelopes as quickly and as quietly as I could. They all seemed to be from chancers whose work we rejected on a regular basis. Couldn't these people take a hint? In one I discovered another snap from the topless poetess, this time holding a labrador puppy and staring sadly (it could have been reproach) into the lens. One of her hands was encircling the pup's neck. Behind her, on a sofa was a bare-chested man wearing a cowboy hat.

'This is hopeless,' Oliver whispered. 'Laughing Boy's going to go to town on us.'

'Just keep looking, it's here somewhere,' I muttered. I now dimly recalled frisbeeing a wad of hand-written horrors across the room a few months back that could have been by our man.

Back at the table, Mad Dog had zeroed in on Winks: '*Stanford?* What kind of nancy-boy fucken name is *that?*'

I started on another pile, a mixture of opened and unopened submissions. ('*Sirs, Having resumed composing again after a recent breakdown . . .*') Oliver was right, this was futile. We were headed for the Ministry of Silly Walks.

'Arts Council? Really? That's very interesting . . .' Mad Dog was saying. Good, they were getting on.

I rifled through the next creative slagheap. Despite the terror of our predicament I found myself marvelling again at the number of souls putting pen to paper in a bid to be heard above *the human fracas*. And not for the first time was I unable to decipher the emotion this engendered. As I laboured I was trying to keep half an ear on the conversation developing behind me. Why on earth was Mad Dog suddenly talking about drama? *The people's theatre*? Did I hear that correctly?

Beside me Oliver had ceased ripping manila and was staring at the wall with his hand cupping the side of his face. I heard a sniffle.

'Oliver, are you . . . are you *crying?*'

'What? No! Just . . . a paper cut.'

'Pull yourself together man – we've got to . . . hang on, what's this?'

I had hit paydirt. A clump of crumpled school jotter-style pages with spidery, left-leaning hand-writing. Five poems: *Ballyclava Blues, The Dead Wo'nt Leave Me Alone, World of Heat* and – on the softer side – *Black & Decker Daydream* and *My Ma*. The spelling was highly unorthodox and they were signed 'By Mad Dog'.

'Come on, you fucken balloons, what's keeping yese?'

'Yep, with you now.'

I took a minute to skim the verses and formulate some vaguely convincing terms of praise – multi-purpose crowd-pleasers like *unashamedly hard-hitting . . . refreshingly visceral . . . bold and iconoclastic* and, if it looked like

73

the author's ego could fend off his paranoia, *works of profound genius*. But as I resumed my seat I sensed there had been a change in direction, a mutation of the group dynamic.

'So you're telling me you have absolute power? You can say yes or no and what you say goes?' Mad Dog was asking.

'Well, yes I suppose I am,' Winks replied loftily. 'That is, I mean, between me and my colleagues. That's what we do.'

Mad Dog's blink rate was increasing as he assimilated some kind of possibility.

'So . . . if you thought something, let's say for example, a *play*, should be put on by a theatre, then that theatre would *have* to put on that play?'

'If they wanted to keep their funding coming in, and by extension, their jobs, yes.'

Mad Dog fell silent. Then he began to laugh, a strange, slow, staccato guffaw, as though someone was trying to start a water-logged tractor. I looked at Winks. He was giggling like a schoolgirl. This was grotesque. Winks was showing off to a man who had come to remove our kneecaps.

Oliver and I swapped incredulous glances.

'Ah Holy God, that's brilliant,' said Mad Dog, swiping a hairy forearm across his damp eyes. 'That is fucken brilliant.'

What happened next could not have been predicted.

(Mind you, this was not your average Monday morning.)

Mad Dog jumped to his feet and in three swift strides had Winks by the throat and the muzzle of the gun pushed hard into the centre of his forehead.

'Now you listen to me Mr Fancypants,' he hissed. 'Do you feel that? DO YOU FEEL THAT? Fucken cold isn't it? Well that's how cold YOU'LL be if you don't do what I fucken tell you.'

He glared sideways at Oliver and me.

'And don't you two get any ideas, you hear me? Or I'll plug ye.'

Oliver moved his head from side to side. I nodded. Fifty thousand volts wouldn't have produced an idea in either of us. I'm not even sure I was breathing.

Mad Dog turned back to Winks, whose eyes were bulging so much they appeared to be smudging the inside of his glasses.

'Right you. This is how it's going to be.' His tone was measured, deadly serious. 'Forget the poetry. *Fuck* the poetry. I have wrote a play. And *you* are going to get it performed. By real actors. At a proper theatre. With all the bells and whistles. Adverts, posters, radio, TV, the lot. And it's going to be good. And it's going to be soon. Very soon. In fact, if this isn't happening by September I will come after you. I will hunt you down and I will make you wish you had never been born. And then I will kill you. Do you understand?'

Winks seemed to be paralysed. Or had he died of fright? With his eyes open?

'DO YOU UNDERSTAND?'

Winks managed the barest of nods.

'What's your wife called?'

'Barney.'

'I will kill Barney too.'

(Mad Dog's brain took a moment to update its files.)

'And it goes without saying, if you tell anyone – ANYONE – about what's went on here today I will kill you. And that goes for you two bucketheads as well. If I get so much as a whiff of pig you're dead.'

He released his grip on Winks' neck and stepped back. The gun had imprinted a perfect O on the Arts Council officer's forehead.

'Are we all crystal here? Everyone on the same page?'

Everyone indicated they were.

'Excellent!' Mad Dog was pleased. He broke into a little boxer-style dance, hopping on the spot, jabbing at the air.

'Now Stanford, me and you are going to take a wee trip to my house where I will make us a nice wee cup of tea and we can have a wee run through my play.'

Winks, it was safe to say, was no longer within his corporeal housing. He was somewhere far away in space and time. Somewhere safe and warm. With the finest soft furnishings.

His vacated body rose now and moved like the Undead to the door, where it stood awaiting fresh instructions. Mad Dog, meanwhile, had tucked his pistol into his waistband and was pulling his jacket on.

'You boys be good now, don't do anything silly,' he warned. 'I'm looking forward to your next magazine.'

With that, the man with the gun took the man from the

Arts Council by the elbow and guided him towards the stairs, tugging the splintered door to behind him.

★

After the others had gone, Oliver and I sat without speaking for a long time. The rain petered out and the sun began to break through the clouds, spilling light across one half of the room. Water from a gutter ticked on the windowsill. In the street a line of traffic had come to a halt, someone's radio up loud – muffled horns, Natalie Cole singing about a pink Cadillac. High overhead, a helicopter pinned to the sky over the Holy Land was droning like a dentist's drill. Quotidien sounds. Diurnal certainties.

'I keep wondering if there was something more we could have done,' I said at last.

Oliver sighed.

'I know what you mean.'

He leaned back in his chair and clasped his hands behind his head.

'I was thinking of having a go at one point,' he said. 'Tackling him. Getting the gun off him.'

'Were you? So was I. That time when he was taking his jacket off?'

'Yes, then. He was definitely off his guard. I think we could have had him.'

'I think you're right. Given the bastard a good hiding.'

Silence resumed as we each indulged fantasies of varying degrees of heroism and brutality.

'Did you see all those tattoos?' Oliver said.

'I certainly did.'

'Some of them were pretty sinister, don't you think – especially that one of Colonel Gaddafi? What's *that* about?'

'Gaddafi? No. No, that was . . . I'm pretty sure that was Elvis.'

'Really?'

'The quiff? The sideburns? Yeah. Definitely the King.'

Singing broke out in the office below, a ragged chorus of *Happy Birthday*.

'So do you think they're at Mad Dog's house yet?' Oliver asked.

'I'd say they're in his kennel right now. Having tea and a . . . run-through. Maybe some raw meat.'

'Poor Winksie. He didn't look too happy.'

'No, he didn't. Though, to be honest, he should have kept his mouth shut.'

'He *was* flapping his gums a bit. Still, it took the heat off us.'

Oliver had recovered sufficiently to make tea. Gush of tap. Click of on-switch.

The sense of movement in the vicinity suddenly made me realise how tired I felt. That was the problem with people like Mad Dog (but not the only one obviously): you were forced to burn energy at the same insane rate in order to withstand their orbital pull. It was very depleting. *Mad Dog* . . . I wondered how long ago he had become his *nom de guerre*, whether he could even remember without effort his given name or, indeed, if anyone still called him by it. His mother? Or had she become Ma Dog?

'You know Oliver, I really think we have to go to the police with this one.'

Something smashed in the sink. Oliver rocketed into view.

'*What*?' He stood there panting. Gorilla face. 'Are you nuts? You heard what Mad Dog said. What he'd do to us?'

'Yes but he can't do those things if he's in prison, can he?'

'In prison for what? An illegal firearm? That'd only get him a couple of years and then he'd be out and . . . Artie, he's not the forgiving type. The clue is in his name.'

'What about threatening behaviour? False imprisonment? Crimes against literature?'

Oliver shook his head.

'I just don't think it's a good idea to get the scuffers involved . . .' He tore open the packet of Choc Delightoes he was holding. 'Look, what's the worst can happen? A crap play gets produced? So what's new? It'll die a death after a few weeks and we'll all be on our merry way.'

I had to admit he had a point. All this would be extremely difficult to prove. Furthermore, it was an enormous risk for potentially very little. Our lives would be in danger – if not immediately, then later and we would have to live with that threat. And then there was Winks: would it be fair to put him in jeopardy? And wee

Barney? It would also, in all likelihood, sound absolutely ludicrous in court.

'There's another reason,' Oliver said quietly.

'And that is?'

'Sammy Niblock.'

Niblock. Of course. This was his patch.

'What about that cup of tea,' I said.

We gave ourselves over to the restorative powers of hot liquid, sugar and carbohydrate.

'Tell you what though.'

'What?'

'It was lucky Winksie was wearing his brown corduroys.'

'*What?*'

'Nothing.'

★

In the days following the Mad Dog incident, neither of us wanted to be in the office. The trauma was too present. Instead, we met up at The Greedy Pig, a café near the university specialising in bulk-feed for students. Officially these were editorial meetings but they doubled as mutual counselling sessions (Oliver was having a recurrent nightmare about an over-sized rabbit in a balaclava). They were also a chance for my co-editor to indulge in what he dismissed as 'temporary comfort eating' but was in fact the servicing of an appetite grossly over-stimulated by the forced intake of milk puddings. I began to suspect that if he didn't have that just-breast-fed feeling he couldn't relax. Luckily, one of The Greedy Pig's specialities was double D-cup Creamy Caramel Desserts.

We called Winks from a phone box to check his corpse wasn't sitting by the side of a laneway with a bag on its head. It was a short conversation: yes, he was back at his desk; no, he didn't want to talk about it; no, we shouldn't talk about it either. I asked him what Mad Dog's play was like but his answer was drowned out by a fault on the line, a high-pitched whinnying sound followed by gusts of static, then rapid beeping.

Eventually, Oliver and I decided we both needed a break – from the incident, from *Lyre*, from each other, from everything. Oliver, after fantasising about a number of exotic locations, finally faced reality and caught a bus to his parents' holiday caravan in Donegal. I'd gone there once with him and a couple of the lads for a weekend of carousing but the only pub for miles around had been closed for renovations and we'd spent the entire time staring out the window at varying velocities of rain. The highlight of the trip was when we saw something moving outside in the mist which we think might have been a goat.

Being similarly short of cash, I reconciled myself to a week or so of peace and quiet in my own flat (*for peace comes dropping slow*) catching up on some reading. Anyway, wasn't the odd spell of solitude supposed to be good for the soul? Or was that just spread around by people who didn't have any friends?

I resolved to be methodical about my reading programme and on day one went along my bookshelves identifying all the famous tomes I'd always meant to read but never quite got round to (had I really skipped *Tom Jones* and *Middlemarch*?); that I'd only skim-read (*To the Lighthouse, Moby-Dick*, and yes I admit it, *Ulysses*), and that I knew I'd have to open one day but really couldn't face (*Crime and Punishment, Pilgrim's Progress, Under the Volcano, Finnegans Wake*). I'd soon amassed a shamefully tall stack, which I sat and contemplated for a while, reflecting on that verse from Ecclesiastes about there being no end to the production of books and how too much study is *a weariness of the flesh.*

After a while I took up the Joyce and began at the beginning. Two guys arguing in a tower. (What in God's name was a Chrysostomos?) They eat breakfast and then this English lad Haines joins them and they dander down to the sea for a swim. Hardly spectacular but more fun for them than a weekend in Donegal. That was as far as I got. It was clear, for the second time around, that at my reading speed it would take at least a year to do justice to this. It struck me that most of my favourite works of literature – *The Great Gatsby, Heart of Darkness* and *The Outsider* among them – were relatively short and I wondered whether this was part of the reason. Books in general were too long. I skipped ahead to Molly's bit. Even that took half an hour. This was where poetry had the advantage: a highly concentrated hit straight into the vein and you were on your way. I listened to my tape of *Graceland* instead and by then it was lunchtime.

In the afternoon I started *Ulysses* afresh and managed

forty-odd pages before finally feeling woozy and succumbing to the ineluctable modality of a good snooze. When I woke up, I discovered that *A Country Practice* was on TV, followed by the weekly matinee which, as luck would have it, was the Hitchcock classic *Rear Window*, with Jimmy Stewart's wheelchair-bound photographer overdosing on voyeurism in his sweaty Greenwich Village apartment.

The following morning, I limbered up for the day's activity with some nostalgic light verse from my much-abused childhood copy of *The Golden Treasury of Poetry*: old favourites like *Jabberwocky*, *Father William* and *La Belle Dame Sans Merci*. By coffee time I'd flicked through (and discarded) two-thirds of the previous day's leaning tower of shame and assembled two new ones. I discovered I'd only read half of the books that had been integral to my degree course, and only half-read the rest. This was turning out to be a useful exercise. After lunch (beans on toast), I continued with *Ulysses*. God it was intense! Hallucinatory almost. The detail. The energy. The flow. The colours. *Paris rawly waking, crude sunlight on her lemon streets . . . Moist pith of farls . . . the froggreen wormwood . . . mouths yellowed with the pus of flan Breton . . . rolls gunpowder cigarettes through fingers smeared with printer's ink . . . sanguineflowered . . . Old hag with the yellow teeth . . . Green eyes . . . the blue fuse burns deadly . . . orangeblossoms . . . breeches of silk of whiterose ivory . . . a dryingline with two crucified shirts . . .* Pure poetry. Every page. Totally absorbed, I read until I realised the afternoon had gone and then feeling thoroughly

Bloomish strolled round to Kavanagh's for a pint and a plate of stew.

On the third day of my holiday, I ran into Mick the Artist (doing some light shoplifting in College Books) who informed me that Johnny Devine's hap – party was back on for Saturday night and that I should definitely get along because it was going to be 'far out'. He wanted to know when the next issue was due and whether we'd decided on the art content because he'd just completed a sequence of lithographs on the theme of industrial accidents that could look quite good. Not that Marty Pollocks's *Penis Parade* wouldn't also be outstanding. His main concern, though, seemed to be that we didn't succumb to the 'bourgeois bullshit' of Heather Turkington, who painted pictures of dogs and white-washed cottages in the Antrim Glens and was at least four times as successful as her rivals.

I bought an ingot of cheese and some just-baked wheaten farls and meandered through the Botanic Gardens in the direction of my flat. A warm breeze was sighing through the pines and redwoods (*Yet still the unresting castles thresh . . .*). College administrators and office workers, released for an hour, were strolling along the sun-stippled paths and sprawling on the grass to eat lunch. In the distance, a young barefooted couple floated a lime-green frisbee to each other. The Palm House came into view, its chambered curves and countless facets like a shimmering deepsea palace risen to the surface. People were moving around in its jungle-spiced interior, poleaxed by the breath-taking humidity, awed by the profusion of life: orchids, bromeliads, banana trees, the silent hullaballoo of leaves. A century ago, thousands of Victorians would have been flocking to behold this wonder of the age . . . I came to a standstill trying to picture the scene.

'Hello Artie.'

Rosie was sitting on the grass, nibbling a sandwich.

'Sorry, I didn't mean to interrupt your daydream,' she said.

She was wearing a soft blue cardigan over a pale green sundress and her face was lightly tanned. She looked beautiful.

'No, no. Just thinking about stuff. How are you?'

'Great. Do you want a bite?'

'Fine thanks.' I held up my paper bag.

I hunkered down beside her and we chatted. I learned that she was thinking of moving out of her flat ('it's very noisy', meaningful look, 'and there's that odd smell'), that she'd finished her final exams and that she'd started a placement, just for the summer, at an accountancy firm on University Road. She came to the Gardens to eat lunch most days, though not usually on her own.

'And how's the work going?' I asked.

She screwed up her face.

'It's a bit tedious, to be honest.'

'Isn't that a requirement of accountancy?'

'That's a popular misconception, accountancy is actually fascinating.'

'Really?'

'No, it's deadly dull. But mathematics is. The complex

mystery of numbers, that's what really interests me. In fact I'm thinking of going on to do postgrad.'

She must have detected some scepticism in my expression because she coloured slightly and her tone of voice tautened.

'Of course, artsy types like you think maths is for geeks – '

I attempted to protest.

'. . . You do. You think it's dry and self-referential, but do you know something? As far as I'm concerned it's a more convincing way for humans to explain the universe to themselves than . . . well, *literature.*'

Her eyes blazed.

'And it might just interest you to know,' she went on. 'That Einstein referred to maths as "the poetry of logical ideas". What do you think about that?'

I'd never thought about it that way before. In fact, I wasn't sure I'd thought about it at all.

Realising I was on the back foot, I reminded her how lack of numeracy had very recently reduced two grown magazine editors to tears and she laughed.

'How's your boyfriend?' I asked.

She swallowed a mouthful of sandwich, frowning.

'Boyfriend? Oh, my *boyfriend.* Oh, he's . . . well actually . . .' She paused, gave me a momentary, unreadable look. 'Actually, we broke up.'

On the grass in front of the Palm House one of the sunbathers switched on a boogie box and Aztec Camera's *Somewhere In My Heart* came bouncing out.

'Really? Oh, I'm sorry.'

'Don't be. It hadn't been going well for a while.'

Suppressing the urge to spring to my feet and attempt a triple salco with full twist, I put on my best we've-all-been-there expression and gazed soulfully into the middle distance – picture-book greens and blues – where some teenage Goths were shuffling around, baffled by the sunshine.

'Listen,' I said, after sufficient silence had elapsed. 'I was thinking, if you need cheering up some friends of mine are having a happening on Saturday night – if you're not doing anything else.'

'Nothing major, but . . . they're having a what?'

'A happening.'

'A *happening*?'

'Yeah, you know, a happening.'

She stared at me.

'Do you mean a party?'

'Yes.'

I could see doubt in her eyes. Mick and his bloody happenings.

'Well, I'm actually supposed to be going out with a friend . . .'

'Bring her. Him.'

'Her. I suppose I could . . .'

We were back on track . . .

'Should be a good party . . .'

'Well . . .'

Nearly there . . .

'Do you good to get out . . .'

'Well . . . Okay, you're right. Why not?'

Success.

We arranged to meet for a drink beforehand in Betje-man's.

★

Over lunch I listened to *I'm Sorry, I'm Cleverer Than You* on Radio 4, then pulled down *The Complete Poems* of Emily Dickinson (*For love is immortality*) and hit the sofa. Unfortunately, The Actor was in residence above and just as I opened the book he embarked on his dreaded vocal exercises – muffled but infuriatingly audible: 'Maaaaa . . . Mayyyyyy . . . Meeeeeee . . . Mowwww . . . Moooooo . . . Blue black bugs' blood . . . Blue black bugs' blood . . . Lovely lemon liniment . . . Lovely lemon liniment . . .' Every few minutes there would be a pause followed by a shouted 'HA!' from the depths of his diaphragm as though he were trying to expel a hair-ball, and then the declaiming would begin again. 'He thrusts his fists against the posts and still insists he sees the ghosts . . . Eleven benevolent elephants . . . Eleven . . .' Past experience told me this could go on for ages so I sauntered up the street to the office. In the fridge I located some usable milk and settled down with a cup of tea to triage the post. Without Oliver's expansive (and expanding) presence, I have to say, the place was oddly quiet.

I found myself replaying the events of that stormy Monday. Did it really happen? Did Mad Dog really walk in out of the rain and hijack three lives? There were few signs of it now, except for a chair facing the wrong way and some duct tape on the door, holding the lock on.

The roll of tape was lying on the floor and as I replaced it in one of the drawers on Oliver's side I noticed an unfamiliar black ledger. Curious, I hauled it out and riffled through. It contained miscellaneous jottings in Oliver's distinctive scrawl, many of the pages stained with tea or chocolate or both. It wasn't marked Private so I started reading.

Much of the first half was taken up by fake signature practice, complete with experimental dedications, for example: '*What ho! Pelly (P.G.) Wodehouse*', '*Keep kicking the pricks, Sam (Beckett)*', '*From one super woman to another, Shirley Conron*', (sic), '*From one super man to another, Geordie Shaw*', '*Hope the op goes well, best wishes, Mary Shelley*'. The quality was up and down but it was good to see he was taking our cottage industry seriously.

Further on he'd turned his attention to honing a slogan for the Sunnyland Farm Bunny prize (I wondered, not for the first time, what on earth rabbits had to do with dairy products) and this was where the real work began. 'Complete the following in no more than 20 words,' he had written at the top of the page. *The Sunnyland Farm Bunny would like to go round the world because* . . . And his first effort was: '*he wants to spread the word about his dairy treats*'. Presumably this was a butter reference. It wasn't bad, but by no stretch of the imagination was it a winner. Worryingly, he appeared to have stalled immediately because next he had scribbled: '*cheese milk cream udders pasteurise churn spread shake drink squirt breasts pudding teats icecream goodness'*.

The next six lines were all scratched out, then inspiration had returned: *'because it's always pouring at home'*. And again: *'because everyone should have icecream from a bunny when it's sunny'*. The line below had been crossed out, but read: *'he's full of the milk of human kindness'*. Hmm. There followed a further three pages of slashed, blacked-out and otherwise redacted text worthy of Laurence Sterne. Multiple indentations suggested frenzied stabbings with a biro. I wouldn't have been surprised at this point to come across an interlude of five thousand lines of calligraphically perfect, *'All work and no play makes Oliver a dull boy'*.

I skipped ahead to the last page that had writing on it. Here it became clear that frustration and self-pity had finally engulfed him. *'The Sunnyland Bunny would like to . . . because back at the farm the shite is past-your-eyes'*. Eh? And: *'Because he's a randy rabbit and he's run out of tail at home?'* Uh-oh. *'He wants everyone to try his cream?'*. Oh dear. Oliver, no. *'He wants to cream on foreigners'*. Oliver, for Godsake.

I went back to sorting the post. Another invoice from the printers, with a little note this time about it being the *third* request for payment. I wasn't sure I cared for their tone. The next envelope had American stamps on it and contained yet another broadside from a frustrated contributor griping that we hadn't responded to the poems he'd sent *fifteen* months ago. *Is this any way to run a* blah . . . What was this? Another demand. From the British

Library's deposit office insisting we send copies of previous issues. A reminder of our *legal obligation*. I lit a cigarette and sat back. It was true, everybody wanted their spoonful.

A clock somewhere was striking the hour. I switched on the radio. '. . . a sixty-year-old woman and a twenty-four-year-old man were killed on the Falls Road earlier today by an IRA bomb intended for a British army patrol . . .' I hoisted my feet onto the desk and practised blowing smoke rings. Through the skylight I could see where two jet vapour trails had intersected and were decaying in slow motion, and for a second I had the sensation it was me that was drifting sideways. The last item on the news was about a farmer who had rescued one of his sheep from a slurry pit and brought it back to life by giving it mouth-to-mouth resuscitation. 'I didn't think about it, I didn't have time,' he told the interviewer. 'I just grabbed her by the ears and did what I had to do.' Though evidently a man of few words he divined, correctly, his audience's need for a tagline and added that his wee sheep had 'had the heart of a lion'. Cut and print! Pure poetry. I stubbed out my smoke. Hope he remembered to clean his teeth. I wondered what it would be like to kiss a sheep. Quite nice probably. Soft lips.

PART TWO

Come live with me, and be my love, | And we will all the pleasures prove | That hills and valleys, dale and field, | And all the craggy mountains yield . . .

For some reason these couplets were drifting through my head as I walked, and I was thinking, he certainly promised a lot in that poem, old Marlowe's shepherd: *melodious birds, fragrant posies, pretty lambs, silver dishes, dancing swains,* and – what has to be the clincher – *fair lined slippers.* The question for the object of his affections I suppose was, *pro tanto quid retribuamus?* This was not a love poem (no wedding rings on the table) – it was a *lust* poem. And that got me thinking about love/lust poetry in general.

There were all the flowery ones, needless to say, and I'd used my fair share of Keats & Co. to advantage over the years but, increasingly, *succinct* was the way ahead for me. (It's what's left unsaid that breaks the heart.) Love, like happiness, it seems, is in sharpest focus when half-glimpsed – in margins and interstices – lending itself to the subordinate clause, the short lyric, the apercu. *On me your voice falls as they say love should, | Like an enormous yes.* Hard to beat that one (verging on zen archery). Who else? Shakespeare's sonnets? Rilke? Whitman? Gravesie, of course, lord of the love lyric: *Love is universal migraine, / A bright stain on the vision / Blotting out reason.* And the other symptoms? Leanness, jealousy, laggard dawns, omens and nightmares. All very familiar. *Could you endure such pain / At any hand but hers?* These are the questions.

And the sexy stuff . . . who were we talking about? That saucy one, *Come Slowly, Eden,* by Emily Dickinson with *the fainting bee / reaching late his flower . . .* How did it go? *Round her chamber hums / Counts his nectars – alights / And is lost in balms!* Oh Emily! And let's not forget Mr Cummings (you couldn't make it up) and his *i like my body when it is with your body.* Very hard to recall, old E.E. How does he put it? *i like kissing this and that of you* . . . blah, blah, something about *slowly stroking the shocking fuzz / of your electric fur . . .* Can't remember the next bit either, goes on about eyes being *big love-crumbs,* and then *the thrill / of under me you so quite new.* Phew. Warm today. I looked up. Trickles of smoke on the hillside. Gorse fires.

I was passing a delicatessen where racks of fruit and vegetables had been stacked on the pavement under a striped awning and sprayed with water. It was fresh and cool under there. Oxygen-rich. I paused to survey the produce, inhaling the earthy scents. I was thirsty so I bought a nectarine to eat on the way. Not counting a strawberry milkshake at Oliver's it was the first fruit I'd had in a fortnight.

Now, where was I? Ah yes, love poems. I briefly

wondered whether I was cynically trawling my archives for something that might be useful with Rosie at a later date, but discarded the notion. She *was* nice though, and the first woman I had found myself thinking about on waking for a long while – usually a reliable indicator.

I had reached the mouth of 'Loyalist Sandy Row' and as I passed across it I could see, further down, men up a ladder busy with decorations to mark the Twelfth of July. The street was already criss-crossed at lamp-post level with lines of red-white-and-blue bunting, looping like an outsized cat's cradle. Strings of dragons' teeth. In the distance, above a clutter of rooftops, a sloping patch of Black Mountain undulated behind a slight heat haze.

So, the Twelfth was nearly upon us once again. Somehow, it had slipped my mind but now I realised why the city seemed quiet: the annual middle-class migration, The Great Escape. In a few days the place would be teeming with banners, pennants and gaudy silks, and the air itself would be shuddering under the onslaught of the mighty Lambeg drum (at 120 decibels, they say, the loudest acoustic instrument on Earth). I remember as a child being taken by my spectacle-loving aunt one Twelfth to 'see the bands' and having to be delivered home early wrapped in a blanket because of the noise of those drums. Always a street away, always approaching . . . Moving through the city like . . . like what? . . . like the id monster in *Forbidden Planet*.

I could see the ladder men unfurling a banner: King Billy on his horse at the River Boyne, framed in dazzling orange. He wore a long black curly wig, a frilly shirt, and a tangerine tunic. His white steed, which appeared to be prancing on water, had a look of the nursery rhyme about it. I moved on towards Shaftesbury Square. Didn't Van Gogh consider orange to be the colour of madness? I traversed the Square and entered Dublin Road on course for the headquarters of the BBC, where, thanks to Stanford Winks, I was due on air within the hour.

In the office earlier in the week the phone had rung – a rare occurrence – making me jump. It was Winks, sounding slightly less feeble than he had the last time.

'Artie, here's the thing,' he said after thirty seconds of niceties. 'Radio Ulster have asked me to go on their arts programme to discuss Dylan Delaney's book but I'm really not feeling up to it. I said you'd take my place.'

'What?'

'It would be a personal favour to me.'

'But Stanford – '

'And I also think it would be an excellent opportunity to promote *Lyre*.'

'Yes, but . . .' To be honest, I wasn't exactly sure why I was resisting.

'And there's a fee of fifty pounds.'

'You're right,' I said. 'It'll be a good profile-raiser for the magazine.'

As he seemed to be in better form I asked him about Mad Dog's play.

'Artie,' he whispered. 'It's an abomination of the first kidney.'

'It's disappointing then?'

'What can I tell you? It's the work of an evil, irredeemably twisted mind.'

'That bad?'

'Artie, it has taken me a full week of twelve-hour days to translate it into recognisable English. My eyesight has been impaired.'

I gathered the play was entitled *Suspicious Minds* and that it told the story of a Belfast hard man tormented by the belief that his wife was helping the other side and even planning to change her religion.

At this point Winks faltered.

'. . . And?' I prompted.

'And so he kneecaps her.'

'What?' (I had a sudden headache.)

'Yes, but then it turns out she was innocent all along.'

I massaged my skull.

'What happens now?' I asked.

'I've handed it over to Tristan Quigley at Lagan and told him to get cracking.'

'Quigley? Whose raison d'etre is the transformation of metaphor into stage reality?'

'The same.'

'And what does he make of it?'

Winks sniffed.

'He absolutely adores it.'

Once at Broadcasting House I progressed through a series of high-security air locks, decompression chambers and lifts to the canteen on the seventh floor where I was handed a styrofoam cupful of coffee (it might have been oxtail soup) and informed that Monty Monteith, veteran presenter of *The Big Arts Show*, would be along presently. I took a seat and pulled out the notes I had jotted on the back of a takeaway menu. Around me, BBC staff, some of them familiar from television, tucked into late lunches or lingered over hot drinks. I tried to filter out their chatter so I could concentrate. Two men, both in leather jackets, stood at a nearby window looking down into the street. 'See that Beemer?' the older man was saying. 'The Troubles paid for that. Overtime. I wouldn't be driving that if there was peace.'

'I hear you,' his companion said. 'I'm thinking of – '

'Artie?'

A well-dressed woman in her mid-thirties with bobbed hair and expensive glasses was standing beside me.

'Yes?'

'I'm Sinead, Monty's producer.'

'Pleased to meet you.'

'Monty'll be with you in a minute, he's just finishing in make-up.'

'Right . . . Make-up? For radio?'

'He likes to look his best. Old school.' She shot me a smile that melted instantly into a look of engrained suffering. 'Are you set? Do you have everything you need?'

I assured her I had.

'Good, see you in Studio Three. Remember, just be yourself.' Sound advice.

I tried to decipher my notes. We were creeping towards show time and I was experiencing a flicker of nerves. Did I actually have anything to say? I'd rehearsed a few phrases but . . .

'Arthur, is it? Monty Monteith. Big Arts.'

Tall, with hair the colour of Guinness foam and attired (I kid you not) in a dinner suit, the great man extended a languorous hand.

'Call me Artie,' I said.

'Good man Artie.' He squeezed my knuckles until they cracked audibly.

He sat down, eased back and spread his knees wide. His face was huge, untroubled by self-doubt, ice-blue eyes accentuated by the burnt orange of his pancake make-up.

'Let me have it Artie.'

'I'm sorry?'

'What are we looking at here?'

'I'm not sure . . .'

'What's the bottom line?'

'I'm sorry Monty, in what sense?'

'The book, it's poetry right?'

'Oh. Yes. Yes, it's a book of poems.'

'So what's your opinion? What do you think?'

I took a deep breath.

'Well, I thought I'd start by saying something about the overall theme being – '

'Wait, what's the title?'

'What?'

'The title of the book.'

'It's called *Postcards From Here.*'

'Right. And it's by?'

'Dylan Delaney?' Was he serious? Surely he knew that much?

He nodded and paddled his hands in a circular motion, inviting me to go on.

'The overall theme being, I suppose – to reverse a famous line of Philip Larkin's – that something, like nothing, happens anywhere. That *place* – by which I mean wherever you happen to be at any one time – is in a sense less important than what happens in the head.'

Monteith suddenly looked very sleepy. I continued.

'And then I thought I'd say something about this being an ingenious, if at times ingenuous, debut. Some might even say *jejune* – ' I didn't really know what this word meant, but I was betting Monteith didn't either. '. . . and that I believe this to be a very convincing statement of intent, the emergence of a significant new voice and . . .'

Monteith's lids were closed. Was he asleep?

'I'm just resting my eyes. Please go on.'

'. . . And something like, you know, if Delaney can sustain this quality into the future then we'll have, um, a real contender on our hands.'

'What about the verses themselves?'

'Individual poems, you mean? I've a few in mind I thought I'd single out for comment, depending on how much time we have.' (I had to be careful here. Delaney's book contained a couple of eye-poppingly explicit pieces – specifically, *Down in Cherryvalley* and *Fundamental Love* – that I'd really rather we *didn't* discuss.)

'Plenty of time.'

'Well generally, they range from short romantic lyrics

such as *The Bad Ferret* to political pieces like *Barricade Your Mind* and longer meditations such as *Ballymena Dancing* that explore social and sexual taboos. Technically-speaking they often employ traditional forms – Popish heroic couplets, for example – to wrong-foot the reader's postmodern expectations.'

'Yes?'

'I also thought, again depending on time, that I'd briefly pick up on his exhilarating use of arcane language, which at times makes the verse read like something out of, I don't know . . . *Jabberwocky.*'

At this point Monteith's eyes flashed open and he stood up.

'Okay Artie, let's do it.'

Studio Three was as hot and airless as a killing jar, and the imitation leather of my chair honked beneath me at the slightest provocation. I was starting to get a bad feeling.

'Slip your headphones on there Artie,' Monteith advised. 'And not too close to the microphone, there's a good man.'

I could see Sinead sitting at a console on the other side of the glass beside an unshaven technician in a lumberjack shirt. She gave me the thumbs up. 'One minute,' her voice said through a speaker on the wall behind me. Monteith, who was studying the back page of the *Belfast Newsletter*, waved at her without looking up. A copy of Delaney's book lay untouched on his desk in front of him where Sinead had left it.

'Thirty seconds.'

Accelerated heartbeat.

'Ten seconds.'

Sub-atomic rush.

The red light was on.

'Good afternoon everyone and you're very welcome to The Big Arts Show,' purred Monteith. 'We have a real *smorgasbord* of cultural canapes for you today, from *fantastic* opera and *fabulous* writing to the first performance of an *exciting* new concerto for uilleann pipes and Lambeg drum so, without further ado, let's get started.'

From having been sonorous but perfectly normal outside the studio, Monteith's voice had dropped half an octave and become quadraphonic. His perfectly-modulated Ulster accent, combined with this creamy, cello-like timbre, was lulling and beguiling, the aural equivalent of being immersed in a bath of warm fudge.

'I have in the studio Artie Conville, co-editor of the distinguished literary magazine *Lyre*, who is with me to talk about *Postcards From Here*, a recent collection of poems – ' He pronounced it poy-ems. '. . . by one of our most promising young poets, Dylan Delaney. Artie, welcome to the programme.'

'Thank you Monty.'

'Artie, this is an ingenious, if at times ingenuous debut, a statement of intent and one some believe could mark the emergence of a significant new voice – ' Hold on, what was this? 'If Delaney were able to sustain this quality, would he, in your opinion, be a serious literary contender?'

I had a sense of falling through many fathoms of dead air. The red light was lasering my nearside retina. My shirt was damp. My leg twitched. The chair farted.

'Yes,' I said. 'Yes he would. Um . . . yeah. I think . . . definitely . . . um . . .' What the hell? What was Monty . . .? (I registered Sinead raising her head, regarding me through puckered lids.)

'Let's talk now about the overall theme of the book,' Monteith suggested. 'It strikes me that what Delaney's saying is – to flip that line of Larkin's around – that *something*, like nothing, happens anywhere. That *place* – by which I mean wherever you are at any one time – is in a way less important than where you are in your head. Does that sound about right?'

This was unbelievable. My mouth was suddenly incredibly dry. I swallowed hard and leaned towards the microphone. The leather parped.

'Yes, Monty,' I admitted. 'Um, yes, it does. I think you've hit it on the . . . er . . . yep, I think that sums it up very well.' There was a ringing in my ears as though someone had just pinged an empty wineglass with a fork. It wasn't feedback. (Sinead was giving me a lynx-eyed stare.)

'Let's move on now to the poet's use of arcane language,' Monteith oozed. 'In places the verse reads almost like *nonsense* poetry, like something out of . . . I don't know . . .' You bloody *do* know, you bastard. Go on, say it. '. . . *Jabberwocky*. It's really quite exhilarating, isn't it?'

I was badly in need of water. Why was there no water? My tongue felt like a Weetabix cake. I raised my arm to dab some sweat and my magic chair did itself proud. (I sensed urgent technical adjustments going on behind the glass.)

'Um, yes Monty,' I croaked. 'It is indeed. Er . . . exactly. As you say. Almost at times like, um, nonsense poetry, like, er, indeed, *Jabberwocky* . . . and um . . .' I felt like I was having a stroke but at least I was managing to say more words.

Then, a sidewinder.

'Some might consider this *jejune* – do you?'

This was it. I was definitely having a stroke. I tried to lick my velcro lips. Monteith was reading the newspaper again. I shifted on my whoopee cushion.

'Well, er, to be honest, um, I'm not sure it's helpful to, um, apply words like jejune to work that is so, er, obviously . . . I mean, um, that has yet to . . . um, in the scheme of things . . . to, er, establish exactly what it . . . er, wants to say and of course, um, by extension . . . how to say it?' My surprise at having reached the end of the sentence caused me to finish on a high-pitched, querulous note.

Monteith breezed on.

'We've been talking very generally so far but I'd like to move, if I may, to the poy-ems themselves . . .' He had *Postcards* in his hand. 'Which range, of course, from romantic lyrics to political pieces, to longer meditations on sexual taboos . . . but there's one I'm looking at right now, entitled – '

An icy tongue tickled the back of my neck. Please no. Don't let it be *Down in Cherryvalley* . . . or worse . . .

104

'. . . *Fundamental Love*, in which the poet talks about *forbidden fruit being the sweetest*, and having beseeched his lady friend to make their love *a tighter fit*, he ends: *Bear with me, we'll get to the bottom of it* . . . Artie, could you take us through this?'

So it *could* be worse. As far as I could see, my choice was this: either I could explain to the God-fearing people of Northern Ireland exactly what the poem was about and secure my future as a leper-hermit on a rock in the Atlantic, or I could waffle. As I mumbled my way around (and under and above) Delaney's most aberrant work I kept catching glimpses of Sinead's red-hot eyes and realised, too late, that I should have asked for cash upfront.

'Now, technically, of course,' Monteith began again. (Please make it stop.) 'The poet often wrong-foots the reader's postmodern expectations by his use of traditional forms. For example he's fond of Popish heroic couplets – isn't this a bit risky? Isn't there a danger he could alienate one half of the community?'

After what seemed like another three hours, during which Monteith cornered me in several more linguistic cul-de-sacs and left me to die in an abandoned ideological mine shaft, we reached the end.

'So there we have it,' he crooned. 'A fascinating collection from a highly promising young poet. Now before we move on to our next item, it just remains for me to thank my guest, *Lyre* editor Artie Conville. Artie, I think it's only fair to give you the final say. Off you go Artie, the last word, then, on Dylan Delaney.'

The last word? THE LAST WORD? You stole all the words, you bastard! YOU ABSOLUTE –

'Yeah, thanks Monty, I um . . . I er . . .' Hold it back, hold it back. 'I . . . er . . . I . . .' All the supercharged, greasy-sweat fury was bubbling up. 'I er . . . I . . . um . . .' Don't let go. It's nearly over. Where were the words?

'Erm, yes, it's . . . er, well . . . His real name's Keith.'

★

The city's social circles were small and overlapping and I next ran into Delaney on Saturday night. He was in the midst of a train of young ladies dancing out of Johnny Devine's place as I was going in. He spotted me immediately. 'Jejune?' he cried as we drew parallel, and again, hoarsely over his shoulder: '*Jejune?*' I was grinning and shrugging and then I was swallowed by the house. He didn't come after me. He had looked a bit peevish but, to be honest, I didn't feel too bad about it. While I had to concede that my performance earlier in the week probably wouldn't make it into any end-of-year best-of radio compilations, I thought that, overall, *Postcards* had received a pretty good review, albeit through unwitting ventriloquy. In fact, it was possible we'd made it sound slightly better than it was.

Devine lived in a large, three-storey Victorian redbrick that stood alone, detached from the rest of its terrace several years previously by a fire that had destroyed the three houses adjacent. Its isolation was a happy circumstance for all concerned as he lived with five other artists, all male, all of them committed to feverish self-expression. In theory, this was supposed to result in a powerhouse of artistic endeavour earthed by a salon of intellectuals constantly discussing the future of human creativity; in practice it meant a lot of drinking and talking bollocks. Drugs were a staple of the house regimen, as signalled by William Blake's famous quotation about *the doors of perception*, inscribed in fluorescent letters on the lintel above the foot of the stairs. (*For man has closed himself up, till he sees all things through narrow chinks of his cavern.*)

Most days would find at least two of the residents semi-deranged on ill-advised combinations of banned substances as the commune drank, smoked, popped and snorted its way towards a vision of the infinite. To be fair though, artistic experimentation was much in evidence: on the obvious spaces, of course – floors, walls and ceilings – but also on more unlikely surfaces such as the television screen, on which had been painted a convincing approximation of Munch's *The Scream*, and the lavatory bowl in the first-floor bathroom which had been transformed with ceramic pigments and cunning use of perspective into the ravenously open mouth of Margaret Thatcher. The 'happening', as advertised by Mick the Artist, was simply the final drive by the housemates to fill any unused 'canvas' with their genius, and to this end they were busy perpetrating 'live art' throughout the building.

It was already past pub closing time when I arrived with Rosie and her friend (a pleasant but withdrawn pharmacist who was drinking a lot without showing it and whose name I didn't catch because she mumbled). Several genres of music were pulsing through the foundations, most immediately Prince's *U Got The Look* from the first doorway we passed. Inside the room what seemed like two or three hundred people were dancing, their movements accelerated to insane speed every few seconds by bursts of stroboscopic light. We pushed on towards the kitchen. In the next chamber, The Pogues' *If I Should Fall From Grace With God* was careering out of the sound system and a number of amorous refugees from the Prince room were arrayed around the furniture.

Once through to the back of the house I managed to fish some bottles of beer out of a bathtub full of ice and the three of us huddled at the side of the fridge. Despite the presence of Mumbles I was making good progress with Rosie, who seemed delighted to be out for the evening and had so far appeared to find most of my jokes amusing.

After Betjeman's we had moved on to a packed Kavanagh's where a folk-rock band called Puckoon performed right beside us, forcing Rosie and I to put our lips almost directly to each other's ears to make ourselves heard. During this strangely erotic parody of kissing I contrived to brush my mouth against the side of hers several times and to bury my nose repeatedly in her hair, which smelled of coconut oil and tobacco. (*Quand je mordille tes cheveux élastiques et rebelles, il me semble que je mange des souvenirs.*) The ease I felt in her company encouraged me to believe that real kissing was only a matter of time.

The kitchen, free of a music source, was fully abuzz with urgent, inebriated chatter, and skeins of smoke were making the air seem three-dimensional. We were discussing with some other guests the merits of *Magnum, P.I.* over *Remington Steele* and arguing about whether there was actually a TV detective called *The Liquidiser* when we were interrupted by one of the artists thrusting his head in through the open window above the sink. His hair had been soaped up into cockatrice-style spikes and he was wearing eye liner. He regarded the assembled drinkers as though he had just discovered us under a rock. We, in turn, stared back at him.

'I am The Walrus,' he announced, and at that moment I knew it was going to be a long night.

'I'm going to see if I can find any food,' I informed the girls. (Counter-intuitively, the kitchen had failed to yield anything edible; not even the fridge, whose contents, while almost certainly organic, were not immediately identifiable as being of earthly origin.)

'Bring some back,' Rosie commanded.

The next floor was just as thickly populated, with most of the landing taken up by party-goers waiting in line to defile the prime minister. I opened a door to a bedroom and shut it again instantly, startled by a volley of angry shouts from low down in the darkness. In the next room, a large group of people were slumped on sofas or sitting around cross-legged while slow-moving, fantastically coloured shapes were projected around the walls and ceiling to the sounds of Brian Eno's *Apollo*. No sign of snacks.

As access to the largest room, the one I felt held the most promise comestible-wise, was temporarily blocked by two artists crashing a set of stepladders through the doorway, I progressed to the next level. Here, the atmosphere was altogether more rarefied; quieter, less frenetic, fewer people. The artwork, however, was more obsessively executed than down below, the entire stairwell being covered in swirling tempera, mixing Renaissance-style scenes of hellish torment and spiritual ecstasy with portraits of popstars and politicians, interweaving depictions of nymph-draped idylls with friezes of bombed-out cities and their scurrying, blighted citizens. It was impressive, if only in terms of the time and labour that had gone into it, but I couldn't see Sanderson adding it to their wallpaper range any time soon.

The first door I tried revealed a bathroom, complete with a bath-full of rubber snakes; the second a tiny room occupied, more or less entirely, by a double bed in which a lavender-haired lady of advanced years was sitting up with the covers drawn about her, sipping something from a white mug. Curiosity got the better of me.

'Who are you?' I enquired.

'I'm the landlady,' she replied. 'Who are you?'

I moved on.

A sign over the architrave at the entrance to the master bedroom warned visitors to *Abandon all hope* . . . This, I guessed, was Devine's room. As I turned to make my descent the door opened and Mick the Artist appeared, wearing a horrid fawn kaftan.

'Conville, you made it,' he said, clutching at my sleeve. 'Good man. Come and say hello to Johnny.'

The room, which ran the full width of the house, was illuminated by a dozen candles and a large lava lamp, the impression of smoky gloom intensified by light-absorbing tapestries and dark daubings on most of the walls. Human figures were sprawled around in various stages of toxicity. The opening chords of a Talking Heads' song I recognised as *Psycho Killer* were emanating from a speaker somewhere. Marty Pollocks was lying under a rug on a chaise longue beside the window, staring stark-eyed at the ceiling. 'My life in front of me . . . My life in front of me . . .' he moaned as I passed.

Devine, dark, muscular, naked except for a pair of crimson Speedos, was propped against a leather beanbag beside the fireplace, presiding over a water pipe of alarming size and complexity. Two companions lay unconscious on the floor nearby.

'Johnny, Conville's here to say hello,' Mick told him.

'Who?'

'Conville? From *Lyre*?'

Aromatic fumes drifted from his ears.

'My *lawyer's* here to see me?'

'No Johnny. Look, it's Artie. From the literature magazine. You remember.'

He looked up. All the circuits in his eyes had blown. He resembled a spent bloodhound being roused for a final push down the trail.

'Hi Johnny.' I held my open hand up and kept it there until I thought I detected a pulse of recognition. He patted the air in front of him, inviting me to sit.

'Dawamesk?'

'Pardon?'

He proffered one of the hookah's tentacles.

'I'm fine thanks, I – '

He wagged the mouthpiece at me.

'Well, okay, but I'm trying to . . .' The smoke went down more smoothly than expected. I exhaled without coughing. Mick receded.

'Dawamesk?' Johnny repeated.

'Pardon?'

He gestured to a tray of what looked like Turkish Delight beside him, small, sugar-dusted cubes of some kind of paste in varying hues of coffee and caramel. I took one. It was sweet and almondy, with the texture of gritty fudge. I put a few in my pocket for later.

Devine cleared his throat as though about to speak, and then didn't. I waited. He seemed quite comfortable for us to sit without talking. Fair enough. I listened to the ambient hum of the room: mumble of voices, clink of glass, grumble of bass guitar. The remains of a fire ticked and sighed in the grate. My eyelids felt slightly swollen.

He held out the smoke-tube again and the pipe made its subterranean bubbling sound. He shifted on his haunches so he was facing me square-on. He had, I noticed, surprisingly hairy legs, given the smoothness of his upper body.

'So you're a lawyer.'

Christ, he was out of it.

'Far from it. I edit a poetry magazine,' I enunciated. 'We had some of your pictures in our last issue.'

Devine was nodding his head and smiling.

'Poetry magazine.' The concept was amusing to him. I watched for a while as his skull attempted to untangle a myriad of thought processes. To stave off boredom I had another go on the pipe and this time a mischievous genie entered my body and began in business-like fashion to tinker with my fine tuning. (What did Baudelaire say? *Wine exalts the will; hashish annihilates it.*)

'How is poetry?' he asked at last.

Right. Yep. You said it Johnny boy. How *was* poetry? Picture of health? A bit peaky? On life support? I suddenly had no idea whatsoever. Why don't we try *why* was poetry?

'It's a bit slow at the moment, Johnny. To be honest. The good stuff anyway.'

Was it just my imagination or was Devine wearing a wig? His hair seemed to be moving. In fact, was it moving to the beat? Surely the smoke wasn't *that* strong?

'Make it faster.' He touched his hair and it appeared to stop.

'Pardon?'

He massaged his jaw.

'Seize the carp.'

'Right. Yes.' A fishing metaphor. Excellent . . .

Devine was definitely off his head. And then it occurred to me: *hang on, maybe he's right.* Is he saying that I, *me*, have got to get into the river? Myself? I think he is.

He's saying I've got to get my waders on and get off this dry bank and into the water. And get wet. Get the fish myself. (I registered another change of background music. Jazz. Horace Silver.) That's what he means! Why am I sorting other people's fish? I could pluck my own from the flux. (*Somewhere a god waits, rod in hand, to add you to their number* . . .) Carp, perch, trout, salmon. The Salmon of Knowledge. (One taste and the scales fall from your eyes?) Why be confined to the river though? Why not push beyond fresh water . . . out into the salty . . . open sea. *By a high star our course is set* . . .

I had a sudden vision of zig-zagging clouds of silver fish seen from below, a sky of aquamarine light above them, a fat, writhing net hauled from the seething swell onto a drenched deck. A memory came back to me of fishing with my grandfather in a rowing boat, with hooks and twine and a toy bucket, looking back at the blurred blue, pink and yellow watermarks of a northern seaside town in the rain. How the herrings, when they came aboard, went frantic trying to swim in air. The smell of brine and seaweed. The gull's cry, piercing the years. *By a high star* . . . Starfish. Sea stars. Asteroidea . . . Pisces. (My birth sign.) Twin fish. The heavenly twins. The constellation of Gemini, Castor and Pollux (protectors of shipwrecked sailors) its brightest stars. The whitefish pollock. ('My life in front of me,' Pollocks lowed at that moment from back down the room, as though from the depths of a dream.) He's saying 'take control'. He's right. He's saying . . . Actually, what *was* he saying?

'I want my money.'

114

'You what?'

'Pay. You pay. Me.'

Bugger. He'd remembered.

'No problem Johnny. S'in the post, should be here any day.'

'Pay.'

'What . . . *now*?' I made perfunctory pocket patting motions. 'I'm afraid I . . .'

The subject of cash was making me nervous and Devine was beginning to look menacing.

'Now. Very now.'

'Johnny, there are no shops open, why don't I drop it round next – '

'You want me to call my lawyer?'

Call his lawyer? Devine had a *lawyer*? This was confusing.

'But Johnny,' I parried. '*I'm* your lawyer.' (I was pretty sure I wasn't, but then again, I couldn't think of any immediate reason why I shouldn't be.)

This stopped him in his tracks.

He gazed wonderingly at me while he nibbled a cube of drug-fudge. He was all at sea. I adopted a lawyerly expression, a challenging mixture of fond avuncularity and cold self-assurance. It succeeded. Whichever islet of reality he was trying to reach, he wasn't going to make it.

'Well, okay then,' he said finally. 'You take care of it.'

'Leave it with me,' I assured him.

I *would* take care of it. I would carry out my jurisprudent duty. Unleash the power of the law. Its pound-per-square-inch force. I would make me pay.

115

'We work in the dark,' Devine said abruptly, his chin jerking upwards.

We were off again. Who? Who worked in the dark? The artists? It *was* pretty dark in here.

I nodded sympathetically.

'Yeah,' he continued. 'We do what we can.' His eyes were actually spiralling, like that snake in the film of *The Jungle Book*.

'Right.' Do what you can for who? Was someone dying? The old lady?

He muttered something I couldn't make out. Something about passion? Or *fishing*?

'What was that Johnny?'

'The rest,' he said, leaning forward to reignite the blackened lumps of space rock in his pipebowl. 'Is – ' His angular, unlined features were lit up by match flare. 'The madness . . . of art . . .'

He slumped back against his beanbag, exhaling as he did so, the longest plume of smoke I had ever seen emerge from a human being.

I guessed that was about it from Johnny. The final turn of the screw. I climbed to my feet (a surprising distance).

'Listen, I'll catch you later, yeah? Thanks for . . . everything,' I said, and began picking my way among the casualties. I looked back. In the half-light Devine had fused with his gorgon-haired water pipe.

'I want my money,' he croaked.

Back in the kitchen, Rosie and Mumbles were watching The Walrus paint vertical rivulets of blood on the fridge. I found my beer and joined them.

'We thought we'd lost you,' Rosie said, with a hint of hostility.

I refreshed the inside of my mouth.

'Sorry, I got . . . waylaid.'

'Lucky for some. Nothing to eat then?'

'No, it's all been scoffed.' (Actually, I'd been concentrating so hard on not tripping over bodies on the way down the stairs I'd forgotten to check the last room.) I put my hand in my pocket.

'I did find these, but . . .'

Before I could finish, Mumbles had snatched two cubes from my hand and was chewing vigorously.

'What are they?' Rosie asked, peering at them.

'Dunno, some sort of Turkish Delight, I think.'

Mumbles mumbled something that sounded like 'cinnamon'.

'Looking at the state of your eyes, I think I'll give it a miss,' Rosie said.

'My eyes? What's wrong with my eyes?' I felt a quickening of paranoia.

'They're very . . . pink.' She was examining my face at close quarters.

I tried to assemble a sentence: something I'd once read about how in some Middle Eastern cultures bloodshot eyes were considered attractive, a signal of desire.

'. . . And they're all weird – they're like that snake's in . . . what's it called . . . *The Jungle Book*.'

Great.

'Anyway,' she said, draining her drink. 'I think I'm going to go. I'm playing squash in the morning.'

She consulted with her mate, who opted to stay.

'I'll walk you home,' I offered.

'You're fine. I'm just going to jump in a taxi.'

'I'll see you out.'

I handed the remaining cubes to Mumbles.

Outside, there was a smell of burning wood and rubber in the air and the sound of several varieties of siren moving in different directions through the city.

'Eleventh Night bonfires going up early?' I said, sniffing.

'Could be,' Rosie agreed. 'Keep the firemen busy.'

We stood in silence, side by side, near the edge of the pavement. My ears were receiving a torrent of night noises, and along with the smoke, I was getting the sweetness of lime trees, street dust, the hops on Rosie's breath.

'Are you escaping for the Twelfth?' she asked.

'Yeah, thought I'd go down to my folks'. What about you?'

'No, I'm stuck in town. We've got a big audit coming up and most of the partners have buggered off on holiday.'

'That's horrible. Are you around tomorrow?'

'Yes. In the afternoon.'

'Can I give you a ring?'

'Okay.'

We angled towards each other. My head was blocking the light from the streetlamp, putting her face in shadow.

Her eyes were a glycerine shimmer. Okay, was this it? Was this the real kiss? It could be. Let's see. I reached out and grasped her arm, gently, near the elbow and drew her fractionally towards me. Easy does it. Was I trembling? A bit. No, actually, more . . . my whole body was pulsating.

'Look, a taxi!'

She leaned sideways and gave a high wave. Much to my annoyance the cab was for hire. Then I wondered why I didn't just go with her. Why hadn't I thought of that? Or had I? On the other hand, if she'd wanted me to go with her, wouldn't she have said so? Maybe she had. But not in so many words. No, she definitely hadn't indicated clearly. In fact, if anything, she'd seemed pissed off that I'd been gone so long (only seemed like ten minutes to me). That was a good sign though, right? That she'd missed me? Or did she just think I was rude? (What on earth had I smoked? It kept coming and going like . . .) My jacket! I couldn't go with her anyway, I'd left my jacket somewhere in the house –

The taxi was shuddering beside us, its engine rattling like a bebop rhythm section.

– Forget the jacket. What's a jacket compared to . . . It was my best one though: buckskin at peak age and texture. Worth going back for. Or was it –

Rosie opened the car door then swung back to me. Taking my face in both hands she kissed me emphatically on the mouth.

'Thanks for a great night.'

I watched the cab disappear, savouring a sense of mild exultation, then turned towards the house which, I now saw, was in a state of advanced decay. The garden, enclosed by railings and a makeshift metal partition at the fire-damaged side, was overgrown with ancient, musky shrubs and sweaty creepers. A heavy tangle of ivy had dragged one of the drainpipes away from the wall revealing wet, crumbling brickwork. The interior though, was alive, the windows aglow, the pounding music like a monstrous heartbeat. Behind the blinds, silhouettes were flickering back and forth as though a series of shadow plays were in a race to the finish. On the top floor the panes were blacked out. Heavy drapes. Heavy funk.

I re-entered the Dome.

In the dance room numbers had thinned, but an electrical storm of lights and technopop raged on. Bomb the Bass. The high volume and the rapidity of the beat hit me physically as I passed, like a strong cross-wind, triggering a tingle of panic. (This in turn led to a quick surge of drug-induced anxiety, reminding me again of my long-held personal reservation about marijuana – namely, in what possible world was a fifty-fifty alloy of lust and paranoia helpful?)

I eased my way back to the kitchen, which was packed tight with red-faced dancers trying to rehydrate themselves with the remaining beer. There was no sign of Mumbles. Or my jacket, which I'd carefully hidden underneath several others on the back of a chair. The chair was bare. The Walrus was just putting a touch of light on the last globule of *Blood Fridge*.

'Looks like something out of *The Shining*,' I remarked.

He finished up and stepped back, cocking his head, to admire his work.

He glanced at me and then back at the fridge.

'Heeeeere's Johnny!' he said, in a passable imitation of Jack Nicholson.

'That's the one,' I said.

He looked at me again.

'No, I mean, here's Johnny.' He indicated with his chin a spot just behind my right shoulder.

I turned. Devine's face, a third of it obscured by mirrored sunglasses, was very close.

'Need beer,' he said.

He was still sporting the crimson Speedos but he'd raffishly teamed them with a pair of plastic sex boots, complete with studs, and . . . my jacket.

'Nice blood,' he told The Walrus.

'Thanks Johnny,' The Walrus said, seeming pleased. 'Should be a brew left in the bath.'

Devine returned from the bathroom clutching a dripping green bottle.

'I know you,' he said as he strode past me in the direction of the stairs. It was a dream-like comment made more to himself than to me and he didn't stop.

I wondered why I hadn't said anything about the jacket. The sunglasses, probably. Why were they so intimidating? An image of 'the man with no eyes' from *Cool Hand Luke* flashed in my brainpan.

With some weariness I climbed the stairs. In the projection room, Bob Marley had replaced Eno, and the giant amoebae had given way to reefs, atolls and bleached tropical islands. The big room I'd omitted to investigate earlier, meanwhile, was the setting for a surprisingly civilised scenario. The stepladder was near the door with one of the artists perched on top of it, painting a winged *putto* on the ceiling. Further down, on sofas and armchairs, a dozen or more people were ranged in a loose conversational archipelago. Among them was Mick the Artist, who beckoned to me.

'I thought you'd gone,' he said, patting the chair beside him.

'Yes. No. Kind of. Came back for my jacket,' I replied. 'Problem is, I just saw Johnny wearing it. Do you know where he is?'

'Johnny? No. He had it on did he?' He sucked his teeth. 'I'd forget about it if I were you. To be honest Johnny doesn't really have a lot of respect for that whole property . . . ownership thing.'

'Yeah? Well I want my fucken jacket.'

Mick had changed out of his kaftan and into jeans and a white tee-shirt and wore a chequered keffiyeh round his neck. He was holding a bag of dry-roasted peanuts which he offered me. I was starving. The bag weighed nothing. I tipped it into my palm and a tangle of pale, nodule-headed stalks tumbled out. Foiled again. I looked at Mick.

'Liberty Caps,' he said with a wink, plucking a loose one from my hand and popping it into his mouth.

'No kidding.'

I chewed one. It was no white truffle.

There was some tranquil music playing, an unidentifiable instrument undulating endlessly through a repetitive sequence.

'Can I ask you something?' Mick said.

'Shoot.'

'You like poetry, right?'

Uh-oh. Surely . . . Had Mick turned his hand to poetry?

'I mean,' he continued. 'It would help, wouldn't it, given what you do?'

'Well, yes.'

Did I like poetry? Was *like* in fact the right word, implying as it did some kind of choice? I *loved* poetry, certainly, but even that was by the bye. Perhaps it was more accurate to say I *needed* it. I was addicted to it. Even that, though, wasn't quite right: it was like saying I was addicted to breathing, or to language. It didn't make sense to say it. It was already in me. And yet it was perfectly clear that poetry was a minority interest, prompting glazed stares, distaste and even outright hostility from most of the general populace, so it wasn't a given – something else was at work. What was it exactly that poetry had? What was its fascination for people like me? Was it innate? Was it a virus? What was poetry for? Or was that like asking what are days for?

'What's the point of it?' asked Mick.

'How do you mean?'

He was eating his way steadily through the dried mushrooms. (So he did like *some* foods.)

'I mean . . . it doesn't really do anything, does it?'

'How do you mean?'

'It doesn't change anything, does it? It makes nothing happen.'

'I think you'll find someone's beaten you to it with that one.'

'What?'

'Nothing. What about art for art's sake?'

'That's just a bourgeois fucken cop-out,' Mick snapped. He prised a fragment of fungus from between his teeth. 'You know, it seems to me that none of your lot are grabbing the bull by the balls. You're just not living in the here and now.'

'My lot?'

'Yeah. The poetry people.'

'And the art people are?'

'We're a bit more political, yes.'

'So art has a duty to be political?'

'Everything we do is political.'

Something many-toothed, elaborate, stirred briefly in the labyrinth.

'Tell me, which Irish poets do you rate?' Mick said.

'Do you mean from the island of Ireland?'

'Yes.'

I gave him my top five and he nodded.

'What about Irish-language poets?'

I said I'd read some very good translations.

'You don't have Irish then?'

'No.'

He scraped at some dried red pigment on his thumbnail, then seemed to have a thought and began rummaging in his pocket.

What now?

He pulled out a large, crumpled sheet that had been folded tightly and, opening it up, handed it to me.

'D'yever read that one?'

It was a photocopy of Paul Muldoon's hallucinatory meditation *Gathering Mushrooms*.

'Of course. Interesting poem.'

'What do you think of what the horse's head says in the last verse?'

I skimmed the poem, or at least tried to; I was having trouble with the words, or rather with the patterns they were forming. Having read it with relative ease several times in the past it suddenly seemed incredibly dense and rich, with a dizzying backhand slice at work in the rhyme scheme . . . and *precise* (so that's how you pick a mushroom – *the nick against his right thumb* . . .). No sweeping generalisations here. *The wood-pigeon's concerto for oboe and strings / allegro, blowing your mind* . . . I gave up trying to read it – relying on my memory of what it was about – and skipped to the end where the narrator's head has grown into the head of a horse that shakes its mane and speaks this verse:

If we never live to see the day we leap
into our true domain,
lie down with us now and wrap
yourself in the soiled grey blanket of Irish rain
that will, one day, bleach itself white.
Lie down with us and wait.

Mick had rolled himself a cigarette, which he now lit. 'Well, what do you think?'

'About what?'

I had become distracted. Devine had appeared at the other end of the room, deep in slow-motion, mutually unintelligible conversation with Mumbles, whose eyes told me all I needed to know (*weave a circle round her thrice*). Devine, looking supremely comfortable in my best buckskin, was stroking Mumbles' upper arm. The situation appeared terminal.

'About what the horse's head says.'

'I'm not sure I'm with you Mick . . .'

Devine had removed his sunglasses and was moving in for the kill, hypnotising Mumbles with his luminous eyeballs.

'What it says about *waiting*,' growled Mick, his bony face drawing impatiently on the roll-up. 'Lying down and waiting. Do you agree with it?'

'Um . . .'

Several things became clear at this point: I realised (but not in so many words) that I had never consciously agreed or disagreed with what the horse's head said, having been more occupied with calculating the direction and velocity of the irony I was sure had been applied to its speech; I divined exactly where Mick's line of questioning was taking us – and that it was somewhere I didn't want to go – and I also understood, with sudden and chilling certainty, that Mick definitely did *not* agree with the nag and was, in fact, not lying down or, indeed, waiting. He was *making something happen*.

Devine and Mumbles were leaving the room. I began

hauling myself out of my chair, an effort that felt like I was consciously defying gravity.

'Where the fuck are *you* going?' screeched Mick.

'Back in a minute.'

When I reached the landing, they had disappeared. They weren't in the projection room. The bathroom was empty. He must have taken her up to his nest. I proceeded up the stairs. *Abandon all hope* . . . Poor Mumbles. But as I approached the master bedroom, my attention was diverted by noises from the chamber next to the landlady's. I turned the handle and was just in time to see Devine, in Speedos only, and Mumbles, in white towelling pants, stepping inside a huge mahogany wardrobe. My jacket lay discarded on the floor.

I seized it and fled.

*

It was with a mingled sense of resentment and relief that I caught the 9:15 out of town on Tuesday morning, the Twelfth. The city, as I made my way to the train station, was deserted, the shops shuttered, the gutters rustling with chip wrappers and lager cans from the previous night's festivities. The drums were already stirring, practice flurries echoing far off: the monster clearing its throat. A terrible vengeance, a furious purification, I surmised with a grim smile, would soon be visited on several thousand hangovers.

I pictured the marchers strutting in formation, the elders, sober and well-rested in their *Clockwork Orange* garb; the younger ones in shirtsleeves, with shattered eyes and roiling innards. The noise. The heat. The weight of the banner. Hands sweaty on the pole. And much distance ahead. (Street miles too, not springy grass; hard on the feet.) Regretting that antepenultimate pint now, no doubt, and that fry-up – surely that wasn't a good idea? Sunlight bouncing off that double yolker; death pallor of bacon; greasy gristle-pap. Breaking ranks, *here, hold this*, just have to . . . *boak* in this litter-bin. Boak it all up. Christ, top of the head coming off. Whoa! Second wave. And again. What the hell was *that*? Don't look. There, feeling better now. Feeling the beat in the bones. The power in the blood. Un-fucken-stoppable. It's true what they say: the sun always shines on the righteous.

The train was almost full – a mixture of day-tripping parade fans and last-minute refugees – but I managed, with an unseemly scurry, to secure a window seat. I pulled a copy of Rilke out of my rucksack and laid it on the communal table. The purple-cheeked, hairy-eared pensioner opposite peered at the book and then at me with suspicion and looked away. Further up the carriage, a group of high-spirited women, dressed to the nines and hellbent on fun, began uncorking bottles of something fizzy and pouring it into plastic cups. The day, which had started off cool, was heating up. Someone opened a window.

We set off, pulling away from the centre and heading north-east towards the shore of Belfast Lough. I tried to read but I had too much to think about and gazed out as the train dragged itself through the remnants of the city's industrial past: the red-brick acreage of the Sirocco engineering works, the once-mighty ropeworks, the shipyard's mustard-yellow cranes, the port from which vast fields of white linen had been spread across the world. *Linenopolis* . . . Brought low by cheap cotton. Samson and Goliath: emblems of hope and might, immense steel sinews made sclerotic by the rush to the skyways. Titans of a golden age. We moved on past neat municipal parks (carved out for exhausted shipyard workers) with their bowling greens and beds of stupefying wallflowers, towards the mudflats and marshland of the inner lough.

I kept detecting an unreality to the landscape (everything was too bright, the colours too primary) that I blamed on the residue of Saturday night's substances. Certainly, a deep, phantasmagorical sleep had not prevented their effects setting the agenda for Sunday, a day that had kicked off with a panic-stricken retrospective of recent events and ended with something similar, neither survey leaving me any the wiser. Monday had been spent entirely in bed.

On Sunday morning I had grounded myself temporarily with coffee and several handfuls of cigarettes and then, to escape the eerie silence of my flat, gone for a turn around the Gardens which, apart from a man teaching a child how to walk, were devoid of human life. On the way back, for something to do, I diverted to the office where a small cache of letters was waiting on the carpet, most prominently an envelope bearing the Arts Council logo. It was a letter from The Hawk, which I read at arm's length through squinting eyes.

In short, he expected the next issue of *Lyre* to appear promptly and to contain high-grade material, preferably of homegrown origin, otherwise he would be forced to seek new editors ('facilitators of more focused abilities') or to pull the plug entirely ('review, with extreme prejudice, the continuation of fund transfers'). So, this was it, the ultimatum I had feared. The situation was now officially grave: there was no possibility of survival on the revenues generated by advertising (paltry) and sales (worse). To add to my dejection, the best the other envelopes could yield in the way of literary value was a discounted subscription to *Ireland's Own*.

As I paced the room I realised it was the threat to replace us that hurt most. *Of more focused abilities . . .* That was the real plum-crusher. After all the hard work. All those envelopes. All those paper cuts. Okay, so Oliver was no French intellectual, but he did put the hours in. When he wasn't busy with Iris. Or on holiday. Or in the pub. Or hung over. Or asleep. And anyway, it wasn't like we were paid a fortune . . .

A police siren that had been in the distance was suddenly nearby. I paused at the window. An armoured Land Rover was bearing down from the direction of Shaftesbury Square, slowing sharply as it approached our building. Its ululations ceased. The vehicle drew parallel with the doorway where it came briefly to a standstill before regathering speed. It disappeared up the street, but braked again, the pads squeaking – then a change of engine tone as it reversed, and it was back, idling, directly below.

I froze. My mind was fizzing with paranoid possibilities. Who were they looking for? Mad Dog? Had Winksie shopped him? Oliver? Had Niblock sweated Iris down? Me? Had Mick or the dope fiends implicated me somehow? As I was sifting through these scenarios, the Land Rover revved a few times and moved off. Something completely unrelated, obviously. I rummaged in 'the kitchen' and found a packet of Fruit Snap Jacks, which I worked through while mulling the ramifications of The Hawk's letter. It confirmed what I had suspected about Winksie's visit, that it had been no routine pep-talk. The Hawk had already been circling.

In the early afternoon, after yet another largely futile trawl through the submissions backlog, I descended to the street. I was halfway back to my flat before I remembered I'd meant to call Rosie and, rather than trudge back up the stairs to where I'd just been, I prised open the door of one of the avenue's malodorous public phone boxes. Sure enough, this one had recently hosted a support group for incontinent wolverines. Trying not to breathe in, I let the first try ring out, then hung up and dialled again. Still no answer. As I put the handset back in its cradle I glanced back and spotted the grey Land Rover, stopped once more – on the other side of the road this time – directly opposite the office. Protective grilles over the windows meant I couldn't make out the occupants or what they were doing but I now had enough justification, in my current state of mind, for being fully spooked. Later in the day Rosie again failed to answer my call and this added to my general edginess. I had the feeling, irrational but distinct, that the city was turning against me.

The train was running parallel to the loughshore now, and would shortly trace a gentle arc away from the water and into north County Down's velvety green interior. We were getting close to my stop. Nearly home. (I suppose I should have let them know I was coming but it was too late now. Anyway, what was that line of Frost's? *Home is the place where, when you have to go there, / They have to take you in.*) The tide was low and various seabirds were at work: gulls and cormorants in the air, oystercatchers and sandpipers tending the rock-pools. A curlew cried out, just audible above the clatter of the rails. Close offshore, some small yachts were scything back and forth in a frisky swell, their sails icy white in the sunshine; beyond them, the Liverpool ferry was making its steadfast way along the lough's centre lane towards the open sea. Beyond that again, far off on the opposite bank, on the hills above Whiteabbey and Greenisland, tiny sparkles from the windscreens of moving cars flashed like random morse. As we plunged out of the sun, under a bridge and into the shade between two steep embankments, the brakes began to take hold (. . . *there swelled / A sense of falling* . . .) and a few moments later I was standing on the platform, back in my childhood.

★

'Hold the bloody thing!'

'I am holding the bloody thing!'

'Hold it with both hands.'

'I *am* holding it with both hands!'

'I'm going to break my bloody neck in a minute.'

'*I'm* going to break your bloody neck in a minute . . .'

'What did you say?'

'Clive, just bang the bloody thing in.'

My father, his paunch overhanging the waistband of his creaking tennis shorts, was balanced at the top of a ladder attempting to nail a wooden trellis to the side of the garage. My mother, oddly infantilized by a raspberry-pink velour tracksuit, was leaning on a lower rung with one hand while perusing a gardening catalogue held in the other. I could tell from the glistening fire-apple of my father's tonsure that it was already hot in the courtyard, a high-walled suntrap whose flagstones would be untouchable by mid-afternoon.

From the window of my old bedroom, where I was standing, I could see across the gardens of the neighbouring houses to a sweep of woods where the land fell away towards the lough. On tiptoes, on a clear day, you could make out the glint of water beyond the trees.

I looked around. Apart from the addition of a filing cabinet that had been wedged in beside my old writing desk, the room was more or less as it had been through my teen years: the obligatory basketball hoop, the Stiff Little Fingers and Clash posters vying for wall space with Man Ray and a blown-up reproduction of the original cover of *Howl and Other Poems*. The doors of the wardrobe were still plastered (the result of some hormone-swamped *horror vacui*) in a collage of photographs and magazine clippings that tracked the development of multifarious interests, from opium poppy cultivation to the Triumph Bonneville. There was a snap of me in my school uniform – it must have been my last day – smiling laconically into the camera with my collar unbuttoned, like there was nothing left to learn. My hair was feathered out at the ears and I was sporting a queasy centre parting that made me appear even younger, even more inane than necessary. (A girlfriend once told me I reminded her of Rob Lowe in *Oxford Blues*, 'but nowhere near as good looking'.)

I heaved the wardrobe doors open, creating a miniature breeze that was laden with the smell of the past: a blend of wood shavings, iodine, and the ghost of some sweet, overwrought aftershave. Swaying on their hangers were several of my old shirts and some jackets, including my school blazer, which I took out and held up: navy blue with the school crest in gold; turquoise thread spelling out the motto, *Fortis Est Veritas*. Several stains on the front I could immediately identify as canteen custard. I hesitated for a moment but couldn't resist. I slipped it on and stepped in front of the mirror. Slightly snugger, but not much. Tighter across the shoulders. A couple more inches of wrist. But the face . . . That was the real time-register: slacker, sadder, half an inch lower on the cheekbones, the eyes warier, slower, the skin tone leached by dehydrating tinctures and sleep debt. My teeth, though – perhaps surprisingly – were still white, and my hair, though shorter, was still a dense thatch of mahogany brown. I pulled a few faces. There was a clatter in the courtyard.

'Hazel, for Chrissake! I thought you were holding it!'

I peered out. My father was standing in the flowerbed, a ladder's length away from where I'd last seen him, rubbing his lower back and doing gorilla face at my mother.

'I *was* bloody holding it – '

'But not with both hands, you . . . silly old trout.'

'Don't you dare call me a trout – '

'Oh shut up, my bloody back's buggered. Owww . . .'

'Shut up yourself, you big bloody baby . . .'

My parents' marriage had many years ago made a leap from relatively standard trench warfare into a psychologically complex game of Battleships. Only they knew the running score, although despatches were readable from time to time in my father's facial expressions (from slightly hangdog to outright Pearl Harbour) and my mother's vocal tone when addressing him (from cool to polar blizzard). As the partnership went on and their mutual failings and foibles became more visible, so the theatre of war expanded, and as they came to know each other's secret bays and sheltering places, so the weaponry – its precision and damage capability – escalated.

In the early days, destruction of each other's vessels was simply a means of securing temporary advantage in stressful situations, for example, when setting off on holiday:

'Clive, did you remember to turn off the gas?'

'Of course.' (Miss.) 'Did you bring the camera?'

'It's in my bag.' (Miss.) 'What about the lilo?'

'Um . . . Yep, s'in the boot.' (Near miss.) 'Directions?'

'Right here.' (Miss.) 'Clive, where's the dog?'

'Ahh . . .' (Boom!)

In time, the targets would become more individually critical, more intensely *personal* (including a suspected but never openly discussed extramarital affair of my father's) and the tactics more cunning. Of the two my father was the less-skilled strategist, which was surprising given his obsession with military history, and the decisive battles of the Second World War in particular. For a man who spent much of his spare time immersed in the dynamics of conflict, he took a hell of a kicking from his wife. (Or had I misunderstood: was it his defeats on the marital front that sent him back to the books?) His other big interest was sport, which he watched in all its forms but played in only one: golf. Out on the links with the boys, that was where my father was truly free. And, to be fair, he had worked hard for his day in the sun.

An accountant by training, he had moved into business in his late forties, opening a couple of sportsgear outlets just as the government began building leisure centres all over the place in a bid to divert young people away from violence. Now he had his own chain, including two sports superstores, and could swing his clubs every day of the week if he wanted, which he didn't because he didn't trust anyone else to run his empire, not even my brother Fenton, who was in charge of a few of the smaller shops. (I wouldn't trust Fenton either.)

My mother, who had worked in a bank before she was

married, played a significant part in setting up the sports-gear business, stepping down once it was established to concentrate on her passion, gardening, and to devote herself to attending charity fundraisers. (She was much more outgoing than my father and in several quarters her pledged attendance at a social event was considered crucial to the planning process.) Eventually though, none of this was enough to engage all of her scattered energies and she opened a shop of her own in the village, selling gratuitous gew-gaws at hilarious prices to people who already had too much. It was an instant success.

I hung the blazer back in the wardrobe and closed the doors. The dialogue in the courtyard, which had eased to a low grumble, now rose sharply with a yelp of genuine pain from my father.

'God's Teeth woman, what the hell are you doing?'

'Keep still you silly man, it's going everywhere . . .'

'Owwww . . . It stings like buggery!'

'For Godsake it's only liniment. Anyway, how would you know?'

'What? I've read reports. Owww, it burns!'

'It'll stop in a minute and then you'll feel better. Sit down there.'

I looked out. My father, his shirt pulled up and his shorts low on his buttocks, was perched on a bench with his back to the house, my mother standing beside him, stroking his hair. She was murmuring something to him. Then he said something and they both laughed and she put her arm around his neck. The pose reminded me momentarily of a photograph that hung in their bedroom: a black-and-white seaside snap from the year they got married – him in shirtsleeves, strong, engaging the lens with easy assurance; his new wife gazing past the camera, her hair blown back, tilting her face to the warm breeze as though it were the future itself. (What is it with these freeze-frames? These postcards from the past? Why do they break the heart so?) More laughter rose from the courtyard. They seemed content enough, the pair of them down there in the sunshine, looking about them at the stone walls and the big solid house, with its mortgage paid off.

Neither of my parents had grown up with money. My mother came from farming stock – strict Presbyterians who believed in hard work, abstinence, and the redemptive power of hessian underwear, and while she had to a large degree managed to out-run her upbringing, part of her would, I sensed – for all her adult worldliness and agnosticism – always expect to answer to the Lord in the final hour, in the spiritual equivalent of a deserted, rough-hewn kirk on a storm-whipped headland.

Her husband, meanwhile, whose Huguenot ancestors had fully understood the value of transportable skills, had emerged from a long line of smiths: ironsmiths, silversmiths, woodsmiths. After the war his father had become a cabinetmaker, second generation, and shaved out a living patently incommensurate with his craftsmanship – an imbalance that wasn't lost on my own father, who secured a university place and from there a snug berth in the world of numerical drudgery.

Needless to say, they found me utterly baffling.

Neither of them was able, for the life of them, to work out where 'the pay-off' was, in what they referred to as, 'the poetry business'. My father, especially, had little time for things lyrical, nodding along tolerantly if the topic ever came up before clapping his hands to signify that enough was enough and trotting out Groucho Marx's quip about how the poem that begins *Thirty days hath September* was his favourite – because it actually tells you something.

My mother was more indulgent of my artistic interests and would occasionally even show support by reciting verses she had been forced to learn at school – usually Wordsworth's *Daffodils* or *The Fairies* by William Allingham. Even so, I think she still hoped I would somehow grow out of it. I caught her sometimes looking at me in the same way as she might regard a plant whose flowers had turned out a different colour to the one advertised on the seed packet.

*

At dinner that evening around the kitchen table, inevitably, the subject of me and my future came up. I braced for the customary probings, inferences and freighted silences.

'So Arthur,' my father began as we passed the baked potatoes around. 'How's the poetry going?'

I bought myself a moment by pouring a glass of Mateus Rose.

'Oh, you know . . . flourishing. What did Goethe say? *A man should hear a little music, read a little poetry and see a fine picture every day so that* – how does it go? – *so worldly cares don't obliterate the sense of the beautiful that God has implanted in the human soul.*'

'What?'

'Oh, nothing.'

No one spoke. I looked up from my buttering operation. They wanted more.

'Yes, we put out a very good issue of the magazine a couple of months back and we're due another in September. It's very popular.'

My father mis-swallowed.

'Really?' he squeaked, reaching for his wine.

'Oh yes,' I said. 'It's definitely, well . . . certainly in the top five arts publications in, um . . .'

'The Province?'

'I was going to say Ireland, actually.'

'Really? You mean . . . including the Republic?'

'Yes. We would be very well regarded.'

My father chewed for a few moments, his forehead flexing. I could tell he was searching deep within himself for some coalescence of pride but finding only the usual nebulous disquiet. He gave up and turned his attention to the tiny portable television that was switched on with the sound down on the worktop beside him.

'Well I think that's excellent, Arthur,' my mother said. 'We're very proud of you.'

I glanced up and caught her giving me the wrong-flower look again. She converted it into a loving smile.

'By the way, I ran into Beefy Campbell's mother the

other day,' she said. 'She told me Beefy's doing very well at the bar.'

'Really? I'm so glad.'

A close-up of Beefy's face loomed. It was the last day of term at the end of second year and he was straddling my chest, trying to strangle me with my own tie. His blubbery lips were distorted with the effort, saliva seething through his dental brace. I could still see his snakey eyes dilating with panic in the moment before I passed out.

'He's with one of the top law firms in London now. Very prestigious. She did tell me the name but I can't – '

'Burke & Hare?'

'No . . . no that wasn't it – '

'Moloch, Belial & Mammon?'

'No, I would have remembered that. It was more – '

'Grynne & Barrett?'

'No, sshh, you're confusing me . . .'

'Was it Cavill & Gouge?'

'Yes! Yes that was it. I knew it was something posh. He's paid a fortune apparently. Anyway, she was wondering if you'd give him a ring when he's home for Christmas. There's just the two of them there now. It's terribly sad.'

Beefy's father had checked out a long time ago; his policeman brother Soupy, who was two years ahead of me at school, had been killed some months previously by a booby-trap bomb under his car.

'Yeah, sure.'

My father made a noise like a dray horse attempting to adjust its mouthpiece.

'Hazel, did Arthur hear Fenton's news?'

'I don't know. Arthur, did you hear Fenton's news?'

'I don't know, *did* I hear Fenton's news?'

Communications between my elder brother and myself were intermittent at best.

My parents raised their eyebrows at each other. My father coughed, and in a sepulchral voice said: 'Fenton has branched out on his own.'

'Yes,' my mother chirped. 'He's moved into the glamour business.'

My glass paused en route to my lips.

'He's become a topless model?'

'No Arthur,' my father said. 'He's opened a tanning salon. In the village. And it's booked solid. And he's opening another in the city centre next month . . .'

So, every member of my family was some kind of shopkeeper, except me.

'. . . If he's judged demand right it could be an absolute goldmine,' my father went on. 'They've really cracked the technology on these tanning machines, you know. You get inside them and they do your whole body at once, like a rotisserie. And the beauty of it is, it's very addictive. Once you've got that lovely golden tan you can't help yourself, you've got to keep topping it up . . .'

Great. My brother was going to be rich. That was sure to improve his personality.

'Are those sunbed things safe?' I enquired, just to take some of the exultation out of the air. 'I thought I read

somewhere that they cook your internal organs or something.'

'Nonsense, they're perfectly safe,' my mother said.
'Pixie Dixon's got one at home she's been using for
years. Never done her a bit of harm.'

'Maybe not on the inside.'

'What do you mean by that?'

'Well . . . look at her.'

'Pixie? What's wrong with her?'

'Are you serious? Look at her face.'

'What's wrong with her face?'

'She's completely overdone it. She looks . . .' I
pronged a baked potato and held it aloft. '. . . Like that.'

'Arthur, that's . . . Do you think so?' Ashamed delight
and loyal outrage tussled briefly for control of my
mother's demeanour. 'No. That's not . . . Pixie's a very
attractive lady. She's – '

'Mother, she looks like she was dug out of a peat bog.'

'Arthur! That's a terrible thing to say – '

'She looks like the Tollund Man. She's the Tollund
Woman.'

'Arthur, that's enough now – '

'For Godsake, would you look at this!' my father
exploded. 'Bloody disgrace.'

I wasn't far from the television but I had to strain my
eyes to make out what was happening on its miniscule
screen. There was a jumbo-sized set in the adjoining room
but I'd noticed my parents seemed to prefer watching the
news on this one, as though the horror itself could be
diminished, choked off, distanced by keeping the images

small and fuzzy. The evening bulletin was running footage of an Orange march being pelted by an enraged crowd. Several youths in sashes were to be seen retaliating. A police Land Rover was lit up by a petrol bomb.

'It can't go on,' my father moaned.

'What can't go on?' My mother's tone was weary.

'All this bloody nonsense. The government's got to get tough . . . the year we've had. And it's only going to get worse.'

'Clive, what are you talking about?'

'Internment. It's the only way – '

'Oh, for goodness sake, Clive. It doesn't work – '

'. . . Round up the chief troublemakers from both sides and put them on ice – '

'Don't be ridiculous.'

'Why is it ridiculous? These bastards stirring up the trouble are walking the streets large as life and twice as ugly. It takes bloody years to gather the evidence and then you can't get a witness to stand up for fear of being bloody murdered . . . I'm telling you, it's the only way.'

My mother tilted her head back and sighed heavily.

'You're getting yourself all worked up for nothing. Calm down. There's no point. There's nothing you can do. We're all just going to have to wait it out . . .' She pushed her chair back and stood up. 'Now, who's for Arctic Roll?'

She began gathering up the plates, while her husband tried to compose himself by staring intently at various objects on the table and I fixed my gaze on a portrait of a severely bilious Asian lady that hung beside the archway to the living room.

Dessert was meted out and we ate in silence for a while.

'By the way,' I said, hacking at my thick coaster of frozen hydrogenates. 'What were you two doing earlier on? It sounded like there was a bit of a palaver outside.'

'Oh that,' replied my father. 'Just a spot of DIY – '

'We're going to have to get a wee man in,' my mother announced. 'Your father can't get it up.'

I struggled to keep custody of my eyes. (On the maternal unintentional double entendre scale monitored by my brother and me over the years this was fairly run-of-the-mill. Our favourite was uncorked during the pudding course of a Sunday lunch when she enquired loudly the length of the table whether her charity's honorary president, a man of the cloth, would like some cream up his end.)

'She means the trellis,' my father said sharply to me. Then to her: 'And I would've had it up if you'd been holding the bloody ladder properly . . .' He trailed off.

'Pass the wine dear,' she instructed. 'Arthur, I was wondering if you'd do me a favour.'

'Of course.'

'Pixie's having an open garden event tomorrow and I really have to go. Would you be an angel and mind the shop for me?'

'Oh, um, actually . . .'

'Your father's playing golf and Fenton's busy. It's just for the morning.'

'A garden party you say?'

145

'Yes. For charity.'

'Which one?'

'I'm not sure. Skin cancer research, I think.'

★

My first split-second assumption – a reflex from living too long in a war zone – was that I was caught up in some kind of rocket attack. In fact, it was simply my first act of the day in my role as shopkeeper: knocking over and smashing a large piece of pottery that exploded as though it had contained a zeppelin's-worth of gas. I had been reaching up to a high shelf to examine an unidentifiable object that now turned out to be a ceramic dustpan encrusted with semi-precious stones. I hid the shards (some of them embedded in a raffia chair ten feet away) in a drawer of the reproduction Welsh dresser on which the object had originally stood, pocketed the startling price tag and shakily took up my position behind the counter of *Knicks 'n' Knacks*.

As I sat down I noticed a frame on the wall beside me. It contained a piece of card embossed with the following: *Lovely to look at, | Delightful to hold, | If you should break it, | Consider it sold.* I was just remarking to myself how varied and inventive were the uses of poetry when the telephone rang. It was someone very elderly enquiring whether our antimacassars were handmade or factory-made. Antimacassars? I attempted to wing it. Were they available in vinyl, my interlocutor wanted to know. What colours? What sizes? Were they machine washable?

Were they self-gripping? (Weren't we all? Silence.) Were they frilled or straight-hemmed? Were the crocheted ones durable enough? And finally – and this was where the jig was up – were they resistant to *all* brands of pomade? *Pomade?* I suggested the customer make the effort to visit the shop in person, then set about acquainting myself more closely with the stock.

Knicks 'n' Knacks was an eye opener. Taken in the round, its contents – the very fact of the *existence* of its contents – necessitated a recalibration of values, acceptance of which, by extension, meant breaking through to a new level of consciousness: *micro*-consciousness. What was most shocking was that someone somewhere had gone to the trouble of visualising, designing, manufacturing and then transporting items so arcane, so rarefied in function a family could pass through several generations before happening upon the opportunity to use them.

What was this plastic tube with metal teeth next to the ornamental saffron mills? A Carrot Gripper. *A Carrot Gripper?* And this? Between the garlic presses and the multi-coloured chicken-leg hats? A solid silver Egg Hole Puncher. And here, below the tortoise-shell sconces, beside the marjoram-scented pin-cushions? A set of twelve mother-of-pearl Butter Curlers . . . I ran my fingers across the slub silk valances, the cashmere napkins (and their amethyst-studded obsidian rings), the gossamer doilies (*Hand-Woven by the Elf People of Carpathia*), and gazed open-mouthed at the diaphanous skeins of fabric suspended, along with the seal-skin pampooties and fur-lined slippers, from the ceiling. Five whole shelves were dedicated to name-place holders and pomanders (*Individually painted by the Java Women's Nostril Collective*); another three to writing-paper (*Made with wood-pulp masticated to order in limited batches by the blind elders of the Okavango Delta*). A large table was taken up entirely by a collection of glass fruit. Some poor bastard had made a model of the *Titanic* out of coconut husks.

By now the fumes from fifty heinous varieties of potpourri were burning through my mucous membranes. I staggered back to mission control. As I mopped my streaming eyes with a napkin (*Personally Embroidered by Pocahontas*), a bell shrilly announced the arrival of a live customer. It wasn't. It was my brother, leaning round the door.

'Telegram for Mongo.'

'Fenton. What are you doing here?'

'Right bro? I heard you'd drawn the short straw,' he sniggered, entering the shop. '. . . How does it feel to be in charge of Knickers 'n' Knackers?'

He stood there, in his purple Ralph Lauren polo shirt, jangling a set of keys. He had my father's broad brow and heavy build, and could look forward to a similarly long struggle with his midriff.

'Fine thanks. Nothing to it.'

'Broken anything yet?'

'Nope.'

'You will. Many been in?'

'Oh, you know . . . *dribs'n'drabs.*'

He paused to pick inside his ear with the longest key, grimacing horribly.

'You still pissing around with your wee magazine?' he asked.

'Yes, and it's very successful. Fenton, what do you want? I thought you were working.'

'I was,' he said, examining the result of his excavation. 'I'm just round the corner at *Sunbirds*.'

'Oh yes, your new venture. *Sunbirds*, is that what it's called? Not bad. Quite poetic. Is it from Arabian mythology? Symbol of rebirth or something?'

'You're fucken kidding right?' He squinted at me. 'I can never tell with you. Sun-birds. Sun and . . . birds? . . . Like chicks? Girls? Suntanned girls?'

'Of course. And how's it coming along?'

'Totally mad. Crawling with women. They can't get enough of that sun-kissed look. Although the blokes are getting in on it too, in fact – ' He patted his pockets. 'You should have a go yourself . . . here, have a complimentary voucher – ' He tossed a card on the counter. 'Don't say I never give you anything.'

'Thanks, but – '

'Take it. Pass it on. It's for three sessions in our latest machine: The Sizzlemaster 9000. I swear, half an hour in that thing – ' He shook his head in wonderment. '. . . It's like a week in the Mojave Desert. Very impressive results.'

I examined my coupon, with its lavish chocolate lettering and impossibly buxom silhouettes on a field of inferno-orange. Fenton consulted his watch.

'Look, what I swung by to say is, when you see our mother you need to tell her Crystal's got new stock in, including croc-skin cotton-bud caddies, *and* she's dropped the price of her diamante crème brulee hammers by fifty percent.'

'What?'

'Godsake Artie, I'll write it down . . . gimme that biro . . .'

Crystal Turkington (yes, Heather was her daughter) was my mother's arch-rival. Her shop, *Dotey Things*, was situated diagonally across the village square from *Knicks 'n' Knacks*, and sold almost exactly the same merchandise. Needless to say, the two women hated each other with life-altering intensity. A tit-for-tat price war had broken out on day one and was supplemented a short time later by a mutual, undeclared quest to seek out the obscurest trinkets, the rarest baubles, the most exclusive designers and reclusive craftsmen; to find the *ultimate* knicknack. Neither of them could picture exactly what that might be, but both knew it would be an object at once priceless . . . and useless . . . and utterly irresistible.

I swivelled in my chair and looked across the plaza at the faux-Dickensian frontage of *Dotey Things,* where several people were milling around, peering in through the window or pawing at the soaps (*Made Exclusively With Extracts From The World's Most Endangered Species*) that were heaped in wicker hampers at the door. The shop was flanked by an optician's on one side and a butcher's on the other, while further along, set back behind black railings, was a church, its classical façade painted an incongruous pink. A banner, hung between two pillars in the portico, read: *And ye shall know the truth, and the truth shall make you free. John 8:32.* In the centre of the stone-flagged square stood the war memorial, a life-size bronze soldier on guard with his rifle at the ready. Around the base of the plinth were chiselled the names of the local dead: Armstrong, Corry, Dunlop, Ferguson, Gray, Herron, Lennox, Mahony, Neeson, Orr, Praeger, Richardson, Shaw, Trainor, Wilson . . . Was this really why two world wars were fought? So we could flog each other taffeta bog-roll covers?

'Okay, there you go. Make sure she sees that,' said Fenton, propping the note against the cash register. 'Now, I'd better get back to my money mine.'

I had a thought.

'Hey Fenton, maybe you'd know – ' I twisted back to face the counter. '. . . What the fuck is an antimacassar?'

He pondered for a minute, his lips working through a series of unvocalised possibilities.

'I'm not sure. Is it . . . is it like a *sloth*?'

After Fenton left, a series of customers insisted on coming into the shop. I sold a garlic press, a set of ivory toothpicks, a glass pineapple, and a sack of potpourri so pungent even the buyer was wheezing and dabbing at her eyes as she fumbled for her cash. The final visitor was a leathery activist in her sixties demanding I display one of her posters in the window: a call to arms ahead of the annual Tidy Towns competition.

'We've been the *second* tidiest small town for three years running.' she explained. 'And it's not good enough. This time around, it's personal – ' She was evaluating with a cold eye my frayed jeans and faded T-shirt. '. . . We're all in this together.'

I promised to put on a tie.

My mother arrived just as I was thinking about shutting up shop and going to find something to eat. I was tired and hungry.

'Sorry I'm late, Pixie had a disaster with her vol-au-vents. How did you get on?'

'Easy-peasy. The till was lit up like a pinball machine.'

'That's wonderful dear. And were you polite to everyone?'

'Positively smarmy . . . Mother?'

She picked up Fenton's note.

'Yes, dear . . .'

'What's an antimacassar?'

'Mmm? Sorry, what?' As she read, she had the look of a field marshal receiving critical intelligence, her face tightening to a fox-like sharpness.

'What's an antimacassar?'

'An antimacassar? It's um . . . it's a cover to prevent gentlemen's hair oil staining the backs of chairs. Why?'

'Do we have any?'

'Don't be silly dear, they went out thirty years ago. Now, you probably want to go and get some lunch. Let me pay you . . .' She opened her handbag.

I made a parodic attempt to dissuade her.

'Nonsense. You've done good work.' She pushed a twenty pound note at me. Just as she did so, her gaze snapped towards the Welsh dresser. 'Oh, I don't believe it!' She took a step forward. 'Someone bought the wig tree!' She beamed at me.

'The what?'

'The imitation Spode porcelain wig tree! I thought I'd never get rid of it.'

'Yes. About that – '

'Aren't you clever!'

'Actually, I was about to tell you. There was a little accident – '

'An accident?'

'Yes. With the . . . with the wig tree. You see I was reaching up – '

'You broke it?'

I became aware of a refrain running through my head, a piece of verse recited sing-song fashion by a small chorus of fairy children: *Lovely to look at, / Delightful to hold* . . .

'Well, it got broken, yes, but . . .' Surely not? Surely she wouldn't . . .?

Her palm was outstretched, her expression grave.

I returned the banknote.

★

Three days later I was back on the train, stretching out my aching limbs (a long session of garden duty) and enjoying the fading afternoon heat through sun-smeared

153

windows. The lough, on my right for this, the return journey, was an expanse of silver dazzle, the cranes and gantries that marked the edge of the city a line of small, dark pictograms in the distance. (*See Belfast, devout and profane and hard, / Built on reclaimed mud, hammers playing in the shipyard, / Time punched with holes like a steel sheet . . .*) The change of scene had, I felt, done me good. Apart from a few misguided attempts to make me work or play golf, my parents had mostly gone about their business, leaving me alone to read books and revisit my record collection. I had eaten well, imbibed moderately, and slept soundly in my childhood bed, reunited with the ancient mattress as though it were a faithful old pet.

At the insistence of my mother half a lasagne and a Tupperware box of cold chicken were weighing down my rucksack. Tucked in the top was a gift from my father. He had called me aside a couple of hours before I left with the air of a man about to hand over something truly significant, the philosopher's stone, say, and I had briefly allowed myself to hope for my grandfather's gold Omega wristwatch, its casing worn to the silky smoothness of a pebble. It turned out to be a golf jersey the colour of arterial blood, featuring on its front a pink, yellow and black interference pattern so shocking I actually took a step back. 'This is brand new stock,' he whispered. 'Top of the range. The boys at the club would kill for it. I want you to have it.'

Refreshed as I was, though, the dread and despair from earlier in the week hadn't lifted entirely, The Hawk's ultimatum returning sporadically in an ominous mono-tone at the back of my head. The prospect of losing *Lyre* was . . . well, not pleasant. Okay, so it wasn't *The Paris Review* or *The Criterion*. It was a small, provincial magazine, with horribly inadequate production values and a readership you could probably squeeze into a minibus. But it was *our* small magazine. It functioned in interesting times, and once in a while we were proud of its contents. There was no doubt that if it came to the crunch I would miss the material benefits – the warm office, the beer money, the free envelopes and, let's face it, the custard creams – but I would mourn much more profoundly the lifestyle to which I'd grown accustomed: *the state of mind.* More immediately, I would have to brace myself for a torrent of unbearably righteous pity from my parents, and a prolonged display of Olympic-standard sneering from Fenton. And then there was Oliver. What would become of him in the outside world?

The train groaned to a standstill. Doors slammed. A man wheeling a bicycle stopped on the platform to exchange banter with the conductor – some rapid-fire speculation about the absence from work of a mutual friend. Then cackling laughter. 'Right Jackie.' 'Right Bob.' Two teenagers carrying fishing gear traipsed through the carriage, followed by a denim-clad woman struggling with a large baby. She paused to hoist it further up her hip and the child, resting its wobbling, outsized head on her shoulder, gazed down at me with scathing incuriosity.

There was no point trying to reason with The Hawk,

that much was clear: his letter had positively reeked of excuse-repellent. He wanted the right stuff and he wanted it right now. But what could we do? We couldn't pluck poetry out of thin air. On the other hand we couldn't just slap our guns and badges on the table and walk away . . .

We pushed on, towards the famous cranes and the clanking sprawl of the docklands: smells of tar and rope and rusting metal; pulleys, tramlines and bridges; Ship Street, Sailorstown, The Rotterdam Bar. Another stop. Cavehill in the distance, its profile like an Easter Island statue on its back, gazing at the sky. Three shiny girls got on, settling instantly into eye games with the fisherboys. The football ground and a honeycomb of houses on the left, and then the approach to the commercial sector. The markets. The courts. Saturday night traffic on the Queen's Bridge. Then a tunnel. Another halt. We lost a few, gained a few. We reached the river, its restless surface glinting blood-red in the last of the light, and as we crossed over – suddenly, from the depths of my reverie – came an idea. It was audacious, dangerous even, but so simple as to be almost poetic.

By the time we disembarked I knew exactly what had to be done.

★

'You do realise what we have to do, don't you?'

Oliver shifted in his chair. Sweat was darkening the

armpits of his cheesecloth shirt and a recent visit to a cut-price barber's had resulted in a hairstyle horribly reminiscent of the one pioneered by puppet middleman Geoffrey in the children's TV show *Rainbow*. On the desk between us lay The Hawk's letter.

'Don't you?' I allowed some sternness to enter my voice.

He didn't reply.

'Oliver, we have to be tight on this. It's a serious move.'

He had gained more weight on his holiday and appeared not to have been exposed to sunlight, his skin so pale it was verging on bluish.

'Oliver?'

Not a flicker.

'Oliver?'

Silence.

'Oliver?'

'Alright, alright!' he blurted. 'I know. Okay? It's been on my mind since I read the letter on my first day back . . .'

'And?'

'Well . . .' He shrugged.

'Yes?'

He tipped his head back and shut his eyes.

'I think I'm thinking what you're thinking,' he said quietly.

Progress.

'I know it's pretty radical but I really can't see any other way,' I told him.

He gnawed at a thumbnail, while I knocked back the dregs of my tea.

'Do you know anyone?' he asked.

'What?'

'Do you know anyone who could help us?'

I stared at him. It seemed I was really going to have to spell this out.

'No,' I said. 'No, we're going to have to do this ourselves. That's the point.'

'Ourselves? Jesus.' His eyes bulged with alarm. He began drumming an agitated rhythm on the tabletop. Then stopped. Some moments elapsed.

'How are we going to do it?' he asked.

For the love of . . . How did he *think* we were going to do it?

'Well, it's probably safe to say it's not going to be easy.'

'Oh sure, these things never are for people like us but, I mean . . . what method?'

(It occurred to me that this could actually be even harder than I thought.)

'Whatever it takes. We're just going to have to grit our teeth and get on with it.'

The fingertip drum solo resumed as Oliver tried to access auxiliary thinking power.

I waited.

'Have you ever done anything like this before?' he asked.

'Not on this scale, no. I tried my hand at some stuff when I was younger, but . . .'

'But . . .?'

'It didn't really work out. I didn't think I was much good at it and after a while I felt I might as well just leave it to others.'

'Really?' Oliver was inordinately agog. He began running his hands through his hair, giving it the look of a cropped fright-wig.

'Wait a minute!' He dropped both palms on the desk. 'What about Mad Dog?'

I stared at him.

'*Mad Dog*? What about him?'

'Couldn't we get him on board?'

'Get him *on board*? On board what? A rocket to Saturn? Oliver, what are you talking about?'

'Well, we know he's got the . . . the means.'

I continued to stare at him.

'The gun! His gun!' Oliver cried. 'He was waving it around. In this room. I'm pretty sure you were here.'

'I was here alright – but what's that got to do with anything?'

'Are you serious?' He did his looking-around-for-the – hidden-camera impression. 'How else are we going to kill him? *Tickle* him to death?'

He was twitching now, like a malfunctioning replicant.

'Oliver, have you lost your mind? Kill who?'

'The Hawk! The Hawk! Who else?'

'*The Hawk?*'

'Yes! We're going to kill the bastard, right?'

I opened my mouth and closed it again. Then repeated the action. No words emerged.

'Right? Artie?'

159

I took a couple of deep breaths.

'I think we're going to need more tea.'

Such was his relief at not having to murder a senior civil servant, I think Oliver would have agreed to more or less any other alternative plan. Certainly, he jumped at my more modest proposal with a gratitude-charged energy that dispelled many of my residual doubts and made me think that maybe, *just maybe*, we could pull it off. What we undertook, on that sultry July afternoon, was as follows . . .

We decided that, in the face of a severe lack of suitable poetry, we would step into the breach and write the stuff ourselves. Given the quality of most of what had arrived on the *Lyre* mat of late, we figured our efforts would, *at the very least*, not be any worse. Moreover, we knew what we wanted.

As our funding conditions stipulated that we couldn't publish in *Lyre* under our own names (such an abrupt outburst of creativity would, in any case, appear highly suspicious) we would invent a poet and attribute the material to him. Our phantom scribe would then account for the bulk of the next issue, with whatever passable scraps we had managed to scavenge from recent submissions taking up the slack. If it worked, we would have succeeded in engineering the magazine's content to meet the required specifications – ie. The Hawk's demands for both topicality and fresh talent – thereby salvaging our editorial careers and avoiding any disruption to our comfortably bohemian lives. Then it was simply a case of delaying until the poetic *corpus* rediscovered its feet and, as the flow resumed, letting our bogus bard fade gently from the scene or even (perhaps more poetically) commit suicide. Voila!

As a plan it had a convoluted but ultimately compelling symmetry; a certain bold beauty. It also had a number of potentially crippling flaws, not least its reliance on our ability to string together a mini-collection of convincing poems in a short space of time. Just the two of us. Me . . . And Oliver. Me . . . And . . . Oliver . . . I suddenly remembered his heart-breaking attempts at a slogan for the Sunnyland Farm Bunny and, just seconds into our strategy, I was having my first crisis of faith. This was insane! It couldn't be done. What was I thinking? We didn't stand a chance. I reached for another Rich Tea Cream Finger. On the other hand, didn't Jack Kerouac write *On The Road* in three weeks? And that was a whole novel. All we needed was a bunch of poems. How hard could it be?

'The first thing we have to do is think of a name,' said Oliver.

'A name?'

'For our poet. He's got to have a name.'

'You're right. That's a good place to start.'

Several minutes of relative quiet ensued, along with the eyeball-rolling, sighing, and pen-clicking that tradition-ally accompanied mutual deep thought.

'Any ideas?'

'Not really. You?'

'No. S'quite tricky isn't it?'

Faint timebomb music from the office below signalled the start of the one o'clock news.

'Shall we get some lunch?'

'Yeah. I'm ravenous.'

★

Rosie, it seems, had been called away on my long dark Sunday of the soul, to the hospital bedside of her beloved Aunt Jane, who had acute angina.

'Well that's nice, but what's wrong with her?'

'You know, it's true, the old ones really are the best.'

'I'm sorry. That was . . . How's she doing?'

'She's . . .' Rosie waggled her hand from side to side. 'Okay. Just. We were hoping she'd be out by the weekend but they're saying now she might have to have a bypass – ' She pointed at my glass. '. . . Same again?'

We were in the back room of Kavanagh's with the rest of the after-work crowd, in that bright hour when pub-world is buoyed by a sense of refreshment earned.

'Why not.'

I watched her take her place at the bar beside the bank clerks and salesmen in their white shirts and skinny ties; how they looked at her (it wasn't just me, she definitely warranted a second glance), and how she defused their leering banter with confident, not unfriendly, ease.

'By the way, how's your mate?' I asked, as she set the drinks down and resumed her seat.

'Which mate, the one you left for dead in Dr Terror's House of Horrors?'

'What?'

She closed one eye and squinted at me as she sipped.

'I think you know what I mean,' she said, wiping her lips with a finger and thumb.

'I'm not sure I do.'

'Let's just say she wasn't quite herself when she woke up.'

'Oh? How so?'

'Well, for a start it was twenty-four hours later; secondly, not only did she not know *where* she was, she couldn't remember *who* she was. On top of that there was some old lady in bed with her. She's still not right.'

'Now hold on a minute!' I protested. An image of Mumbles in her snowy pants came back to me. 'The last time I saw her she was climbing into a wardrobe with the host in a state of undress and, believe me, the look in her eye said they weren't coming out any time soon. What was I supposed to do?'

'That's as maybe.'

'Hey, she's a grown woman. Free will and all that.'

Rosie gave a sceptical snort.

'What, you don't believe in free will?'

'Do you?'

'I will if you will.'

She laughed.

We both lifted our glasses and drank.

'I meant to ask you, how did it go back at the farm?' she asked.

'Oh, fine thanks. Yeah. The usual . . . Slow dying.'

'Come on, it can't be that bad.'

'I'm exaggerating . . . slightly.'

'They're your flesh and blood. Weren't they pleased to see you?'

'Hard to say. I suppose so. They're all very busy with their own lives, very focused on achieving . . . making money and, you know, being successful, in the conventional sense, and, um, I'm not sure they really get what I'm up to.'

'What *are* you up to?'

I considered for a minute. It was a reasonable question. And one I'd asked myself often enough. Her eyes were on me.

'I don't know.'

She looked away.

'I'd be lost without my family,' she said. 'We're very close. My sisters especially. We tell each other everything.'

'Everything?' I enquired with a gratuitously raised eyebrow.

She shot me a glance.

'Yes. So you'd better behave yourself.'

Just then the swing doors flew open and an affectation of actors led by Tristan Quigley swarmed in and clustered round the end of the bar. All of them were dressed in shades of black except for the director who was wearing a faded blue smock.

'. . . Of course, by then,' Quigley was saying. 'Sir Laurence was making such a fuss I had no choice but to pull out . . .' He was surveying the room as he spoke, and having spotted me waved with a rolled-up script.

'Gin and tonic, tons of ice,' he called over his shoulder as he advanced theatrically towards us.

'There he is! There's the big radio star himself!'

'Hello Tristan, how're you doing?'

'Never mind me, what about you? Tell me, what did you think of Monteith? Isn't he a dreadful old tart?'

'I think he has his own distinctive style. Tristan, this is Rosie.'

'Hiya Rosie. Are you artsy-fartsy too?'

'No.'

'Artie, did you hear we're working on a new production?'

'I did hear something about a compelling new play,' I said. 'How's it coming?'

'Fantastic.' He closed his eyes in semi-ecstasy. 'I think it's just about the most exciting thing I've ever done. I've never seen the guys – ' He gestured towards the bar where his players were practically eating their drinks. '. . . More energised.'

'Sounds interesting,' I said.

'Oh, it is. It's called *Suspicious Minds* and it's about . . .' He paused for thought, biting his lower lip with his upper front teeth. 'You know what? In a way, the story is secondary. It is, quite simply, a parable for our times.'

'Intriguing,' I said. 'And what do you know about the author?'

'I haven't met him yet but Stanford says he's an unforgettable character. Street cred oozing from every orifice.'

'I think I'm going to be sick,' Rosie said under her breath.

'But, you know, the key thing for me is that this is *new*,' Quigley went on. 'It's fresh, it's raw, it's painful, it's not the usual boring old tea & scones stuff we've been force-fed for years. Do you know what I mean?'

I nodded. 'I'm looking forward to it already. When do you open?'

'Middle of next month, fingers crossed. But here, look at me, getting all worked up about myself. What about the magazine? When's the next issue? S'been a while.'

'Same. Mid-September. Fingers crossed.'

A goateed sylph at the bar was miming an offer to deliver the director's G&T.

'No, I'm coming now,' Quigley mouthed. Then to us: 'I'd better get back. They probably want me to pay for the drinks. They're like children really. Will we see you on opening night?'

'Absolutely.'

He rejoined his parched artistes.

'Do you think that play could be as bad as it sounds?' asked Rosie.

I considered for a moment.

'Yes.'

After an hour of two-fisted drinking the volume of declamatory babble from Quigley's crew became un-bearable and Rosie and I were forced to de-camp to a nearby bistro, where we washed down platters of garlic-soaked molluscs with cheap Chablis. From there we progressed to the green-leather comfort of The Merchants' Lounge, where we found Boyd Monroe and Marianne Trench sharing an upmarket Graves. Monroe (looking initially shifty, I thought) hailed us from their nook. '*What wind blows you thus . . .?*'

'Why, the wind that bloweth all the world besides: desire of alcohol.' I responded.

'We are of like minds, then. Won't you join us?'

While Monroe went to the bar for extra glasses and another bottle, I introduced Rosie to Trench, who was a little the worse for wear.

The two women exchanged pleasantries.

'How's the poetry going?' Trench slurred at me.

'Cliterogenically,' I said.

She blinked at me. The wine had taken some of the haunted quality out of her visage, and there was even a slight lustre to her print-weary eyes. I was slightly confused. I wondered why one of the city's most upright and industrious intellects was hobnobbing with a louche and indolent creature like Monroe.

'Identify the quote,' she said, holding up an unsteady forefinger. '*Like a piece of ice on a hot stove, a poem must ride on its own melting.*'

'Robert Frost!' cried Monroe, returning amid chimes of glass.

'Oh Boyd! I was asking the young people. I know *you* know.'

'It's a lovely definition, though, isn't it?' Monroe said, pouring the drinks. 'Kind of like a duck being cooked in its own fat. Or a squid in its own ink.'

'That's right, spoil a wonderful simile with carnivore pornography,' Trench scolded.

'Sorry Marianne.' He made a face at us. 'Vegetarian,' he mouthed.

He pushed the drinks across the tabletop.

'Mmm. You know, just saying that has made me hungry. Anyone else hungry?'

'We just ate,' Rosie said.

'Anything nice?'

'Sea creatures fried in butter.'

Trench groaned.

'Yum.' Monroe proffered his hand. 'We haven't met. Boyd. Artie's old tutor.'

'Rosie. Potential girlfriend.'

They shook.

'How *was* Artie back then?' Rosie asked.

'Oh, unfair question. Artie, what were you like?'

I shrugged.

'Let's see . . .' Monroe stroked his chin. 'What can I say? He was . . . interesting. Full of promise. Definitely one of the the brightest to come my way.'

I protested, but Rosie was already looking at me with an expression of humorous surprise.

'A model student? Who would have thought it?'

'Oh no, I didn't say that,' Monroe laughed. 'He was quite the contrary. A prime example, in fact, of why the university system doesn't work.'

'In what way?'

'Basically, he never showed up,' he said, grinning at me.

'You didn't have a water-tight attendance record yourself,' I reminded him. 'Anyway, I would've turned up more often if your lectures hadn't been so damned boring.'

'Me too!' cried Monroe. 'Now, what shall we drink to?'

Trench raised her glass. 'Let's drink to potential.'

'To potential! Going for gold!' Monroe trilled.

We clinked and drank.

'*Nothing gold can stay*,' Trench murmured.

As the night wore on, Rosie became mellower and sweeter, like peaches marinating in brandy. We were sitting close together on the slippery leather banquette and her body, when I leaned into it, was soft and warm, her outer thigh answering pressure from mine. The high-quality wine (which Monroe paid for) seemed to lift everyone's game and there was much eager badinage. Even the analytic Trench shook off her customary *douleur* to reveal a deceptively nimble wit, disorienting her younger, court-holding colleague several times with a flurry of jabs from left field.

Later, we found ourselves in a taxi heading for the docks and more sympathetic licensing hours. In Carolan's (it might have been Muldoon's) the ambience had been supercharged by a psychobilly band whipping new life into old tunes. As we arrived they were just finishing a joyous version of *Ruby (Don't Take Your Love to Town)*.

'Excellent. Live popular culture!' Monroe declared with glee.

We nuzzled into the crowd until we found a resting

place and, magically, refreshments appeared. Everything was hilarious. More drinks materialised. After the official musicians stepped down an impromptu talent contest began and a sparkling Monroe, pint in hand, took to the makeshift stage, managing half of a surprisingly mellifluous *On Raglan Road* before losing his balance and crashing sideways into a table of Dutch tourists.

'More stout?' he enquired, appearing unfazed in front of us.

'Boyd, you've had enough,' Trench admonished.

'My dear Marianne,' he said, rubbing her arm and smiling. '*You never know what is enough unless you know what is more than enough.*'

'And, my dear Boyd,' she replied. '*If the fool would persist in his folly he would become wise.*'

By now Rosie was regarding me with candid desire.

'I think we should go,' she whispered in my ear.

'Aren't you enjoying yourself?'

'Yes. But I want to enjoy myself more.'

We said our goodbyes (Monroe made a token bleat for us to stay) and slithered into the back of a taxi.

'We'll go to my place,' Rosie said. 'I have to get up in the morning.'

By the time we'd finished our first kiss we were there, standing in the street. Fumble of keys. Swarm of darkness. Threshold. We embraced while still moving and tumbled onto the sofa, Rosie on top, my leg between her legs. Her hot mouth was sweet and garlicky. I grasped her shoulders and pushed her up so I could unbutton her shirt.

'Wait, not here,' she hissed. 'The bedroom.'

170

She led the way, clothes fluttering to the floor in her wake, into the inner sanctum of gossamers and girl-smell, where we plunged into goose-down three feet deep. Rosie, naked except for her briefs, was breathing noisily and her lips trembled as they met mine. Her body was full and smooth and lithe, and fluttered where I touched it. The inflow of sensory data was dizzying. *i like my body when it is with your body.* My fingers sought the elastic of her underwear . . .

And then it started.

Thwack! 'Ohhhh . . .'

Rosie froze.

Thwack! 'Ohhhh . . .'

'What the *fuck* is that?'

Thwack! 'Owww . . .'

She sat up.

Thwack! 'Ohhhh . . .'

We both looked at the ceiling.

Thwack! 'Ohhhh . . .'

'What on earth . . .?' said Rosie.

But I already knew what it was.

'Pleeease officer . . . offence . . . anything . . .' (Female voice, muffled but plaintive.)

Thwack!

'Madam . . . like to . . . however . . . rules . . .' (Familiar male voice, regretful but gruff.)

Hysterical giggling.

Thwack! 'Owww . . .'

Rosie turned to me. Even in the half light I could see the horror in her eyes.

'Artie! Do something!'

'Like what?' I clasped my hands behind my head. Bloody Oliver.

The snippets that were clearly audible ('will be taken down', 'cavity search', 'truncheon') suggested the dialogue was unfolding predictably enough, the splat of a hard, flat implement connecting with human flesh increasing in frequency as the emotional pitch of the voices tightened. Then, sounds of a scuffle; something heavy hitting the floor. The talk dropped to unintelligibility. More cackling. A low, electrical buzzing started up and a few seconds later, a rhythmic squeaking. The buzzing accelerated, producing (or not) a squeal of what might have been surprise. Then a new sound. Like a panicked bull seal in a tankful of jellyfish.

'I can't take any more of this,' said Rosie, in some distress.

'It'll stop in a minute,' I soothed. (I was trying to stay positive but the mental imagery was taking its toll.)

From above there was suddenly the impression of many feet moving chaotically in a confined space (had they introduced livestock?), bronchial panting, then an abrupt surge in both the volume and speed of the buzzing, the squeaking *and* the seal panic.

Rosie clambered out of bed.

'It's too awful,' she announced. 'I'm going to sleep on the sofa.'

Overhead, someone began castrating a warthog.

★

My co-editor appeared well pleased with himself when he rolled in late the next morning whistling the theme from *The Dambusters*.

'Ah! Here's himself and pepper on him,' I said, with all the false bonhomie I could muster.

He gave a cheery wave without pausing and diverted straight to 'the kitchen'.

'Kettle's hot,' I called after him.

I watched from behind the typewriter as he placed his mug on the desk and settled himself, ripping open a packet of Sprinkle Crinkle Crunches.

'Good night?' I enquired.

He grunted. He was focused on dunking.

'Nothing too *punishing*?'

He looked up.

'No, took it pretty easy. Quiet night in with Iris.'

'Sounds very *disciplined*.'

His hand twitched, and a chunk of stodge sank into the milky depths.

'Bugger . . . What about you?'

'Oh, I had a *spanking* good time, thanks.'

'Were you with Rosie?'

'Yes. Well, she does tend to *dominate* things these days.'

'Indeed,' he said uncertainly.

'I hope that doesn't *smack* of weakness on my part.'

'No, not at all, it's a great thing to have a lady in your life.'

I gave up.

'Listen,' I told him. 'We need to get cracking with our

plan. When you've finished your . . . *breakfast*, why don't you try and come up with a name for our poet. I was thinking this – ' I tossed a map-book of Northern Ireland across the table. '. . . might help narrow it down a bit, provide a few ideas.'

He began flicking through it.

'Not sure I'm with you,' he said.

'Just close your eyes, stick a pin in and see what you come up with.'

He pored over it.

'Isn't that how The Wombles got their names?' he asked.

'I don't know. Is it?'

'Yeah, remember? Uncle Bulgaria? Orinoco? Tomsk?'

'Well, there you go, it worked for them. Now, I have to get on with what we need in the way of material.'

On my sheet I had typed a number of categories:

* Urban Angst
* Identity
* Death
* Violence
* Violent Death
* Rural Practices
* Ancient Rites
* West of Ireland Pastoral
* Love Lyric
* Ancestral Voices
* Mushrooms

To these I now added, 'Love Across the Barricades'.

I unspooled the page and fed in another. Right, a poem. How hard could it be? Let's see . . . Blank verse or heroic couplets? Terzains, quatrains, sixains, or ottava rima? What about a hudabrastic? Rime royal? Spenserians? Sapphics? Ouch. Slight headache. Let's stick with vanilla: blank verse, iambic pentameter. And a title. Off the top of my head I typed, *A Belfast Breakfast*.

I took a couple of breaths. Tried to focus. Here we go.

The city wakes to the smell of –

What? Napalm? Fear? *Doughnuts*?

I thought for a moment. Two syllables – just write.

The city wakes to the smell of autumn –

That'll do. That's set the tone.

Turfsmoke and leaf-rot, a moon-haunted sky

Not bad. I took a swig of cold tea.

Coming to light above slumbering hills.

Slumbering hills? Mmm, not great. Fix it later. Now, need a domestic scene.

My father, first up, mixes milk and oats
Together, sets the pot on the heat –

Hang on, let's cook with gas. More atmospheric.

. . . sets the pot over blue flame,

Good, that's brekkie under way. What would he do next? I stared at the ceiling.

Listens for life-signs in the sleeping house.

So far, so good. But where's it going?

'Artie?'

'Not now Oliver.'

'Artie, what do you think of Kells Magilligan?'

'Who?'

'As a name for our poet.'

'No.'

'Kesh Clogherbog?'

'No.'

'Teemore Gillygooley?'

'Oliver, no.'

'What about Clabby Madden?'

'Oliver, I'm writing a poem here. Keep trying.'

Where was I? Yes, could do with a bit of free association.

Porridge, he muses –

Comes from *pottage*, doesn't it? But what *was* pottage exactly? I consulted the dictionary. 'Soup or stew. Middle English from Old French *potage*. That which is put in a pot.' Hmm, not particularly helpful. Ah, here we go, 'oatmeal . . . pease pudding . . . A mess of pottage: something of little value, from the exchange by Esau of his birthright for a meal of lentil stew (Genesis 25: 29-34)'. That'll do nicely.

Porridge, he muses. By way of pottage,

Esau's lentil stew –

No, that's not right.

Esau's . . . priceless stew?

No, that's not right either. What about costly?

Esau's costly stew. Found in the stomachs

Of neolithic corpses. (Thanks Seamus.) *Staple fare*

Of . . . what? Jailhouse? Workhouse? Hospital?

Of workhouse and sanitorium.

Phew. Hard enough. I munched a Crunch.

The molten gruel starts to heave and sigh
Molten lava. Volcano. Liquefied metal . . .
Craters and steam-gouts, a shipyard foundry –
Local reference, good.
Volcanic birth pangs of a new planet . . .
Hey, where did that come from?
He kills the heat. Leaves it aside to rest.
Making me hungry. Quick breather. More chai.
(Three cups of tea and half a packet of biscuits later I
had roughed out the next few lines.)
He is savouring this time, this headstart
On the day, for soon it will be someone else's.
Hint of class politics. No harm.
Outside, deliverymen rattle crates
And bring yesterday's – something *– news*
Horrible? Predictable?
And bring yesterday's undigested news:
'Guess what? We still don't understand each other.'
Running out of puff here.
The streetlamps fade. The dreamers are stirring.
Now the last line. The punchline. Something chunky.
But resonant. Something –
'Artie.'
Block him out. Concentrate.
'Artie.'
Just need one more . . . Nearly there. *Morning has
broken* – no, dammit. *It's the dawning of the age of –*
bugger!
'Artie?'
I dragged my eyes from the page.

'Yes Oliver?'

'What about Shrigley Macosquin?'

With a degree of discipline unheard of in less pressurised circumstances, we stayed in the office at lunchtime and ate sandwiches (supplemented in Oliver's case with a selection of homemade fools and mousses from his refrigerated stash). Despite an increasingly assertive hangover, I attempted another poem, this time about a 19th century damask loom I had once seen in action at the Ulster Folk Museum. It started well enough – *He works the yarn like a virtuoso, / Pedals and strings like some strange piano* – but quickly foundered on lack of technical knowledge: chiefly, which was warp and which weft? And where did that leave woof? I earmarked a few rhyme possibilities (shuttle/subtle, brocade/blockade, flax/attacks) and put it aside until I could get to the library.

Oliver, meanwhile, had boiled his poet names down to a shortlist of six, which he wrote out on a sheet with a black marker pen and pinned to the door: Tynan Galbally, Gortin Pomeroy, Derry Kinawley, Moy Trillick, Tyrone Dunseverick, Glynn Seskinore. By the publication date, we assured ourselves, a process of elimination would have revealed the winner.

Chuffed with his map-work and invigorated by several jugs of lime-flavoured milkshake, Oliver volunteered to try his hand at a poem. I suggested something on the theme of forbidden love, which seemed to excite him. In longhand, tongue protruding, he began.

For myself, I thought, a sonnet. Good to have the discipline of form. But on what topic? I scanned the room. On the wall near the bookcase was a poster advertising an exhibition, long past, of artefacts from the *Titanic:* a jade and sepia-tinted photo montage including the stupendous vessel itself; its white-bearded captain; a cut-away of its massive central propellor, and spectators at its launch from Queen's Island (truly that was the era of the hat). I gazed at it for a while, at the faces staring back out of the photographic mist, at the doomed unsinkable liner framed by showers of silver light. An hour later I had completed *Ship of Fools*.

'What rhymes with husband?' Oliver demanded.

I thought for a moment.

'Hatband?'

He peered at his notebook, muttered something inaudible and resumed his labours. I rose and crossed to 'the kitchen' to refill the kettle. I was pleased with the start we'd made. If we could maintain this pace surely we would have enough in a couple of weeks to harvest at least a solid dozen? And it would be useful, I was thinking, if one of them was long, fifty lines or more, to fill up a few pages. That might be one for Oliver. I glanced over. He was staring into mid-air in a rictus of horrified wonder, as though witnessing something supernatural. Then again, perhaps my hopes were too high. Of course, there was always the possibility that this enforced creativity might unlock something deep within him, that he would turn out to be some kind of poetic idiot savant. I looked again. He already had the haircut.

When he left the room to perform one of his notorious three-act bowel movements I had time to run my eye over his work-in-progress. It was indeed on the theme of illicit passion and, while syntax and imagery were somewhat tortured in places, it had achieved some rhythmic momentum, and a certain emotional honesty.

We spent that Saturday with no clothes on,
Mostly in bed, but also on the sofa, and then
In my bathtub listening to Van Morrison
Singing about Jimmie Rodgers.
Your breasts were like two Jammie Dodgers.
You felt guilty about your husband
As you reached beneath the suds and
Took me in your hand. Poor bastard,
Back at home, alone, watching 'Grandstand'.

The next few lines had been amended to the point of disintegration and then scored out, the only legible words being *feather* and *hatband*.

Was it good? Sometimes it was hard to tell with poetry. It wasn't as bad as it could have been – there were definite signs of some kind of facility – but it seemed safe to shut down the sleeping genius possibility for the time being. In fact, it was beginning to dawn on me, depressingly, that when it came to creative partnerships through the centuries Conville and Sweeney were probably leaning less towards Wordsworth and Coleridge or Eliot and Pound and more towards The Krankies.

I devoted the remains of the working day to devising

likely-sounding titles for pieces we might write; an exercise that was oddly exciting, each one containing its own perfect unwritten poem.

The Stubble Burners
Dark City
Morning Star
No Man's Land
Lagan Delta Blues
Put Out More Flags!
Schrodinger's Cat
Atlantic Visions
Evening Star
Mushrooms (On Toast)

★

By Friday, despite a couple of failures of nerve, our poetry factory was hitting its stride, the air fairly crackling with brain activity. By the middle of the following week it was at full capacity. We obtained a second typewriter and our clacking duets, when the muses favoured us, were deafening. Gradually, out of blizzards of paper, pages bearing squares and oblongs of print began to accumulate. Oliver, fortified by milky treats, applied himself with unexpected vigour and produced (with some micro-management) several passable lyrics and an affecting elegy for the owner of his local off-licence, who was run over by a drunk driver. He was also working on Sunnyland Farm slogans on the sly (I spotted a particularly tortured one over his shoulder about how the rabbit wanted everyone to *hare* his *warren-ing* about dairy substitutes and *cotton on* to the luxury of full fat etc) but I said nothing. I decided to take on the required long poem myself and, selecting *The Stubble Burners* from the title list, embarked on what I hoped would blend an account of the impact of industrialisation on rural life in north-eastern Ireland with a meditation on humankind's need to impose order on nature, while also hinting that the whole thing was underpinned by a complex extended metaphor. It was no picnic.

Outside the window July had subsided into bloodshot August, and in the street below, the bad news on the sandwich boards in front of the newsagent's increased in frequency and brutality, flicking past as though in a film: IRA Kills Parents & Child 'By Mistake'; Two Catholics Shot Dead By PAF; Provos Murder Two Protestants In Belleek; Eight Soldiers Dead In Bus Attack . . .

During that period we rarely left the office. I met Rosie a couple of times for a drink after work but she was distracted by having to go early to visit her aunt, who was back in hospital, and at the weekend she was called in to babysit her inept father while her mother came up to town. Oliver had little to distract him either as Iris had been dragged away by The Mongoose for their annual fortnight in the Algarve. We took it in turns to shop for sundries at the mini-mart across the road and ate take-away food most nights. Eventually we gave up going home and kipped in sleeping bags on the floor. As the discarded pizza boxes and Chinese containers (not to mention Oliver's empty milk cartons) accumulated, space became a problem. Hygiene had already established itself as a real worry. So had Oliver's appearance, which was now – thanks to medieval hair, chronic sunshine deprivation and a diet of lactose, sugar and junk food – that of a bloated Nosferatu. I made him promise that when the magazine had been put to bed he would eat some vegetables. His skin, even though so etiolated it might have been bleached, seemed to absorb rather than reflect light . . . which reminded me.

'What's this?' he asked as my brother's complimentary Sizzlemaster 9000 coupon swished to a standstill in front of him.

'Free suntan.' I said. 'Put some colour in your cheeks.'

Once it had generated a critical mass of basic material, the character of our factory mutated into something more akin to a forge, as we melted the less distinct stuff down and hammered it into shapes we imagined would be pleasing to The Hawk. The work was even more exhausting than we had envisaged and as the production deadline approached (our cheap but slow printing outfit needed a two-week turnaround) we were reaching the end of our mental reserves. The pending file now boasted nearly thirty poems, only a third of which were pure guano. Half of the remainder were actually good, or at least not immediately recognisable as counterfeit: we had built in enough ambiguity, musicality and pretentious allusion to keep the experts busy for the foreseeable, should they be so inclined. We even had a space-hogging epic in *The Stubble Burners*, which had taken so many wrong turns I despaired of ever getting to the end of it but I'd ploughed on and, after a final bad-tempered and occasionally weepy afternoon, punched a full-stop on the last of a ball-busting seventy-five lines.

We hunkered down for a final edit, augmenting a core of twelve works by exciting new talent Tyrone Dunseverick (the name seemed to us to possess a certain mist-wreathed Hibernian glamour) with the best ten poems from the slush pile. The same day, as luck would have it, a controversial poetess finally responded to one of our begging letters with a clutch of erotic sonnets we were confident would arouse intriguing, subterranean emotions in the kind of jaded middle-aged man that sat on funding committees, say. Padding material included an unctuous but largely unintelligible review by Boyd Monroe of *Erato's Labia* and a series of lithographs by The Walrus entitled *The War On Kitchen Appliances* (including a particularly upsetting bandaged toaster). All that remained now was to publish . . . and be damned.

PART THREE

'Fantastico. Absolutely top notch.'

Stanford Winks was on the hotline.

'You've had a chance to look through it then?'

'I certainly have. More importantly, so has The Hawk.'

'And?'

'And he's over the moon. I've rarely seen him so excited. Where on earth did you find this Dunseverick fellow?'

'It's just a question of knowing where to look really. In a way he was just waiting for someone to put him on the map.'

'Well bravo to you guys, he's a godsend. And those dirty sonnets! Mama mia!' He let out a strangled snort of laughter. 'Not my cup of tea, needless to say, but the suits upstairs – even the accountants! – are suddenly *very* into literature, if you know what I mean.'

'Somehow I thought those might be of interest.'

'Listen Artie, while I have you – you *are* coming tonight, aren't you?'

'Coming? Where?'

'To the opening night.'

'The . . . what?'

'Of the play. *Suspicious Minds*. It opens tonight, God help us all.'

'Well, unfortunately – '

'Free tickets. And a wine reception afterwards.'

'Yeah, I'd like to but – '

'Artie, you've *got* to come,' he hissed. 'Moral support. Your man'll be there, that mad bastard, excuse my French . . .'

'Maybe Oliver could – '

'Excellent! Both of you then. I'll put your names on the guest list.'

To celebrate the success of the magazine, my co-editor and I hit Betjeman's for a slap-up lunch.

'Here's to *Lyre*,' Oliver said, raising the first of several expense-account pints.

We clinked.

'And long may we sail in her.'

Late morning light was illuminating the bar's rich interior, lapping at the ceiling, racing around the polished surfaces of our snug. We drank deeply. It tasted good. (A plate of Strangford oysters arrived in front of us.) We had met the challenge. Disaster had been averted and we were back on course.

The theatre was nearly full and the volume of pre-show chatter, its pitch raised at least a semi-tone by first-night anticipation, had plateaued at a quiet roar. The curtain would be going up shortly and I was beginning to feel self-conscious about the vacant seat beside me. Where the hell was Oliver? I performed another elaborate watch consultation and survey of the auditorium. We were in the third row, closer to the stage than I would have liked, and that ancient tingle of audience-participation-fear was making itself known. Earlier, in the theatre bar, I had seen several familiar faces: Quigley, in what appeared to be a matador's outfit, practically running on the spot with nerves; Monty Monteith, in a paisley cummerbund, inhaling brandy fumes from a balloon-glass, and – with a short-circuit of heartbeat – Mad Dog himself, leaning against the back wall watching the punters file in, a peculiar, sneering smile on his lips. He was wearing a black leather jacket with the collar turned up, and his mullet had been freshly coiffed and pomaded.

There were a number of agitated seat refugees accumulating in the aisle, and I was aware of a couple of them eyeing Oliver's unclaimed space. Where was he? I twisted around again for another scan. Bloody theatre. Still, if it was true to form I would probably be asleep by the end of the first scene. Always a high-quality snooze with drama. Why was that? Collective body heat? The lull of scripted conversation? Didn't Sean O'Casey make sure to include a gunshot late in the play to wake everyone up? Different, of course, if there's a chance of full frontal nudity . . .

I registered a displacement of air and a weight landed beside me.

'Jeez, you're cutting it – ' I began, turning back, but instead of Oliver's full moon visage I was face to face with Grainne McCumhaill.

'I take it there's no one sitting here,' she said, pulling off her beret and arranging herself.

'There is now,' I replied with a phoney grin.

Not a flicker.

'I didn't know you were a theatre fan.'

'Just doing my cultural duty,' I chirped. Bloody Oliver.

Opening her programme, she began intoning in a low voice. Was she reading aloud or cursing me in medieval Irish? I couldn't tell. The house lights were doused and the narcissistic din was replaced by a diminuendo of rustling and coughing.

'Do me a favour,' I whispered to McCumhaill. 'Wake me up if there's any nudity.'

Even in the darkness I could feel the sting of her glare.

There was silence as the curtains parted and then a fusillade of lager cans detonated along the front row where Mad Dog had installed his friends and family. Onstage, illuminated only by the grey-blue strobe of a television set, a bear-like, tattooed man in a vest was slumped in an armchair. He had a cigarette clamped beneath the crow's wing of his moustache and he sported a classic 'Weeping Willow' (a cheer of recognition erupted at the front). He seemed to be getting upset at something someone was saying onscreen. He argued with the voice for a while, then started to swear. Very angry. He hunched forward in his chair, his face a kabuki mask of fury. At last he grasped the heavy glass ashtray he was using and flung it at the TV which, after a few uncertain seconds, exploded and gave off copious smoke. At this point, a handsome, sleep-deprived woman in a fraying housecoat entered stage right and remonstrated with the man. They fought. The lights went down. In the next scene they began slogging through a gruelling passive-aggressive breakfast . . . I nodded off.

At the interval I met Winks at the bar.

'Well Stanford, what do you think?'

He grimaced.

'Isn't it ghastly?' he groaned. 'I can't believe – Hi Tristan!'

Quigley had appeared in front of us, quivering like an unweaned fawn.

'Well Stanford, what do you think?'

'Tristan, it's an absolute triumph. A tour-de-force.'

'Oh thank God you like it. What about you Artie?'

'Tristan, I can honestly say I was transported.'

'Just wait till you see the finale!' he cried, his eyes shining. 'Oh look, there's the author . . .'

He shimmied into the crowd. Winks blanched and took a hungry pull on his gin & tonic.

'Don't worry Stanford,' I said. 'You've given him what he wanted. You're in the clear.'

'I bloody hope so,' he replied with a shudder.

We resumed our places and the second act got under way with a clever split-stage device whereby we could see the reactions of the man as he listened in on his wife making mysterious telephone calls. He then went down the pub and voiced his suspicions to a friend, portrayed by Barney, somewhat incongruously, as a Sobranie-smoking sophisticate. This tragedy of errors continued until once again I succumbed to sleep.

Sure enough, I was jolted awake by the sound of gunshots, opening my eyes just in time to see a pair of blood-streaked female legs being dragged out of sight stage left. In the next scene, the man was again deep in his armchair. He seemed depressed. Then the phone rang and he had a conversation that appeared to clear everything up. Whatever it was that had resulted in the destruction of his wife's kneecaps, it was a big misunderstanding: she'd only been having an affair! (With the Barney character, as it turned out.) The man was laughing now, up and prancing and punching the air.

Cue music: spangling guitar over a frisky high-hat. The whole cast scuttling back onstage to sing the title track. To my horror, the audience began climbing to its feet. Participation! The front row was belting out the lyrics. It was contagious, and soon everyone was at it – even McCumhaill, who was bopping from side to side waving her beret in the air. It crossed my mind that she might try to embrace me and I cast around for an escape route, but the aisle was packed now too. I was caught in a trap! I couldn't walk out!

We hit the chorus, a key change that took an unexpectedly heavy toll on the collective vocal chords. The place was throbbing with bodyheat. Much to the delight of the punters at the front the leading man was attempting an ungainly Elvis impersonation. Then, at the back of the stage, his wife appeared, on crutches, inching forward, blinking in the spotlight. Faces around me began to crumple. People were openly sobbing. I watched through the protective cage of my own clawed fingers as she struggled towards us, wobbly on her shattered pins, gurning a spectrum of emotions . . . The noise, through *nine* curtain calls, was almost unbearable.

★

As soon as I walked in I knew something was wrong. Oliver's features were an even whiter shade of pale than usual and a half-eaten Snapjack lay abandoned by the phone.

'Winksie's been on the blower,' he reported. 'We got trouble.'

I sat down. What now?

'Okay, let me have it.'

It transpired there had been an early morning meeting up on the hill at which The Hawk had shared the results of his latest brainstorming session. Of these, the highest priority was a plan to expose schoolchildren and other innocent members of the community to real live poets in, what was described in Council-speak, as 'a bid to demystify the creative process'. Unfortunately, so impressed was he by what had been showcased in the latest *Lyre,* The Hawk wanted Tyrone Dunseverick to 'spearhead the initiative'.

'Holy shit. What did you tell him?' I asked.

'Well I said it was most unlikely,' Oliver stammered. 'I said Tyrone was a very private person . . .'

'Yes, and?'

'Who probably didn't like children . . .'

'Righ-hht. And?'

'And that he didn't even live here.'

'Good. Hang on, what? Where did you say he lived?'

'Um . . . Tyrone.'

I stared at him.

'You said Tyrone lived in . . . Tyrone?'

'He was yapping at me. I was flustered.'

'And what did he say?'

'He said the Council would pay travel expenses.'

I thought for a few minutes. Oliver did a bit of pacing.

'Well, it's quite straightforward,' I said. 'We'll just have to tell him no. We'll just say Tyrone is deeply focused on writing new stuff and he can't possibly waste time going around the country explaining himself to pesky kids . . .'

I rang Winks and apprised him of the situation. He understood completely.

'There,' I said. 'That's that. Another crisis dealt with. Now, let's get the kettle on.'

We selected some books and settled to a little light forging.

Ten minutes later the phone rang. It was Winks again.

'Listen Artie, I've just been up to see The Hawk and I told him what you said . . .'

'Right.'

'And he's not having it.'

'Pardon?'

'I'm afraid no isn't an option on this one.'

'What do you mean?'

'He wants Dunseverick.'

I took a deep breath.

'Well he can't have him. You'll have to get someone else.'

'He doesn't want anyone else.'

'What's so special about Dunseverick?'

'You want my opinion? I think he detects real fresh potential in him, and you know he's got a crazy idea about some kind of poetry . . . *renaissance* here? A second wave of heavyweights? I think he might just see your man as the catalyst he's been waiting for . . . Just a theory.'

'Well, it's not happening.'

'Artie, he's insisting.'

'He can't make him.'

'No, but he can make you.'

Not for the first time in recent weeks did I find myself opening my mouth without any words to vocalise.

'You're not without charm Artie,' Winks said. 'I'm confident you can persuade him. I'll send over the dates and venues shortly.'

A crisp click on the line marked the end of the conversation.

'We could kill him.'

'For Godsake don't start *that* again.'

'I don't mean The Hawk. I mean Tyrone.'

We were back in Betjeman's, in our favourite snug near the side entrance, the pints in front of us barely touched.

'We can't. In all likelihood we're going to need him for the next issue,' I pointed out.

'Oh yeah. Forgot about that.'

The door to the street was still open, despite the autumnal chill, and an intermittent breeze was depositing scraps of litter in the vestibule with a dry tinkling sound.

'I hate to admit it,' I said. 'But we could be well and truly snookered here.'

We lapsed again into morose silence. The previous day's jubilation in this same booth now seemed cruelly fleeting. Why did everything have to be so difficult all of a sudden? From our cubicle I could see the usual afternoon drowsers on their stools at the bar (most of the lunchtime trade had drifted back to work) and they looked as though they hadn't a care in the world. A radio that had been talking to itself in the background cleared its throat and began to get excited about the three-thirty at Lingfield, stirring a couple of them into an upright position. Two men entered, one of them calling for drinks, the other glancing idly around the interior. He made eye contact and raised a hand in greeting. It was Barney. I waved back.

'Who was that?' asked Oliver.

'Wee Barney.'

'Who?'

'Winksie's partner. You know, the actor?'

'Never met him.'

'Man of few words.'

The race started and quickly hit its stride, the commentator keeping pace with evangelical fluency, holding the narcoleptics spell-bound. The barman too, stood in reverential hush, polishing the whiskey glass in his hand to brilliance while the incantation built towards climax.

Then the final furlong, the men hunched, heads cocked, one of them using his folded tabloid as a crop to pound the side of the counter '. . . *And it's Cyrano de Bergerac by a nose* . . .' Explosive swearing. The barman guffawed and turned towards the optics.

'You know,' Oliver said. 'I've been thinking.'

'What have you been thinking?'

'Well . . .' He faltered.

'Go on.'

'We invented this Tyrone character on paper. Out of nowhere . . .'

'Yes?'

'Well, I'm wondering . . . What's to stop us inventing him in the flesh as well?'

'I'm not sure I'm with you.'

He was looking at me intently. I could see the thought process occurring live in his face, like clouds moving beneath his yoghurt-coloured skin.

'Why don't we get someone to *be* Tyrone Dunseverick?'

'To be . . . Tyrone Dunseverick?'

'Yes.'

'You mean like . . . an actor?'

'Yes.'

I took a gulp of my stagnating stout; wiped away the yellowing foam. Oliver was staring at me with shiny, expectant eyes. Was this a viable idea? Could it be done? Could we do it? Could we get away with it?

'No. We'd never get away with it.'

'Why not?'

I thought for a minute.

'For a start, this is a small town. Everyone knows everyone else. Especially in the theatre world.'

Oliver issued a hiss half way between a derisive titter and a weary sigh.

'Have you never heard of make-up? The ancient art of disguise?'

He leant back and rested his arms, crucifixion-fashion, along the seat ledge, watching my reaction. I practised a musical scale on the table top. Had he actually got something here?

'I'm still not sure it could work,' I said.

'Why not?'

'Because it would require absolute confidentiality and I'm not sure that's something human beings are capable of.'

'Wouldn't that depend on how much they needed the cash?'

The door to the snug squeaked open and a newspaper was thrust into view. I took it and pressed a coin into the hovering flytrap of fingers.

'I suppose that might be a factor . . . Okay, say we could actually swear someone to secrecy, who would it be?'

'What about wee Barney?'

This was typical of Oliver: have one bright idea and immediately sabotage its credibility with a half-baked follow-up.

'Do I really need to tell you why not? For one thing he lives with Stanford Winks, for another, he's probably not

196

in urgent need of dosh. No, what we need is an impoverished unknown.'

'Who has no scruples.'

'Precisely. Although they wouldn't necessarily need to know the full story.' Despite myself, I was warming to this scheme.

I began flicking through the paper. The usual blend of shove-ha'penny politics and provincial feel-good. On page five, I noted, 'Lovely Linda from Limavady' was pleased with her Harvest Fayre pumpkins. Insanely so, judging by the photograph. A phrase popped into my head and began repeating itself. *Lovely lemon liniment . . . Lovely . . .*

'You know what?'

'What?' Oliver was groping abstractedly at his doughey jowls as though he'd just discovered them.

'I think I know of someone who might fit the bill . . . Hold on, what's this?'

Page seven was given over entirely to a review of *Suspicious Minds*, complete with cast photographs and an insert of Mad Dog cupping his chin and scanning the horizon with poignant intent. Beneath the headline, She Ain't Heavy, She's My Wife, my darting eyeballs were subjected to a gush of rapturous prose that included the phrases, 'a theatrical experience like no other', '*Shadow of a Gunman* meets *Viva Las Vegas*', and 'this pistol-packing mama will run and run'. This couldn't *be*! Was this really happening? I read on. '. . . unashamedly hard-hitting . . . refreshingly visceral . . . dramatic writing of the highest order . . .' It bloody *was*. The country's most influential theatre critic had adjudged Mad Dog's play 'a triumph!' A hot mixture of impotence and disbelief swept through me. Was this the way it was? Was this *really* the way things were?

★

Later that week I called at the door of my upstairs neighbour. I had earlier heard him arguing with our landlord, so I knew he was in.

'Good evening . . . William, is it?' (I'd seen his name – William Fisher – on the envelopes that accumulated in the hallway.) 'Artie from downstairs. I was wondering if I could have a word?'

Fisher's flat was smaller and even more untidy than mine; strewn with books and bottles and at least a dozen makeshift ashtrays, all spilling over. I noticed a selection of wigs hanging on a hatstand beside the fireplace, like a tree full of sleeping marmosets. He apologised for the mess and, sweeping a heap of magazines off the sticky corduroy sofa, invited me to sit.

'You're the poetry guy, right? I've been meaning to drop by and say hello for ages. You want a cup of tea?'

'Um – '

'Good, 'cos I don't think there's any milk.'

He flopped into the armchair opposite, letting out an involuntary sigh as if just being upright had necessitated a tap on reserves. He was tall and thin, a few years older than me, with black hair and a long, handsome face defined by thick eyebrows and a pronounced chin. There were dark signs of insomnia beneath his eyes and he had the kind of undernourished look that would have your mother rummaging for her Shepherd's Pie recipe. So far, so good.

'Don't worry about it,' I said, extracting a book from under me. It was a copy of *The Jew of Malta*. 'Ah, the mighty Marlowe: *infinite riches in a little room*. I believe you're an actor? How's it going? Plenty of parts up for grabs?'

He ran a hand over his lugubrious features.

'No, not really. Well . . . yes and no. Depends who you are.'

I nodded supportively.

'S'a bit of a closed shop round here, to be honest. A tight scene. You really have to be in with the right people. To tell you the truth I'm thinking of getting out.'

His voice was of a richer timbre than had been evident through the ceiling and slightly husky from heavy smoking. This was also good. And his diction was precise. All those infuriating vocal exercises, no doubt.

'Really? Where would you go?'

'London. The West End. That's where the real action is – ' He gazed over my shoulder and was briefly lost to a dream of neon and applause. '. . . Real creativity. Real talent. Loads of money. One of these days I'll get up off my arse . . .'

Just then he did something peculiar with his chin, or perhaps, more accurately, his chin did something odd, because I'm not sure he was aware of it – a twitch downwards and to the left, twice, as though tugged by an invisible string.

'Are you alright?' I enquired.

'What? Yes, fine. Slight hangover. Nothing major. What about you, how's the poetry going?'

'Oh, you know how these things are: it's either a feast or a famine. At the moment it's neither one nor the other.'

We both realised simultaneously that what I had just said was completely meaningless. I smiled. He smiled. The silence edged towards vacuum.

'Well Artie, what can I do for you?'

This was it. Time for the pitch.

'I was wondering,' I said, keeping it casual. 'If you'd be interested in a little freelance work.'

He shifted in his chair, stiffening his posture, and reached into his shirt pocket for his cigarettes.

'Possibly.' He proffered the pack.

'Thanks. It's kind of a one-off. Pretty specialised,' I warned.

He shrugged.

'We've all got bills to pay – ' He struck a match and leaned forward. '. . . What had you in mind?'

I began sketching out our unusual requirements, watching as I did so, his expression mutate from one of rapt curiosity into one of simian incomprehension. (To be fair, his understanding may have been impeded by some strategic vagueness and verbal acts of omission on my part.)

'. . . So, you see, Billy – '

'Please. Call me William.'

'So you see, William, secrecy is absolutely vital here. It won't work otherwise.'

He said nothing. Taking a final drag of his cigarette, he ground the stub out in a jamjar lid and sat back.

'So. What do you think?' I asked.

He rubbed at his eye. His chin spasmed. It dawned on me that this was a permanent feature. Was it a problem? I decided it wasn't. In fact, it struck me that it might actually add a useful grace note to our poetic persona: an outer manifestation of inner tumult. (Did it also explain why he wasn't getting parts?)

'Isn't all this a bit . . . deceitful?' he said.

Uh-oh. A scruple.

'That's an interesting word to use William,' I remarked, tilting my head and fixing on a particularly bad landscape above the mantelpiece. I took a moment. 'But let me put it to you this way: doesn't all art depend on a kind of deceit? I mean, isn't acting itself pure illusion?'

'Yes, but . . .'

'The creation of something false in order to reveal something true?'

'Um . . .'

'Look William, it's probably best to see this job as a kind of artistic – ' (I nearly said 'happening'.) '. . . Experiment. An experiment whose success depends on *your* skills as an actor. It's a challenge, I admit, but – '

He was on his feet waving at me to shut up.

'I'll do it. How much will you pay me?'

Despite my fear of haggling (an arts education had left me singularly ill-prepared for the world of money) we went at it like a couple of cattle dealers, with Fisher pressing for fifty pounds per appearance and me keener on something around the thirty-five mark. Eventually we agreed on forty-two pounds fifty and sealed the deal over the dregs of a bottle of Sporran Dew that Fisher located behind the sofa. As the Chinese proverb says: *A wise man is never bound by his principles.*

Winks' promised schedule arrived in the post the next morning. In all, Dunseverick was down for half a dozen engagements before Christmas, the first of them the following afternoon – a little sooner than we'd expected. Winks had also included a note requesting a photograph of our man for the Council's in-house newsletter, which brought into even sharper focus the fact that . . . well, that we didn't know what Tyrone Dunseverick looked like. This was an obvious problem and possibly one we should have solved before my verbal contract with Fisher. However, if we'd learnt anything in the last few weeks it was that stuff didn't just happen: it required prime movers, discipline, and effort.

So, first things first. We knew, purely from the point of view of disguising our actor, that our bard pretty much *had* to have a beard, and I had reached certainty about one specific element of his attire, but that was about it. We gathered from the bookshelves all the volumes by male poets that had authorial pictures somewhere on their covers (Oliver, bless him, included Stevie Smith) and spread them out on the desk.

Boy, there were some beauties! Beards, I mean. From Sir Walter Raleigh's *contemptus mundi* Van Dyke, to

Henry Wadsworth Longfellow's Dutch Elongated, to Walt Whitman's electric-grey Hibernator. These guys knew about facial insulation. (Alfred Lord Tennyson's Maltese appeared to have been excised from a dead Airedale.) There's a theory that beard fashions blow in on the tail-winds of ferment and upheaval, and thus we see the clean-shaven look favoured by the Romantics (you might have thought that rambling man of the woods William Wordsworth was a dead cert for fuzz) giving way to seventy years of pogonotrophic magnificence following the European Revolutions of 1848. The huge Victorian face-bush finally met its end during World War One, kiboshed by a ban on beards in the military (hygiene? gas mask efficiency?), although moustaches must have been permitted, at least for officers, going by the famous portrait of Wilfred Owen.

In the remainder of the hell-for-leather twentieth century, between the mass marketing of the Gillette Safety Razor, the influence of cinema, the Beatnik goatee (hello Mr Ginsberg), and the counter-culture protest beard (hello Mr Ginsberg again), all bets were off. Most of those who had attained heavyweight status by mid way, William Butler Yeats, Robert Frost, Robert Lowell, Wallace Stevens, T.S. Eliot, Philip Larkin, for instance, seemed to have spurned face furniture, the odd ones out being perhaps John Berryman and Ezra Pound (Spade and Ducktail respectively).

We were beginning to narrow it down. It seemed that what we were looking for lay somewhere between the Italian False Goatee of Dante Gabriel Rossetti and the

Short Velutinous of Lawrence Ferlinghetti. Given that Dunseverick was, for various reasons, under thirty, we couldn't have anything too gone-to-seed: no Garibaldis, Van Winkles or Old Testament Prophets, for example. At the same time the nature of his poetry – sensitive urban soul drawn to seek the deep heart's core in rural tranquillity – meant that anything too cultivated, anything that smacked too strongly of the dandy, would strike a bum note.

We turned our attention to eyewear, and here we had more practitioners but less range, the style of spectacles dictated in those days largely, I imagine, by the relevant national health boards. Robert Lowell, Patrick Kavanagh and Allen Ginsberg seem to have had a time-share on the same lead-framed pair. Larkin gazes sadly out from behind twin cathode ray tubes. The exception is Yeats, whose aerial-thin rims are in keeping with his cold, finely-tuned face. This was a dilemma. Was Dunseverick a vanity-free heavy-duty man? Or a studious aesthete with just a hint of self-regard?

These impressions could all be balanced, offset or corrected, of course, by his outfit, and here it was my firm belief that there was no room for vacillation: it had to be tweed; the primordial, rough-hewn, wheaten-flecked fabric favoured by the Irish literary figure for generations. The tweed jacket transcended age, build, religion and class while whispering ambivalently about all of them. The right one would be the bedrock of Dunseverick's identity, his backbone, his armour.

To this end and with categoric instructions, I sent

Oliver off to his favourite charity shop armed with a fistful of petty cash. Meanwhile I rang Winks to try and play for time. No dice. However I did manage to negotiate the itinerary down to three appearances on the basis of Dunseverick's need to finish a career-defining sonnet sequence. The requested photograph of our poet, I blithely assured him, was forthcoming.

Early the next morning we convened at Fisher's flat to start work on our creature. To his credit, Fisher had raided the backstage lockers of the youth theatre where he helped shift scenery and stocked up on crepe hair and grease paint. He had also already chosen from his personal wig-tree two contenders for the poet's barnet (a component of the costume Oliver and I had overlooked). One was a nut-brown mass of Swinburnian curls that could be parted girlishly off-centre, the other an unkempt shock of beige tufts the texture of Alsatian fur. We decided to leave the hairstyle decision till last and set about constructing the all-important beard.

Who knew this would be such a painstaking task? After an hour of pasting, trimming and bickering, and an entire bottle of theatrical spirit gum, Fisher looked as though he had been bobbing for apples in a vat of pubic hair.

'It's not my fault,' he moaned. 'Normally this is the make-up artist's job.'

Oliver returned from Fisher's bathroom, into which he'd disappeared forty-five minutes earlier.

'What, did I miss the cunnilingus competition?' he asked.

'Very helpful, thank you Oliver. Let's see you do better.'

We applied several more layers of gingery fluff, and not helped by the unpredictable convulsions of Fisher's chin, eventually managed to pare the resultant bush down to a half-credible embryonic Hibernator. It wasn't what we'd discussed but it would have to do.

'Right Oliver, clothes. How did you get on?'

'Oh, I think you'll be pleased,' he said, and rummaging in the binbag he had brought with him, hauled out not just a jacket but a whole suit of heavy cloth on a hanger. It was tweed alright, the unrefined variety, so rough it was actually painful to the touch, and of a colour best described as 'stagnant green'.

'Ten quid,' Oliver cooed with pride. 'And bagsy I have it when this is over.'

'It smells,' Fisher said, holding it at arm's length. 'Like some old boy lay dead in this for quite some time.'

Oliver affected not to hear him.

'And here's your shirt.'

An off-white dress shirt with yellowing frills down the front landed on the chair.

'I thought it was like something Shelley would have worn,' Oliver explained.

Fisher took his costume into the bathroom and closed the door. (We heard a shout of disbelief followed by choked outbursts of swearing.)

Oliver rootled in his bag again.

'What do you think of these?' he asked, passing me a pair of heavy, black-framed spectacles. 'Fifty pee.'

They were classic Larkins, made, apparently, of some form of onyx, with scratched, biscuit-thick lenses. I tried them on. It was like viewing the world through pond ice. It hurt. I held my hands in front of my eyes. Smears of pink. Oliver's face loomed at me like a reflection in a fairground mirror.

'Well?' he enquired.

'I can't see a thing. Show me the others.'

'Actually, that's all I could find.'

'You gotta be – '

A large algae-coloured shape was pulsating in the doorway. I removed the glasses. It was the actor. Wearing his poet suit. We stood for a few moments in silence, taking it in. I had to admit, it wasn't an easy look to carry off, but Fisher was as close to getting away with it as could reasonably be expected. The jacket, apart from a certain brutality to the cut of the shoulders and a slight flare at the midriff, was a success. It looked authentic. It had *gravitas*. Unfortunately, the same could not be said of the trousers. To begin with, they were too short. The suit may once have been the property of a big man, a broad man, but it had not belonged to a tall man. These trews stopped three-quarters of the way down Fisher's legs, leaving exposed an alarming span of bony white shank. Length, though, was not the whole story. Their real drawback lay in the construction of the crotch area, where a substantial weight of material had been invested in a foot-long welted fly. Over the years the strain of this feature had fatigued the surrounding fabric, dragging the gusset down to about knee level. From the front this made it appear as though the wearer had been cursed with an absurdly short lower body; from the rear it invited the suspicion that the breeches were cradling a grotesquely overburdened nappy. The overall impression at this stage was of D.H. Lawrence in the role of Toad of Toad Hall. Those flaws aside, though, it wasn't bad.

'The jacket's good,' I said.

'Yep, yep, the jacket's working,' Oliver agreed.

'Really? It's okay?' There was anxiety in the actor's voice. 'What about the trousers?'

Oliver and I exchanged glances.

'They're fine. A little short, but we can fix that. Oliver, do you still have those Doc Martens?' I asked.

'Yes, but – '

'Great, we'll pick them up on the way. Now let's do the hair. We're against the clock.'

Fisher squeezed his own lank mane under a mesh skull-cap and pulled on the first wig, the Alsatian. The colour mis-match with the beard was interesting, but there was a whiff of the shock-treatment lab about the style.

'Mmm, a little bit serial killer. Could frighten the kids,' I concluded.

He donned the Swinburne which, although just about on the sane side of unruly, chimed with the frilly Shelley shirt for a much gentler effect.

'Oliver, the spectacles, if you please.'

Fisher eased the glasses on and staggered slightly sideways.

'Holy shit! I can't – '

'Don't worry,' I soothed. 'You'll get used to them in no time.'

There was no doubt about it: the Larkins pulled the whole ensemble together, completed the picture. The question was: what was it we were looking at?

Our venue was a boys' secondary school twenty miles from town where, we'd been told, our impending visit would have shiny-eyed sixth-formers hopping from foot to foot gagging for culture. In the taxi, Dunseverick practised declaiming some of his poetry. If you closed your eyes and focused on his grave, actorly voice it actually sounded like . . . poetry. It was only when he'd read out one of the weaker efforts (a Crapsey cinquain by Oliver about an injured blackbird) that I realised he could probably make a tax demand sound good. Tendons were twitching in the driver's neck and after a while he yielded his verdict. 'Too fucken modern for me,' he announced. 'I'm more a fan of your old-fashioned . . .'

It began to drizzle and he flicked on the wipers. The trees on either side of the road had lost most of their green now and started on the slow burn from ochre to copper, the colours blurring in the rain. The year had passed its tipping point. (*Lord: it is time. The summer was immense. | Lay your shadow on the sundials | and let loose the wind in the fields.*) We pushed on into the countryside, glimpsing now and then drumlins beyond the hedgerows, tractors at work against a mercurial sky. I was experiencing intense pangs of seasonal change: a feeling not unlike the late stages of convalescence; a sense – nagging, elusive – that something invisible was somewhere preparing to swarm.

But there was something else as well, a commingling of excitement and melancholy that may simply, of course, have been underlying fear. We had set in train, after all, events that required careful management and that were fast gaining their own momentum. It had become clear in recent days just how vulnerable our plans were to circumstance, to outside interference, to chaos, and how easy it would be for it all to spin out of control. The unreality of the current situation was not lost on me: one glance over my shoulder, at the Poet From Another Dimension mumbling to himself in the back seat, was enough to elicit something close to panic. How to make it stop though?

It was still raining when we reached the school. While I waited for the driver to compose a receipt, I watched Oliver help Dunseverick up the front steps. Technically blind, and severely hindered by his pendulous bags, the poet was forced to adopt an Orangutan-like gait in order to haul his, it had transpired, outlandishly large boots up and over each obstacle. That he was making such heavy weather of relatively unchallenging terrain was not reassuring. (Nor was my observation of him on several occasions that morning taking needy gulps from a blistered hip-flask.)

We were greeted in the foyer by a young, prematurely-balding teacher in a chalky gown. He seemed surprised that there were three of us.

'Oh, I, we weren't expecting . . . Mr Winks said . . .'

'It's alright,' I told him, gesturing to my left. 'There's only one poet.'

He stared uncertainly at Dunseverick, who sniffed in his direction like a new-born rat, and then at us again.

'We're just his minders,' explained Oliver.

The man nodded, clearly confused.

'Publishers,' I corrected. 'We're his publishers. But we also take care of his engagements, you know how it is with these artists, they're not great at the organisational side of things.'

'Ah, good. That's . . . Shall we get started?'

He bade us follow him along a corridor, then stopped.

'Listen, I should tell you. There's been a bit of a mix-up – ' He treated us to a toothy rictus. 'I'm afraid the seniors are actually away on a field trip, up at the Giant's Causeway, looking at rocks or something. But luckily the first-years have a free period . . . I hope that's okay?'

We proceeded towards the assembly hall past class-rooms and laboratories from which drifted nostalgic vapours of camphor and sulphur, disinfectant and dead vegetables. The jungle sounds that we'd noticed on arrival – the yelping, screeching, grunting and hooting – grew louder. I looked back at Dunseverick labouring behind us in his lead boots. His beard was twitching with independent life. He halted outside the toilets.

'I'm just going to . . . I'll just be a minute,' he informed us.

While we waited our guide gave us a brief and tedious

history of the school. I didn't hear a word. My mind was flexing through possible scenarios in the event of discovery. Would I be able to make a run for it? Pass it off as a joke? Blame it all on Oliver?

Dunseverick reappeared a few minutes later, his chin temporarily sedated.

'You okay, champ?' I enquired.

'Never better. Now, let's do some poetry,' he replied. He shuffled onward, leaving in his feeble slipstream the fumes of some potent but unidentifiable spirit.

The first-years spotted his trousers immediately but luckily Dunseverick was too focused on clambering onto the stage to worry about the merriment. Our chaperone, on the other hand, whose survival *depended* on the early detection of anarchy, moved in to shut it down. Eventually, the boys were cowed into a receptive silence and the talent stepped up to the lectern.

'*Poetry is a mirror*,' he boomed. '*Which makes beautiful that which is distorted.*'

What was this? Ad-libbing?

The first-years stared up at him.

The poet adjusted his glasses.

'When I was your age our English teacher used to start the class with that line. Does anyone know who said it?'

A hand went up.

'Yes?'

'Your teacher?'

Exaggerated laughter.

'Boys! Boys!' Their keeper was on his feet. 'That'll do, thank you . . .'

'No,' said Dunseverick, with a quiver of the chin. 'No. It was a poet called Percy Bysshe Shelley. Does anyone know anything about Shelley?'

Another hand.

'Yes?'

'Sir, was he very very smelly?'

Uproarious cackling.

'Boys! Boys! That'll do! Childish . . .'

Dunseverick's chin jerked twice, three times.

'Perhaps we'd better just get on with the poems,' he muttered.

Thank God.

'The first one I'd like to read is called *Ship of Fools* and it's about – '

Something small and hard ricocheted off the base of the lectern. The teacher jumped up and scanned the front row. Falcon eyes. Snake eyes. No one cracked. He wagged a warning finger and sat down again between Oliver and me.

'. . . About a famous ship called the *Titanic*, which, as you all know, was built in Belfast . . .'

There was a murmur of apathy.

The poet took a breath, consulted his typescript and realised he couldn't see. Hoisting his glasses up and outwards so they were poised just above the bridge of his nose, he peered downwards and began.

'Could it be, the whole disaster pivots
Not on fire or ice, or ignored advice,
But on the quality of the rivets?'

Apart from an occasional slur, he was reading it well. Slow and generally clear, with a slightly Shakespearean style. And was it my imagination or was he trying out a soft Tyrone accent? Definitely something going on with the intonation. His audience tired of coughing and fidgeting and settled into a trance-like condition.

'. . . *That a ship, unchristened, would be all at sea,*
Regardless of religion or technology.
'*Nearer, My God, to Thee.*'

He rattled on through his perilously limited repertoire (we'd told him not to attempt *The Stubble Burners*). After a while I tiptoed outside for a refreshing cigarette. It had stopped raining and there was a faint layer of steam on the surface of the playing fields. From where I was standing I could see into the assembly hall and the top third of the poet above his pulpit. Even blurred by the condensation on the windows the look wasn't quite right. I began to think about adjustments . . .

As I re-entered the venue Dunseverick was concluding his reading with my favourite of his poems – or rather, his favourite of my poems.

'*The streetlamps fade. The dreamers are stirring . . .*'

He paused for effect, squinting into space through his mysterious lenses. His beard twitched.

'*Let's pretend it's the morning of the world.*'

He waited a beat. Two beats. God he was good.

'Thank you. Thank you very much.'

The appreciation was slow to come and fast to fizzle out.

The teacher hovered over his seat.

'Well boys I'm sure you all agree that was terrific stuff. Very enjoyable. And now I think Mr Dunseverick might be willing to take a few questions . . .?'

He sought confirmation from the stage but none was forthcoming. I looked at Oliver. We hadn't thought this far ahead. It struck me it could be treacherous terrain.

'Okey-dokey then.' A fresh rictus. 'Who has a question for . . . our guest?'

Several hands.

'Sir, where do you get the ideas for your poems?'

Nothing too challenging there.

The poet burbled for a few minutes about feelings and dreams, and about how poetry was everywhere and how (without giving examples) he never knew quite when it would strike. His questioner was blatantly unimpressed.

'Anyone else?'

'Sir, can poetry be any good if it doesn't rhyme?'

For some reason Dunseverick had to think about this one.

'Interesting question. And the answer is yes, certainly, it can. Some of Shakespeare's greatest soliloquies . . .'

At this point our balding mediator was distracted by something in the corridor and excused himself to attend to it. The atmosphere changed.

'Sir, are you a Catlick or a Proddydog?'

'Pardon?'

Another small-calibre, high-velocity missile cracked against the podium and shattered. And again. Someone farted.

'Sir, your trousers look very heavy. Are they full of cack?'

'*What*?'

A fight broke out in the second row. The noise rose to incipient riot level. A Kola Kube whistled past Oliver's ear.

'Little bastards,' he growled.

'Sir, sir . . .'

Dunseverick was confused by what was happening and raised his spectacles the better to see.

'Yes?'

'Sir, what's wrong with your chin?'

'You cheeky fu – '

A sucked pear drop hit him in the eye.

'Ow, Christ – '

'Boys! Boys! That's enough now! That'll do!'

They shrank back in their chairs. The tumult died. Their tamer had reappeared, accompanied by a familiar figure in a Burnt Umber corduroy suit.

'Boys, this is Mr Winks – ' Cue sniggering. '. . . From the Arts Council, and he's here to take some pictures of you and Mr Dunseverick for the Council magazine. Isn't that exciting? Now, I need you all to form into lines by height . . .'

I engaged Winks in conversation while Oliver helped Dunseverick down.

'Didn't expect to see you here Stanford.'

'No, well I thought I'd bring the mountain to Muhammad. How did it go?'

'Excellent. He's a natural. The kids really connected with him. Ah, here's the man himself – ' There was no avoiding it. '. . . let me introduce you.'

The bard proffered an imperious hand, which Winks took while involuntarily performing a kind of mangled curtsey.

'Glad to meet you sir, we're all big fans of yours up at the Council,' he gushed.

The writer grunted. Tears were streaming from his injured eye.

'Are you alright?' asked Winks. 'Your eye seems . . .'

'Oh, it's nothing,' said Dunseverick, with a dismissive wave. 'I often get overtaken by emotion when I read my work . . .'

(This guy was good. He *should* have been on the stage.)

Winks was instantly smitten.

'I can understand that, of course. Your poetry strikes me as particularly personal, heart-felt, it has a passionate intensity – '

He was interrupted by news that the first-years were ready for their close-up.

'Would you mind? It's for our next internal. Won't take a minute.'

The poet approached the clustered arrangement of boys in front of the stage even more gingerly than his trousers would allow. I noticed Winks do a double-take on his badgerish rear view.

'That's lovely. Good. If we could just get Mr Dunse-verick in the middle,' the teacher called.

Winks unwrapped his camera and began fiddling with a pack of flash bulbs.

'Okay, stop moving around,' the teacher directed. 'Boys, I will expel the next person I see mooning, is that clear? Are you alright Mr Dunseverick?'

The poet dabbed at his bubbling eye socket.

'Right. I'm ready,' said Winks from behind his lens.

So, giant Dunseverick posed with his tiny tormentors and, much to my deep unease, his mad-haired, bushy, broken-eyed image (the only one on the roll free of rabbit ears or devil horns) entered the annals.

*

With Dunseverick's first public appearance out of the way, and his next not due for several weeks, life in the *Lyre* office returned to its customary gentle pace. We showed up late, broke early for lunch and mostly read or dozed in the afternoons. We sent off letters to poets begging for new material, and every couple of days Oliver would ring round the publishing houses to blag review copies of the latest releases. After a while I started tinkering with some new Dunseverick poems for the next issue (there hadn't been much pick-up in contributions) and my co-editor resumed his quest for a Sunnyland Bunny slogan. The competition's closing date was fast approaching and he embarked on a final milk binge, struggling in each morning with sacks of homemade puddings and ices, and whipping up tall creamy beverages at every opportunity. I helped him out where I could (drawing the line at the egg nog) but the man himself was a living appetite-killer; a slurping, belching, waddling cautionary tale.

And all for what? Could he even remember? The various elements of his futile endeavour, it seemed to me – his desire to escape, his hunger to see the world, his addiction to comfort food – had fused into a mirage of elsewhere, an illusion that was threatening to blind him to his earthly blessings. What was so awful about here anyway? Okay it had been a bit tempestuous of late but we had prevailed, and now we were no longer under pressure. At least not in the way others were. The guys on the clock. The suckers.

The luxury of our relaxed itinerary had been underlined by a conversation with Rosie. I telephoned her office to arrange a drink after work and, get this: she didn't have time to talk to me! She was too busy! As I regarded the vacantly purring receiver, I was reminded with a jolt that the time zone in which I had operated for most of my adult life – a realm where half a day could be soaked up by a view from a window or a book plucked idly from a shelf – was not where the general public lived. Not even having a spare minute to shoot the breeze? *No time to see, in broad daylight, | Streams full of stars, like skies at night*? Unthinkable. Of course, I understood the principle (I had taken a little philosophy, after all): someone had to fetch the water from the well, blah blah, this person had to be rewarded, etcetera, this led to the exchange of commodities, blah, and ultimately the trading of time for money, and so on and so forth. This was a fact of life, and devising a way to juggle the two, it seemed, was to locate a string through the labyrinth. It was just that I personally wasn't ready to negotiate that particular balance of payments yet.

Neither was Oliver, needless to say, although the dictates of his stomach, his wardrobe, and his mistress-entertainment budget meant his need for cash was greater than mine (most of the review copies landing on the mat these days were being whisked directly to the second-hand book merchants, sometimes still in their Jiffy bags). Sometimes I wondered if his surrender to a nine-to-five could be that far off.

One person who was suddenly *not* short of the folding stuff was Mad Dog, a blow-up of whose moustache (and sideburns) had accompanied the incredible news that *Suspicious Minds* was transferring to the West End.

'This ex-community-worker-turned-playwright came out of nowhere to bow-wow the Northern Ireland arts world,' the news reader chirped. 'Now it's the turn of London audiences to pant for his unique take on life, love and loyalty. I think it's safe to say this Dog has taken the biscuit. Let's hear now from the director . . .'

Rosie and I were watching this in the saloon of The Pen and Quill, where we'd called for a swift drink on the way to the cinema (Wim Wenders' *Wings of Desire* – her choice).

'I thought you said his play was crap,' she exclaimed.

'It was. At least the bits I was awake for were,' I said.

Quigley appeared onscreen wearing a polka-dot cravat. It was a four-week run, he told us, and it was already sold out – a record, apparently, for an unknown provincial production moving to the West End.

'This play is, quite simply,' he revealed. 'A parable for our times.'

There followed some gritty footage of Mad Dog roaming the streets of his native city in the rain, pausing tragically before murals of monster-warriors feasting on the entrails of their enemies, emoting outside pubs as they disgorged lost souls into the night, brooding over glistening roofscapes from the heights of Cavehill. It may have been due to the weather but his hair was unusually pompadourish, and he was sporting a strange, cape-like garment that swirled out behind him in the long shots.

'What's with that cape, is he a fucken superhero now as well?' I growled.

'What's eating you?' Rosie wanted to know. 'At least he's doing something.'

There was an edge to her tone.

'What's that supposed to mean?'

She shrugged. 'Nothing.'

'No, please, go on.'

She shot me one of her unreadable looks.

'I'm just saying that, you know, no matter what *you* think, he's being successful. And that's better than nothing. That's all.'

I was pretty sure that wasn't all.

'Are you saying I've got nothing?'

'On the contrary you've got a lot. It's just . . .'

'Yes?' I could feel a prickle of heat on my neck, blood-static in my ears.

'Well, you've got potential, that's obvious – to do what I'm not absolutely sure – but you're not using it. You seem content just to stay in the background and make others look good.'

'That's not really . . . Like who?'

'Poets. This new guy, Tyrone whatsisname, for example, that you say everyone's talking about.'

'Dunseverick.'

Yes. Why can't *you* be Tyrone Dunseverick?'

(Reviewing this conversation at a distance I realised there had actually been a moment of high ground at this point, from which I had weighed the possible consequences of full disclosure and, despite a clamour of internal dissent, plunged on regardless.)

'Let me tell you something about Tyrone Dunseverick . . .'

Clearly, it was a mistake to tell Rosie the truth. I know that now. I think I knew it then too but, as I say, I went ahead anyway. Why? Why indeed. This was a question I would puzzle over at some length. This, and why I had been quite so shocked at the cold judgmentalism of her response. What had I expected? Approval? Admiration? *Respect?* Was it possible I was somehow *proud* of the entity I had brought into the light? I mean, who was I kidding? Rosie, I had to admit, was on the money: our strategem was not a masterclass in stylish anarchy, it was 'devious, dishonest and – ' (perhaps most stinging of all) '. . . *juvenile*'.

There were other home truths that found their target in our row that night, not least the accusation that I was a moral coward of the first water, paralysed by fear of failure. This I hotly denied, of course (shouting about psychobabble and cliches), but later in the pounding silence of my room I began to wonder. *Was* I hiding from reality (whatever that was), and if so, what *was* it I was afraid of? The word juvenile kept coming back. Juvenile . . . infantile . . . puerile . . . Wait a minute! Was I *jejune*? I paced. I smoked. I stood at the window. I stood smoking at the window. I turned the radio on. The end of the late news: 'Gunmen . . . feud . . . punishment . . . dead . . .' I switched it off. Tried to read. A book at random from the shelves. . . . *And so it stays just on the edge of vision, | A small unfocused blur, a standing chill | That slows each impulse down to indecision . . .*

Eventually though, even the words of the unblenching Larkin became just that: words. On paper. And I fell asleep.

★

Rosie and I didn't speak again for a while after the dangerous-truth-telling session. My pride was hurt. But whether she was right or wrong (she was right) wasn't the point: I still couldn't see a way to abort the Dunseverick project. We had no choice but to follow through.

As luck would have it the poet's next appearance turned out not to involve children but around twenty members of a cross-community Women's Group who met once a month in the back room of their local library. Officially, their purpose was 'to raise consciousness via the embrace of modern culture' but in reality it was an excuse to eat cake and trade tales of spousal imbecility. They regarded Dunseverick with some concern (I overheard one of them remarking that he could do with 'a good dose of Shepherd's Pie') and began fussing over him immediately. Oliver, who had spent the entire journey gripped by fear that we were entering an ambush of feminists, saw he was among sympathetic women more or less the same age as his girlfriend and relaxed.

The bard, in particularly crapulent condition but managing to pass it off as artistic angst, rumbled through his set. Apart from a minor loss of chin control during *Lagan Delta Blues* and a barely perceptible unravelling of the beard as he cast his eyes to the heavens at the end of *Put Out More Flags!*, it was without incident. We moved on to the Q&A. The ladies wanted to know where he got the ideas for his poems. Why didn't he write more about love? Didn't he have a girlfriend? Would he like one? (Ribald laughter.)

Perspiring freely (and worryingly for us, given his prostheses), our man of letters was then taken by both arms and led to a long trestle table laid out with hot drinks and treats. The silver-haired lady manning the teapot seemed oddly familiar.

'What'll you have son, a wee eclair? Or a wee tray bake? Those wee vanilla slices are lovely, so they are. Go on, have two, you're looking a wee bit peaky.'

Mystifyingly, given that thanks to a hasty beard job he resembled a child's Etch-a-Sketch drawing of a werewolf, Dunseverick proved irresistible to the women. Oliver and I watched in amazement as they clustered round, jockeying for position, now and then one of them finding an excuse to stroke his sleeve. ('Are you *seeing* this?' Oliver squeaked through a mouthful of caramel square.) The poet, initially daunted by the attention, began to enjoy it, indulging his fans with sardonic apercus they in turn contrived to find hilarious. (He delivered these with a peculiar waggle of the head that I hoped was affectation rather than the emergence of a new affliction.)

Eventually, after Oliver had collected the price of twenty copies of *Lyre*, we extracted Dunseverick and took a taxi back to town. It was Halloween and the streets were teeming with vampires and demons, fireworks crackling along the skyline like gunfire. Several times before we reached the pub our way was blocked by gangs of drunken monsters, a couple of whom mistook Dunseverick for one of their own.

Installed at the bar with a large whiskey and a chaser of stout, the poet seemed delighted at how things had gone with the ladies, positively pumped up on feminine feedback.

'One of them even slipped me her number,' he purred, removing his Larkins.

'Really, which one?'

'The small good-looking one.'

We were stumped.

'Sorry, *which* one?'

'You know, the wee blonde serving the tea.'

★

We had entered November ('the Norway of the year', as Emily Dickinson once remarked) and there was an icy edge to the wind that chased the remaining leaves along the avenues. The city turned up its collar; people began withdrawing to the fireside; the pubs kept their samovars constantly at boiling point to meet the demand for hot whiskies. In the parks, the trees were black tangles of arteries against thin grey sky.

At the office, the building's antediluvian heating system, with its church organ-sized radiators, seemed to have jammed on, and as a result Oliver and I were spending more time there than in the meat lockers of our respective flats. Despite that, we weren't making much headway with the next issue, inspiration on the Dunseverick front having all but dried up.

Relations between me and Rosie, which had remained frosty longer than expected, had, I felt, begun to thaw. And then, during a telephone call she casually mentioned she'd been offered a place on a training course. In London.

'Great. Are you going to take it?'

'It's at the LSE, I'd be a fool not to.'

'Absolutely. When does it start?'

'Next week.'

'That soon? I see. How long?'

'About a month.'

'Really? That long?'

There was a silence.

'Look Artie, I'm going to be pressed for time, things to sort out at home and stuff, so I probably won't see you before I go. Okay?'

I sat for a few minutes afterwards, staring at the phone, listening to desultory gusts of hail against the office windows. (I was alone. Oliver had headed off after lunch, lugging a bag of books.) I felt oddly bereft. It seemed the flare-up with Rosie may have been more serious than I realised, more than just a shot across the bows. More, in fact, of a point-blank opinion, that I was actually irredeemable. In fact, (I was blinking rapidly now), was she cutting me adrift? I overcame the urge to ring her back.

Images from the previous few months flickered past. One day in particular: a Sunday afternoon in September, following the Lagan out of the city. We had risen late and eaten well at a café (our appetites sharpened by our earlier labours) before strolling through fields and woods to join the river. The air still had the soft quality of summer, and smelled of meadowsweet and mallow and silt. We felt good in our skins, healthy animals at large in a benevolent world. As we rounded a bend, suddenly, from the iridescent shadows under the trees on the opposite bank, a kingfisher broke cover and shot low-down over the water past us and back the way we had come. We both saw the flash of blue-green – stood stock still – caught his intense singularity of purpose; a microsecond drawn out. Rosie turned to me in wonder, and in her eyes, in the reflected light, I saw all the colours of the riverbed, and something else as well: a green-blue blaze like the ghost of the bird itself, and I thought –

The phone rang and I snatched up the receiver.

'Artie, it's Stanford. Have you got a minute? We've had an idea . . .'

Those guys up on the hill had far too much time on their hands, it seemed to me. The plan they'd hatched, Winks and The Hawk between them, was this: instead of our next scheduled issue of *Lyre*, we were to publish a booklet, a chapbook of Tyrone Dunseverick's work; a nicely-produced edition of, say, twenty or so poems, with a modest print-run of, say, a thousand. A collector's piece. The budget would allow for a little strategic advertising and, even better, ('to help give the lad the leg up he deserves') for a public reading and a launch party.

'We're not talking champers and caviar here, just nibbles, say, and the usual glass of wine, you know the sort of thing.'

I did.

'Well?' Winks's voice was breathy. 'What do you think?'

I wasn't sure it mattered *what* I thought so long as I agreed. As for the plan itself, it was something of a double-edged blade. On the one hand it did away with the need to squeeze out another problematic magazine, on the other it meant our phantom would become further entangled in the material world and, more worryingly in the short term, be subject to intense scrutiny by just the kind of people we would be wise, *say*, to avoid.

'I think it's a brilliant idea,' I said.

Which is exactly how I put it to Oliver the next morning.

Looking on the bright side, we already had the dozen poems that had appeared in the last *Lyre*, so in theory, the back of the job was almost broken. We reckoned that to make our chapbook convincing we needed another ten solid pieces. There were a few possibilities left over from our previous frenzy that might pass muster with a bit of surgery, and I'd made a start in recent weeks on another couple that showed promise. That left just five poems to write from scratch. Put that way, it didn't seem too bad. Time, however, was tight.

We knuckled down, Oliver attempting to rehash the left-overs while I pondered the new. It has to be said, it didn't get any easier. Oliver had turned in a love lyric (of sorts) and a piece set in the mountains of Donegal (*Bluestack Lightning)* that we were counting as a West of Ireland Pastoral. I had almost completed one about a Woolworths store being blown up (*Burnt Sugar*) but had accepted my mushroom poem (*The Morel of the Story*) was unlikely to see the light of day.

Dunseverick's final engagement before the big launch was at an old people's home in the north of the city. It should have been child's play, but when we arrived at Fisher's flat that morning there was a problem.

'I can't do it.'

He was sitting in his armchair clenching a can of Headbanger Extra and smoking in a particularly urgent fashion, the red-hot tip accounting for nearly half the length of his cigarette. He was unshaven and his hair was greasy.

'Easy there, big fellah,' I soothed. 'What is it you can't do?'

'This – ' he gestured floppily with his fag hand. '. . . This morning. I can't do it.'

Oliver and I were seated on the sofa opposite. Oliver got to his feet. 'Why don't I make us a nice cup of coffee?' he mumbled, and headed for the kitchen.

'William, it's just a touch of stage-fright,' I said. 'Happens to everyone. You'll feel better when we get you into your costume.'

'No. No, that's not it. It's . . . you see – '

'Yes?'

'I've got another job.'

His chin fluttered. He mashed out his cigarette and tossed back the remains of his can. (Watching him drink high-voltage soup this early in the day was making me feel distinctly queasy.)

'What?'

'I've got another job,' he repeated, more defiant this time.

'But William, we have an agreement. Today's been in the diary for weeks.'

'I know, I know, but this is important.'

A sequence of clatterings concluded in the kitchen and Oliver appeared in the doorway.

'I can't find the milk,' he said.

'There isn't any,' Fisher conceded.

Oliver turned on his heel.

'Ours is important too,' I said.

'Yes, but yours is temporary. This other one could be regular.'

'What exactly is this other one?'

Fisher explained that the previous month, in a bid 'to starve the terrorist and the hijacker of the oxygen of publicity on which they depend', the government had banned groups believed to support terrorism from broadcasting directly on the airwaves.

'And?'

'Well, instead, the media companies are going to dub their voices using actors.'

'*What?*'

'Yeah. I know.'

Oliver had arrived with the black coffee.

'Dubbing voices? What are you talking about? Porn films?'

We ignored him.

'You mean,' I said. 'We'll hear their words but it won't be them actually speaking?'

'Yes. No. It'll be actors reading transcripts.'

I was conjuring images of grown men being operated like ventriloquists' dummies (not for the squeamish). Except the dummies were telling the ventriloquists what to say. Except they'd already said it. But no one was allowed to hear them . . . It was too confusing. And surely it made even less sense on the radio?

'Hold on, let me get this straight. We'll still see spokes-men for whatever band of militants on the screen with their lips moving but it won't be their voice coming out?'

'That's right.'

'It'll be yours?'

'It could be. If I play my cards right. That's why I can't be Dunseverick. I've got a recording spot at the BBC and if I don't show up, that's it – every out-of-work actor in town's going to be on it like a cheap suit.'

So that was his game.

'William, is it a question of money?'

'No, of course not! How could you say that? Give me some credit. This is an opportunity for me to expand my horizons, to get in with the right people, start building a name for myself. You know how hard it is to – '

'We'll double your fee.'

'You're on.'

I regretted my offer as soon as it was out of my mouth. It was an expensive way to avert this particular crisis and I should have at least tried to haggle. Ah well, I'd worry about the money later. I was still having trouble getting my head around the idea of having an actor read some-one else's pre-spoken words over silent footage of that person saying those words in the first place; how this would decrease the killing and maiming, and how, ex-actly, anyone was being deprived of any kind of oxygen. Apart from those wasting their breath. I gave up.

While Oliver assisted Fisher with his hairy transmo-grification, I thumbed through the latest issue of *Grea-sepaint*, which carried a double-page spread on the West

End phenomenon that was *Suspicious Minds*, complete with a competition to win tickets to 'the hottest show in town' and meet the 'Top Dog himself'. There was a picture of the author in his cape attempting a smile. As he should, the standfirst trumpeting that the play was 'the box office cash machine of the year'. I read (and re-read moving my lips) that it had been confirmed the play was moving to Broadway (*Broadway!*) for a six-week run, with none other than Sylvester Stallone and Meryl Streep mooted for the leading roles. It was also believed, the article said, that discussions were under way to take the show on a tour of trouble-spots in the Middle East as part of a U.S.-funded conflict resolution programme. I rubbed my eyes. And, as if all this weren't enough, a side panel disclosed that the playwright's autobiography, *Hard Man Out*, was being fast-tracked by a team of ghost-writers in time for Christmas. I swear to God, you couldn't make it up.

The old people's home was a converted Georgian mansion deliquescing at the end of a long driveway amid dank horse-chestnuts and immense rhododendrons. Ominously, the receptionist could find no mention of our visit in 'the book'.

'Are you sure it's today?'

'Yes.'

'That's strange, you know, 'cos we only had the puppet man yesterday – ' She ran her finger down the page again. 'I have to say, the puppets went down *very* well . . .'

She asked us to take a seat, and disappeared in search of the administrator. The place was stiflingly warm and smelled of suet. We could hear the murmur of distant voices, the rumbling of the building's ancient digestive system. On an easel nearby was propped a wooden noticeboard of the kind you might see in a school or a church, with slots for words. It said, Today is: Thursday; The weather is: Frosty; The next meal is: Lunch.

'That's all the information you need, really,' Oliver observed. 'If you think about it.'

An assortment of residents came and went, moving at fish-tank speed. They paid us scant attention. Then, a very old, hairless man in heavily-taped spectacles and a maroon dressing gown shuffled into view, propelling a Zimmer frame. He glanced at us and grunted, then stopped and trained his crusty eyes on Dunseverick.

'Fitzie? Is that you Fitzie?'

The poet squinted in the direction of the old boy, who was doddering towards him at full tilt.

'Fitzie?' The man's voice was reedy, breathless.

Dunseverick looked bewildered.

'Fitzie, is that you?'

'I um . . . What?'

The old man came to a rocking halt, peering at Dunseverick, uncertain now.

'Fitzie?'

The receptionist returned with the administrator.

'Sorry about that,' the older woman said, as the young-er one eased our new friend away. She smiled. 'Listen, there was a bit of confusion with the staff changeover and you just slipped through the cracks but they're ready for you now.'

'What the hell was *that* about?' Oliver whispered to me as we followed her.

'I have no idea,' I said. 'He seemed interested in the suit. Maybe it was Fitzie's suit.'

The reading took place in the 'day room' (as opposed, presumably, to the more sinister 'night room') and was timed to coincide with tea & biscuits doled out by inanely upbeat nurses in pale blue scrubs. The inmates accepted their elevenses with good grace but seemed unnerved by Dunseverick who had recovered from his earlier encounter and was keeping himself busy with a little light sparring practice on the sidelines. (This he abandoned when a stray punch dislodged a basket of boiled sweets from the top of the television.)

After two false starts, the first interruption due to a bout of hearing aid adjustment, the second to an 'incontinence event' (in the audience), he managed to get his repertoire under way. Despite a degree of premium lager-fuelled gusto, his performance was greeted with impassive silence throughout. He finished, and with some apprehension, opened it up to the floor.

We listened, in the subsequent void, to little more than the tinkle of cup on saucer, the hiss of surgical stockings and the faint static of various bronchial conditions. This, for what seemed a very long time. And then, from the back of the room . . . not a question about the metaphysical provenance of the poet's inspiration, no, not even a query regarding the whereabouts of the

235

crowd-pleasing puppets; instead, a hesitant, piping voice: 'Fitzie? Is that you Fitzie?'

No one was saying much on the return journey. I tried to raise morale.

'Well, that wasn't *too* bad, all things considered. I think it cheered them up.'

In my peripheral vision I detected Oliver giving me a hard stare from the back of the taxi. The poet coughed.

'Miserable old gits,' he muttered.

I let it go and gazed out the window instead. We were in a part of town I didn't know: leisurely avenues swinging down the lower slopes of the mountain to connect with the dense mesh of the city centre; on either side, Victorian redbricks with white-frosted roofs against a cold, cobalt sky. The driver twiddled again with the heating control but it was refusing to give out more than a tepid breeze. He swore and tugged his scarf up over his nose.

We reached a junction and began a steeper descent before changing tack again and heading in a direction that would eventually take us back to our stamping ground. We were on a tree-lined road. Up ahead I could see cars at a standstill and a soldier kneeling on the pavement cradling a rifle.

'Army checkpoint,' the driver confirmed.

'*Cry "Havoc"* . . .' I declaimed in my actor's voice, turning to bestow an ironic grin on my fellow passengers. '*And let slip the dogs* – '

The expression on Oliver's face stopped me short: a

wide-eyed, haunted look of fear as he peered intently past the driver's shoulder at the approaching roadblock. His hand, as he raised it to straighten his hair, was trembling. I sobered immediately. I had caught a glimpse of the world through someone else's eyes, Oliver's, and it turned out that all my assumptions were wrong: it was shockingly different to mine.

'Afternoon gentlemen, could I see some identification please.' These words, delivered in a flat northern English accent, were accompanied by a draught of icy air that instantly converted the car's interior temperature to that of the exterior. The soldier, no older than us certainly, and probably younger, was pink-cheeked and his nostrils were glistening. The driver passed his licence through the window. It was occurring to me that the rest of us might have difficulty producing comparable documentation. I knew *I* wasn't carrying anything more valid than a video shop card. And then I remembered the last member of our party: the poet Tyrone Dunseverick. Or was he the actor William Fisher? My head was so numb I couldn't decide.

'Just pull your muffler down there sir so I can – That's great, thank you.' The soldier handed back the licence, then stooped, breathing wreaths of vapour, and surveyed the passengers. He lingered momentarily on the bearded one.

'What about you chaps? Any I.D. on you?'

There was a chorus of mumbling and some token pocket patting but nothing tangible.

'Names?'

We all stayed in character, including Dunseverick. He came back to Oliver.

'What's your surname again, sir?'

'Sweeney.'

'And where do you live, sir?'

Oliver stammered out his address.

'And what do you do, sir?'

'I, um, I, uh, I'm an editor.'

'Really sir? And what do you edit?'

'Um, I can show you, if . . .' Oliver indicated the bag on the seat between him and Dunseverick. The soldier leaned closer.

'What you got there?'

'Magazines.'

'Go on then.'

Oliver reached into the bag and fished one out. He held it towards the soldier.

'He – ' Oliver pointed at me (almost accusingly I thought). '. . . He's the co-editor. Like it says at the front. And he – ' He gestured to his side. 'His poems are in there.'

The soldier riffled through the magazine.

'Stay here,' he commanded.

He marched over to his unit's armoured jeep. A window was wound down and the magazine received through it. Our inquisitor waited, blowing on his hands and stamping his feet. Now *he* was answering questions. A discussion was taking place.

Meanwhile, in the taxi, we waited. Alone. *Tra-la*. A siren sounded, back up the hill, like the cry of a distressed beast, echoing through the afternoon. Here we were, halfway along a street in the capital city of a disputed province on a small island in the Anglo-Hibernian archipelago on the edge of the vast Atlantic, and none of us had any means of identifying ourselves beyond our names in an obscure periodical. Not to mention that one of our number didn't actually exist.

Eventually, our go-between trotted back.

'That's fine, gents, you may continue your journey.'

He tossed the *Lyre* in through the window.

'By the way,' he said, ducking down to address Dunseverick. 'No offence sir, but the Sarge said to tell you he's more a fan of the good old-fashioned . . .'

We pressed on towards safety.

'That could have been smoother,' the driver grumbled, pulling his scarf up again. He said something else but the only word I made out was 'tip'. No one responded. After a few minutes he activated the radio and did a sweep of the stations. It was only mid-afternoon but already lights were coming on in the shops. The sky had an odd, yellowish glow to it. The needle halted at a weather forecast. Sure enough: 'scattered snow showers, possibly lying on higher ground'. We dropped Dunseverick, as requested, outside an off-licence, and Oliver and I called it a day.

*

The picture was a reproduction of Canaletto's *London, Seen Through An Arch of Westminster Bridge*, with its

239

softly-lit, swooping-bird's view of the teeming Thames and the city swelling along its edges; the palest blue sky, St Paul's in the distance. Morning or evening? Difficult to tell. Apricot tinge to the clouds. Evening? I read the reverse again: *At Tate yesterday – fantastic! Not much spare time though – too busy! Home for Xmas. Rosie.* Medium-size, easy-flowing, curvaceous script. But no love, I noted, no kisses. Nor was there anything for me in the *home for xmas.* It didn't say *see you* at Xmas, for example, it was just a statement of fact. Or was I over-parsing?

'Christ, it's Baltic in here,' Oliver exclaimed from the doorway. He scuttled over to check the radiator. The system had ceased pumping out heat several days earlier. 'Still not working,' he reported. No kidding. He pinched the neck of his duffle coat tighter and approached the desk.

'Well?' I said.

He had just been down to the artists' collective to check on progress with the artwork for Dunseverick's chap-book, which was to be entitled simply *Twenty Poems.*

'S'all under control.'

'Really? They've come up with some good ideas?'

'Kind of.'

'What does that mean?'

'Actually only one of them came up with an idea.'

'Only *one*? Lazy bastards.'

'Yeah. Mick. So I went with it. There was one other but it involved King Billy being weird with his horse and . . .'

'Okay. Well?'

'What?'

'What is it?'

'Oh, you'll like it. Very minimal. Very dark.'

'Good . . . Whaddya mean dark?'

'Well . . . black actually.'

'Black?'

'Yes.'

'Just black?'

'Yep. Pure black.'

'All over?'

'Yep. Well, the way he put it was, look at *The White Album* by The Beatles, how successful that was. Controversial at the time but an acknowledged design classic now.'

'I suppose so . . .'

What he was saying made a kind of sense but there was something about it I didn't like. My mind was elsewhere, though. I was shuffling through our file of Dunseverick material. The typescript was due at the printers that afternoon and it seemed we were a couple short of the titular twenty. I was going to have to make up the number with some of Oliver's left-overs.

'Oh, and another thing,' Oliver said, blowing on his hands.

'Yes?'

'I've got some people to help out at the launch, you know, serving the snacks and so on.'

'Really? Who?'

'Well, you know the Belfast Mime Cooperative have their place next door to the artists? Down at the collective?'

'Yes.'

'One of them called in when I was talking to Mick and . . .'

'Yes?'

'Well, Mick suggested . . . demanded, actually . . . that . . . Anyway I think it's a good idea. It gives them a bit of exposure and we get free waiters. I think they feel a bit neglected, those mimers.'

'I suppose so . . .'

I had a sense of things slipping beyond my control again. Oliver's initiative had reminded me that my parents were now on the guest-list, the result of my having secured Pixie Dixon's catering service for the launch (I was planning to put the discount-for-friends towards Fisher's increased fee). Needless to say, the bush telegraph had been instantly tripped and a few minutes later my mother had been on the line. Still, at least she'd promised not to tell Fenton.

It was so cold in the office that our exhalations were hanging at eye-level, like fog, and there were frost flowers on the inside of the windows.

'For Godsake Artie, put the kettle on, I'm freezing to death here.'

'No.'

'It's your turn. Go on.'

The pressure in the tap was low and it took a while to draw off enough water. 'The kitchen' was even worse than usual, the scabrous smears, spatters and encrustations made somehow more ghastly by their glistening film of ice, like seeping bacterial growths glimpsed in the beam of a caver's torch. I connected the flex and flipped the on-button, recoiling abruptly from a flash of blue, and a sound like a Christmas cracker being pulled. A wisp of pungent smoke curled in the air.

I picked up my gloves from the desk.

'Oliver, the kettle's fucked,' I informed him. 'Let's go to the printers.'

★

On the day of the big launch, I was jolted awake by a reverberating double boom in the street below. Shock waves scurried up through the building's exoskeleton into the floorboards and along the legs of my bed. A beat later, the window panes rattled. I braced for sounds of falling debris but none came; instead, a shouted conversation followed by the ignition of a large diesel engine and an articulated lorry, its shipment discharged, pulled away. I caught my breath, rolled over and squinted at the clock: bloody early. In the digital gloaming I lay back and regarded the familiar network of cracks in the ceiling. Like the suture lines of a human skull. I already felt weary, weighed down by a complicated burden, overwhelmed by the length of the day ahead. There was something else though, something physical. What was it? Idly, I ran my hand over my face, checking its crannies with my fingertips . . . eyebrows, cheeks, chin . . . all normal, and then, on the second pass I found it: a tight hotness at the end of my nose. Surely not? Not today? It *was*. A spot. I sprinted to the mirror. Dammit!

Hang on though, no need to panic yet. There *was* something going on there, definite volcanic activity, but it wasn't critical. My teen years had seen much, *much* worse: profile-transforming Night Screamers as big as ping-pong balls; Pulsators that were visible to ships at sea. The key thing was not to mess with them . . .

As I sat down to tea and toast my nose was pounding like a bull's's heart, the brute at the end of it double its original size thanks to my half hour of mirror work. After breakfast I managed to find some out-of-date nappy rash cream left by the previous residents and rubbed it in, and then set about trying to borrow a car. Pixie Dixon, suspecting (astutely enough) a bohemian lack of commitment to prompt payment, had phoned me the previous evening to demand cash upfront, and despite my smarmiest assurances, had remained insistent. Eventually, Monroe came up trumps with his prized, but clapped-out Triumph Stag and I set off for Pixie's Spanish-style farmhouse in the Narnian hills above Belfast Lough.

Once in motion, the car, an ill-advised convertible, proved to be little more than a large and elaborate air filter and when I reached my destination I was so chilled I couldn't speak. Pixie, by contrast, having just stepped out of her home solarium, looked like someone in the viewfinder of a thermal imaging camera. While I waited at the buttoned-leather kitchen island for her to rustle up an invoice, her be-frizzed poodle Pepe happened along and, with the minimum of foreplay, began to roger my calf, his front legs clamped urgently around my trousers, his teeth bared in a snarly grin of lust. Grateful for the warmth, I did nothing to discourage it. I took a sip of the coffee the hostess had wrung for me from her state-of-the art Express-O-Matic. It tasted like industrial run-off but again, it was helping with the defrosting process. Pixie returned with the docket. 'Stop that Pepe!' (Pepe quickened his pace.) I noticed she had slipped into a distinctly diaphanous robe.

'There, that's the business out of the way,' she said. She was standing with the light behind her and I was trying hard not to assimilate the information being transmitted. She smiled. Put her hands on her hips.

'Now, would you like me to hot you up?'

'Um . . .'

'Or is there something else I can tempt you with?'

I was having a sudden memory of something Fenton had mentioned once about a close encounter in a cloakroom at one of my mother's parties. At the time I'd dismissed it as adolescent fantasy but I was getting a definite trepidation now that Pixie was about to spring a Mrs Robinson on me. When she busied herself with the Enigma machine again, I managed to dropkick Pepe behind the Aga, then made fast for the hallway, shouting a vague 'cheery-bye' as I closed the door on the escalating sounds of her devilish percolations.

Back in town, I was taken by a whim, and instead of turning into Monroe's street I kept going, pressing on past the whispering avenues and parks of south Belfast and out into the meadowlands. Once free of the city, I knew where I wanted to be: Rosie and I had spent an afternoon there in the early days, when the world was in full bloom.

At the top of the hill I parked and killed the engine. Rosie's postcard was in my pocket but I left it where it was. I knew what it said. Or rather, what it didn't say. I blew on my seized-up fingers. How did it come to this? No girl, no money, no prospects. Nothing, really, to show for my adult life, except a ridiculous deception involving a poet made of smoke. I thought about making a run for it. Monroe's banger would probably take me as far as the ferry but would it last until London? Unlikely. I stepped out into the icy dampness and lit a cigarette (the ninth of the day). I zipped up my jacket, wishing again that I'd worn a scarf, and squeezed through the turnstile that led to the ancient circular earthwork known as the Giant's Ring. Which giant, I wondered. Finn MacCool probably. It usually was.

Up on the grassy embankment of the circle I paused. Deasil or widdershins? Below me the enclosed plateau of the ring, as flat as a golfing green and as wide as a stadium, resounded with mysterious silence, generated, one could almost imagine, by the megalithic tomb that squatted like some huge stone toad in the centre. A rook (it might have been a crow) called from a solitary tree on the far ridge. How many Neolithic man hours had it taken to carve this out? And to what end? It was more than a burial ground, that much was clear. Sun worship, perhaps. Or human sacrifice. Around me the countryside endured in the wintry air, a breeze frisking the hedgerows, birds floating across a pale sun. Mist was shrouding the woods opposite, like in those lines of Plath's: *On their blotter of fog the trees | Seem a botanical drawing. | Memories growing, ring on ring . . .*

I finished my cigarette and set off, widdershins. In the distance were the hunched shoulders of the hills above Belfast. As I walked I was oppressed by the weight of this place, its burden of primitive belief, aware that I had no faith, religious or otherwise, to compare with that of my ancestors. Except for Poetry and even that, I realised with a flush of shame, I had betrayed – defiled even – with my recent antics. If he were still alive, my gentle, fearless grandfather, who fought in wars and built a life from scratch with his bare hands, what would he think of me?

I stopped to gaze down over the Lagan valley; tried to picture how many summer suns had rolled across this landscape in the centuries since the druids held sway. There was a sudden movement in the scrub nearby: a blackbird pecking at dry twigs. The light was beginning to fade. It was later than I thought.

By the time I returned Monroe's car to its proud owner it was nearly dark. At the office I found Fisher, alone, at the window. My arrival startled him and he attempted, clumsily, to conceal something under his jacket.

'Jeez, you scared the shit out of me!' he said.

He had the suit on, but no glasses and, I noticed, only a thin layer of fluff where his beard should have been. He seemed unsteady on his feet.

'Where's Oliver? Why aren't you ready?' I demanded.

'Gone to the shop,' he stammered. He pointed at an empty spirit gum bottle. 'We ran out of glue.'

'How're you feeling? Did you get a chance to look over the new material?' I asked.

'Indeed I did. Rehearsed it earlier. No worries.'

Heavy footsteps sounded on the stairs, the door flew open and Oliver entered. Not, however, the Oliver I'd seen the previous day. Not ghost-pale Oliver in Cubist planes of white and cream. This was quite a different Oliver.

'What the fuck's your game?' he cried on seeing me. 'Did you forget what's happening tonight?'

He stood at the desk, glaring at me as he struggled to pull a bulky object from his pocket.

'We've been here for friggin' hours, you know. You could've lent a hand. Where the hell have you been?'

He held up a large tub of maple syrup-coloured glue.

'William, I'm afraid I could only get Bondo-Stik.'

Fisher grunted. Oliver turned back to me.

'Well?'

'Yeah, sorry, I had to, er . . . I um . . .'

'You had to what?'

'I, uh . . .'

It was no good. I couldn't concentrate. Except for the elliptical white discs framing his eyes, Oliver was a spectacular shade of pink. Fuschia to be exact.

'Oliver,' I said. 'What the fuck happened to your face?'

'What?' His hand jerked towards his cheek but stopped short. 'Oh that . . . I er . . . I used that voucher you gave me.'

248

The Sizzlemaster!

'I wanted to look good for tonight. But I might have overdone it.'

I stepped forward to get a better look. At closer quarters there was more complexity to the palette than was first apparent, with graduated bands of magenta and scarlet between brow and scalp, and rich char siu tones on the ears. A swathe of leprous blisters provided lizard-ish texture across the nose and upper cheeks, while slicks of emergency exudation glistened at his temples where the weaker skin had broken down. The mask-like effect where the goggles had been added a dash of albino raccoon.

'No, it's not too bad,' I said.

Oliver, meanwhile, was examining my snout.

'Speaking of which, what's the story with *that*?'

'Just a spot.'

'Yeah, well you might want to put a dab of something on it.'

(This from a man who would be wise not to fall asleep in a baboon enclosure.)

'Guys don't you think we ought to get me ready?' Fisher enquired. 'We're on in a couple of hours.'

The construction of Dunseverick's beard, a labour-intensive task at the best of times, was significantly complicated by the Bondo-Stik which, it soon became apparent, had the resinous tenacity of pine sap. Before long we were wearing crepe hair mittens and the scene, viewed from a certain angle, resembled a team of were-wolf beauticians at work on a particularly challenging client. The glue also gave off dizzying fumes that interfered with our perception of time, further slowing our progress. Fisher, it was clear, had been refreshing himself throughout the day and slept through most of the operation.

'By the way Oliver,' he burbled during a waking moment. 'I forgot to say, someone rang for you while you were out.'

'Oh? Who was it?'

'Actually, I didn't get a name.'

'Man or woman?'

'Man. He said it was quite urgent and wanted to know where he could find you.'

Oliver froze.

'What did he sound like?'

'Dunno . . . business-like?'

'Business-like?'

I could see where Oliver's paranoia was leading him.

'Anyway, he seemed like a decent fellow so I invited him along tonight.'

'You *what*?'

'Yeah, he said it would be a nice surprise for you.'

Oliver said nothing. He sat down. A new layer of sheen lacquered his face.

'Oliver, I know what you're thinking but I'm sure you're wrong,' I said, plucking a stray tendril from Fisher's chin. 'I bet Niblock doesn't even know you exist.'

'Did I fuck up?' Fisher asked.

'Not at all. Nothing to worry about,' I assured him,

adding: 'Listen William, you need to stop scratching or you're going to end up with a wonky beard.'

'I can't help it,' he moaned. 'It's devilishly itchy.'

The poet's suit, I noticed, was beginning to smell *very* bad. Too late to do anything about that now. I briefly wondered whether we should demand the surrender of the hipflask that bulged in his inside pocket but decided it was too late for that too. The fact was, it was too late for a lot of things. The die was cast. The hour was upon us . . .

It was showtime.

The launch was to take place in the City Hall, where Winks had secured one of the civic reception rooms through a friend who worked there. Half way along the Dublin Road it began to snow and by the time we reached the baroque splendour of our venue the pavements were almost white. The flakes were swirling around the pale green glimmer of the building's central dome; falling through the *sfumato* glare of the Christmas lights that looped across the facade. The ground was slippery under foot and it took both Oliver and me to assist the poet up the front steps. Once inside the building, even more effort was needed to propel him up the steep marble staircase to the upper floor.

In the Great Hall, preparations – to our mild surprise – seemed to be in hand. A low stage and a podium had been set up at one end, and Pixie's food and drink laid out on trestle tables between the Corinthian columns on either side of the room. Under the towering stained-glass windows half a dozen white-faced Marcel Marceaus in striped T-shirts and high-waisted trousers leapt into poses of exaggerated welcome as we entered (I'd forgotten about Oliver's arrangement with the Mime Cooperative). At the back, early arrivals – among them several academics including Monroe and Trench – were hovering around a table laden with the latest *Lyre* publication, sipping Norwegian Cabernet.

'Thank God,' I said to the others. 'The books are here.'

We gathered to inspect *Twenty Poems*. It was, indeed, black. Blacker than anything I'd ever seen.

'Jeez Oliver, I'd assumed there would at least be a title on the spine,' I remarked.

I opened one and was immediately reassured: chunky point-size, nice fonts. The poems themselves looked convincing on the page. Interesting, I thought, how the formality of print confers authenticity . . .

'Artie, a quick word?' Mick the Artist was at my elbow. There had been fresh alterations to his physiognomy: a silver bolt through his septum; a tiny crucifix in his left eyebrow.

'Hi Mick, what's up? Great cover, by the way.'

He drew me to one side.

'Yeah thanks. Listen, there's a slight snag. The printers have fucked up. It seems the ink's not quite dry yet.'

I looked down at my fingers. Sure enough. I glanced around, noting for the first time the Sea Devil's smudged mascara, Monroe's black eye, Trench's koala bear nose. That overweight chimney sweep was Cornelius O'Toole. A flush of solar wind swept over my skin and I shivered. Had I caught a chill? (I was also beginning to suspect my pimple was upgrading its status to Pulsator.)

'Great. That's lovely Mick. Very helpful.'

'What can I say, it's a bummer. But, you know, maybe if these guys paid their workers better they'd get better results.'

He melted away. Monroe strolled over.

'Looking good Artie, my boy. Another triumph.'

I thanked him, trying not to stare at his shiner. He was smiling expectantly at Dunseverick who was beside me peering at his chapbook.

'Of course, you haven't met,' I said. 'Boyd, this is Tyrone Dunseverick, the star of the show.'

The academic and the poet shook hands.

'Congratulations,' Monroe said. 'It must feel good to be so much in demand. Tell me, is it true the man from Faber & Faber's here?'

Before I could digest Monroe's unhelpful rumour, Oliver loomed, beckoning urgently.

'Have you spotted it?' he hissed.

I studied the Hitler moustache that had been added to the nuclear testing ground of his face.

'Yes, Mick just – '

'There's one missing!'

'What?'

'There's only nineteen!'

'What?'

'*Twenty Poems* is a poem short!'

'You gotta be fucken kidding me . . .'

I scrabbled through my copy. Seventeen, eighteen . . . It was true. Bloody printers.

'Oliver,' I told him. 'Whatever you say, say nothing.'

The room was filling up. I snatched a glass from a passing Marceau, dispatched it and hailed another. All the artists were in: The Walrus, Heather Turkington, Pollocks, Devine . . . Who was that with Devine? It couldn't be. Mumbles! Who would've thought? (The sight of her triggered an ache of longing for Rosie.) And there was Monty Monteith, striding across the floor in his dinner suit, closely shadowed by a Marceau parodying his pompous gait. I hoped the mimers weren't going to be trouble. In the corner was Grainne McCumhaill (was that a new beret?) with the counter-feminist from Trench's launch. Dylan Delaney, his arm around a young lady I recognised from the bar staff at Kavanagh's, caught my eye and saluted. No sign of my parents yet.

Winks and Barney pitched up on my blind side.

'Congratulations Artie, another sterling production,' Winks purred, squeezing my arm.

'Thanks Stanford.'

'Contents-wise anyway,' he added. 'I'm not mad about the cover.'

'Black,' Barney announced. 'Is black.'

I could think of no immediate response. (Also, my attention was momentarily sidetracked by the sight of Dunseverick relieving a Marceau of an entire tray of drinks. Where was Oliver?)

'Don't mind him Artie, he completely overdid it last night.' Winks regarded his partner with a curled lip. 'I think he might still be a bit twisted.'

Barney swatted away an imaginary fly.

'Special occasion?' I enquired.

'Launch of Mad Dog's "autobiography",' Winks explained with a limp bunny ears gesture. 'Free bar all night in Betjeman's.'

'Say no more. And what state was the great man in?'

'Actually, he nearly didn't make it. He and Quigley were delayed on the way back from the Big Apple. I take it you heard the play is transferring – ' He broke off, raising his eyebrows. '. . . And lo! Speak of the devil and he doth appear . . .'

I turned my head. There in the doorway – almost too bright for the naked eye – was Mad Dog, resplendent in a white spandex jumpsuit and rhinestone-studded cape. ('Bloody hell, it's the Archangel Elvis,' Winks muttered.) His collar was turned up to meet the vast pubic wedges of his sideburns and his mullet had been primped and teased to roughly the size of a small car. He removed his glitter-encrusted sunglasses. The general hubbub faltered; ceased. He surveyed the gathering. Silence echoed off the vaulted ceiling. He replaced his sunglasses. Adjusted his collar. Satisfied that he had been sufficiently beheld, he surged forward into the room, trailing in his wake the elfin figure of Quigley, also in white, and lastly, my bewildered parents.

They spotted me and rushed over in their matching leisurewear, pursued by a pair of silently prancing Marceaus.

'Artie, who on earth was that man?' my mother demanded. 'Is that the chap with the book?'

'That's, um . . . He's uh . . .'

'Bloody spit of Colonel Gaddafi,' my father murmured.

'We haven't missed it, have we?' my mother said. 'I couldn't get your father out. He just wouldn't come. I kept telling him we'd be late.'

'Not at all, you're just in time,' I replied.

'You know what he's like Artie, always fiddling with something just as you're trying to leave.'

Her husband shot me a look of immense weariness.

I instructed them to stay in the same spot while I went in search of drinks and canapes. When I turned around Fenton was standing there, jangling his car keys.

'So this is what you're up to,' he smirked. 'Very grand.'

'Fenton, what the hell are you doing here?'

'Thought I'd come and have a laugh at the culture vultures,' he said, inspecting the crowd. 'Fuck me, talk about the great unwashed. Look at these people!'

'There's an explanation, Fenton, but I haven't time now. Please, do me a favour and keep mum and dad stocked up with snacks and booze?'

'Yeah, okay, seeing as it's you. By the way, you know you've got an absolute cracker on the end of your nose? I mean, a real humdinger! It's . . .'

I found Dunseverick behind a pillar at the back of the hall, three-quarters of the way through his tray of wine.

'William, what are you doing?'

'Artie?' He peered over the top of his Larkins. 'Oh hi. Nothing . . . just settling the nerves. Spot of Dutch courage. It's a big crowd.'

'It is. And it's an important crowd. We can't afford to fuck this up. Are you sure you're okay?'

'I'll be fine. Really. No worries. I just wish – '

'What?'

'I just wish this beard wasn't so bloody itchy.'

'You're just getting used to the Bondo-Stik, that's all. Try not to scratch, and in an hour or so it'll all be over.'

I negotiated my way back through the throng (which, to my dismay, was swelling by the minute), managing to body-swerve both Devine and McCumhaill but almost colliding with Mr Big Arts himself.

'Artie isn't it?' He extended a massive hand. His sea spume hair was speckled with black. 'Monty Monteith.'

'I remember.' (*I remember* . . .)

'How are you?'

'Fine thanks Monty. In a bit of a hurry though, I've – '

'Artie, just so you know, we're recording tonight's proceedings for next week's programme – that's my technician over there – and we'll need an interview with the poet . . . What's his name?'

'Tyrone.'

'Tyrone . . .?'

'Dunseverick.' I felt a quickening throb in my hooter.

'. . . With Tyrone Dunseverick afterwards.'

'That's fine Monty. Shouldn't be a problem – ' I began edging away.

'Perhaps you and I could discuss his work briefly?'

'I'd love to, Monty but I've got to . . . Sorry I'd better – ' I pointed at Oliver who I'd spied on the other side of the room and scuttled away.

Oliver was sitting between the bookstall and a mini-exhibition of the artists' latest work, demolishing a platter of devils-on-horseback. He'd removed his coat and, much to my horror, was wearing the golfing jersey I'd passed on to him – the one my father had handed over with such solemnity. It was even more hideous than I remembered. On Oliver it was tight, and its volatile mix of synthetic fibres crackled at the slightest movement, sending static electricity rippling like St Elmo's fire around his armpits.

'I thought you were supposed to be keeping an eye on our man,' I scolded.

'I am. I was. Where is he?'

'Over there, swimming in his own personal wine lake. We need to get him onstage before he goes under.'

'Righto. I'll get things moving.' He set his plate down. 'Where on earth did all these people come from?'

'Beats me,' I said, tearfully probing the end of my nose. 'By the way, you're going to have to take that jumper off – my dad's here.'

'No can do.'

'What? Why not?'

'Nothing underneath.'

After much goading and shepherding we managed to persuade the crowd to face the stage. Oliver and Dun-severick and I took up our positions and when a proper hush had been achieved I stepped up to the microphone. My nose was really hurting and I was feeling increasingly feverish. I had the impression that the Great Hall itself was breathing in and out, and that the audience now numbered in the thousands.

'Every once in a while a poet comes out of nowhere, fully formed,' I read from my script, pausing while someone executed a complicated cough. 'With a topicality of perception that delights the critics . . . whose voice fills a specific gap in the collective imagination – '

There was a squeal of metal on marble to my left, a door slammed and a familiar, pony-tailed figure in frosty-wash denim tottered up the aisle. Discerning no immediate spare seat, he slumped in a cross-legged position against a pillar and peered blearily about him. I resumed.

'. . . Whose sensibility is tailor-made for the needs of our time. We celebrate tonight, ladies and gentlemen, one such poet . . .' Some women at the front were nodding and smiling at me encouragingly: Dunseverick's fans from the cross-community group. One of them was actually knitting. '. . . A writer who, I feel it's fair to say, has been imbued with more than one person's share of talent . . . who inhabits a space inaccessible to the rest of us – ' The Marceaus, I noticed, were picking out words at random and interpreting them in mime. Were they mocking me?. '. . . between the physical and the ethereal. We should cherish such visionaries while we can, for who knows when this – ' I gestured feebly, aware now of someone sniggering, '. . . *insubstantial pageant* will fade, leaving *not a rack behind.* As The Bard once said: *We are such stuff as dreams are made on* . . . ladies and gentlemen, I give you the dream-poet himself . . . Tyrone Dunseverick.'

Vigorous applause broke out. I descended and stood with Oliver at the side of the stage while our man approached the lectern. Away from the spotlight I could see the audience properly, including my parents, who had been joined by Pixie Dixon. My father was staring hard at Oliver's chest. Damn! He'd clocked the jersey. His face, I registered with a pang of guilt, was a repository of disappointment, hurt and betrayal. Fresh pain pulsed through my schnozzle. The clapping subsided. There was a brief delay while Monteith's technician untangled a cable, and the reading began.

There was no doubt about it, the poet was drunker than I'd ever seen him. His journey to the pulpit was a stop-motion epic complete with diversionary side-steps and haltings at imaginary crossroads; his white-knuckle grip on the sides of the lectern suggested his vertical hold was all but gone. None of this was overly worrying in itself: generally speaking, poets were expected to be drunk in public; it was deemed necessary in order for them to tolerate ordinary people. What *was* of concern was the increasing frequency with which he was scraping at his beard. This wasn't good. Nor, once he had mustered sufficient focus to read, was his diction.

He kicked off with *Ship of Fools*, a piece we at the factory liked to think of as a failsafe box-ticker, and proceeded to annihilate its carefully-paced cumulative impact with slurred intonation and a novel new style of emphasis that seemed to favour prepositions. He followed up with an unintelligible version of my linen weaving poem, *Seamless*, before moving on to Oliver's heart-felt *Elegy For The Drink Shop Man*, which he belted out at a jaunty pace as though doing *The Ballad of William Bloat* at a wedding reception. All the while, his fingernails were creeping back to his face, scratching at chin, jaw, throat with a harsh sandpapery sound that evoked wincing all along the front row.

'This next piece is called *The Stubble Burners*,' he announced belligerently.

Oliver and I looked at each other in alarm. Surely not? Not the long one? While the poet paused for an extended scrabble at his beard I cast around for an excuse to shut him down. Nothing suggested itself. From where I was standing I could see the fiery inflammation of his skin beneath the hot tufts of fake hair, possibly even some pinpricks of blood. His face was contorted. He let out a moan of anguish followed by a sighing rush of expletives.

'*Crows drift in the smoke above Carson's field,*' he began.

'*Black flags at season's end. Another kind –* '

More scratching. Signs of restlessness in the audience. Only seventy-three lines to go.

'. . . *Of scorched earth policy as dusk descends . . .*'

Another itch break. More weight-shifting in the crowd.

'*Cool dawn-light, and cattle raise their heavy heads . . .*'

There was no way we were going to get through this. I would have to act. But what to do? I considered a few possibilities. Start a fight? Feign a heart attack? And then, half way through the second stanza, Dunseverick saved me the trouble.

'Holy crap!' he exclaimed, swiping through the pages. 'Folks, this poem is way too long. I'm going to leave it for you to read at your leisure – ' He flicked ahead. 'Ah, here we go, here's a shorter one . . .'

He'd chanced upon Oliver's first attempt at a love lyric. I had forgotten I'd been forced to throw it in as a filler. Unrevised.

'*We spent that Saturday with no clothes on* . . . Ohhhh Jesus! Oh my God . . .

'*Mostly in bed, but also* . . . For fucksake . . . *on the sofa, and then*

'For the love of . . . *In my bathtub listening to* . . . Ouch! . . . *Van Morrison* . . .'

As he succumbed to the full ecstasy of relieving his torment, his audience stared in horrified bafflement; even the Marceaus temporarily ceased their mugging. A group murmur started up, growing in volume like an approaching swarm of bees.

'. . . Christ Almighty! . . . *Singing about Jimmie Rodgers* . . . Arrghh!'

I had to act. It was now or never . . . but I was just as transfixed as everyone else.

'*Your breasts were like two Jammie Dodgers!*' Dunseverick shrieked, and in the next moment we saw him lose all control. He dropped to his knees with a terrible cry, clawing at the wiry fuzz that gripped his face, ripping at it, tearing it off in blood-stained hanks. He paused, twisted off the Larkins and flung them across the stage. With a high-velocity yelp, off came the moustache, leaving behind a wet stripe of crimson. Clumps of side-burn fur began dropping to the floor. Next his frenzied hands clutched at his head, found the mop of Swinburnian curls and sent it spinning into the midst of the assembly. As the wig descended someone screamed, and immediately after, another voice could be heard, shouting something indistinct. I craned for a better view.

It was Mumbles. She was pointing at the stage, at the genuflecting figure of Dunseverick. She was very excited.

'What's she saying?' demanded the Sea Devil. 'We can't make her out.'

'Something about a tissue, I think,' O'Toole ventured. 'Or maybe a fissure?'

But what *was* she saying? Johnny Devine was beside her, leaning close, his ear to her mouth. He looked up, grave with hermeneutic responsibility.

'She says this guy is Chinwag Fisher!' he reported. 'She says she was at school with him. And he's definitely not a poet!'

A profound silence fell in the Great Hall. In his pool of light the actor knelt with his head bowed. He was still picking at residual scabs of glue, but his itchy fever had abated; the madness had lifted; he was finally at peace. I imagined the tumult of opprobrium that began then with howls of 'Imposter!' and 'Fraud!' and built rapidly to a thunderous onslaught of booing and hissing sounded to him distant, like the soft roar of the ocean, the indifferent crash of waves on shingle.

My suspected chill, meanwhile, had established itself as the onset of something much sweatier, and the rhythmic pain in my nose had added an extra beat. The noise of the mob was inducing in me a sensation of acute anxiety. I was just wondering how to remove myself quickly and permanently from the scene when several things began to happen.

First, a dark shape detached itself from the shadows at the side of the hall and swooped towards the spotlit glare of the stage. Startled, the multitude ceased its baying. With a flap of expensive coat fabric and a shrill bark of rage, The Hawk landed heavily in front of the unsuspecting Fisher. For several seconds the two men locked eyes, Fisher goggling in shock and fear, The Hawk fixing on his prey with cold fury from beneath the brim of his Homburg. The ragged actor was then seized by the lapels and wrenched to his feet. As he started to drag his victim towards the exit, The Hawk swivelled his head in my direction: 'I'll be back for you later, Conville,' he hissed.

Then there was more. The swing doors had barely settled when they shot open again and six policemen entered at a jog and fanned out along the edge of the crowd. They were promptly joined by their sharp-featured superintendent, who stood stroking his moustache and scanning the room with small, darting eyes. Beside me, Oliver whimpered in terror. With a gesture to his men Sammy Niblock strode forward and the line of uniforms made their way into the body of our nonplussed gathering. Oliver clutched at my sleeve. 'Don't worry,' I said. 'My dad plays golf with loads of lawyers.' But Niblock didn't appear. I had lost sight of him but now I could hear snatches of his words: '. . . you under arrest . . . did violate the terms of your parole . . . leaving this jurisdiction . . . United States of America . . .' There were sounds of a scuffle and the mob fell away to reveal four cops struggling with a burly figure in a glittering white cape. Mad Dog, predictably, wasn't going to rock down to the jailhouse quietly. Niblock, meanwhile, had identified Tristan Quigley, and from what I could make out, was apprehending *him* for aiding and abetting Mad Dog's field trip to New York. After some token flailing and screeched demands for a lawyer Quigley *did* go quietly, a policeman on either side of him and two Marceaus behind, acting out their own pantomime arrest while a third (less imaginative than his colleagues) pretended to be imprisoned in a glass box. With much grunting and swearing, Mad Dog was finally subdued and hauled out to the waiting meat-wagon. Niblock followed up the rear. As he passed us, he slowed his step (nearly causing a Marceau collision) and jabbed a finger at Oliver. 'I'll be back for you later, Sweeney,' he growled.

Oliver, already in a state of near paralysis, was distraught. I tried to lighten the mood.

'You know Oliver, it's true, he really does look like a mongoose.'

'*What?*'

'His face. It's kind of ferretty.'

Oliver stared at me tearily.

'What are you talking about?'

'Niblock. He has a weaselly demeanour.'

'For Godsake Artie, don't you get it? He knows everything! I'm fucken dead!'

I feared he was right but I didn't know how to respond. The way I saw it, we were both finished. The hall was in uproar now. If only I could wake up and find this had all been a bad dream . . . just a bad dream . . . like in a film . . .

But wait a minute, it *was* a dream! Because there, at the door, was a giant white rabbit! Or was my fever worse than I thought, and now I was hallucinating on top of everything else?

'What the fuck am I going to do?' Oliver sobbed, sitting down on the side of the stage and putting his head in his hands.

The giant white rabbit was conferring with a Marceau. Christ, I was seeing a woman in a red bikini now as well! The Marceau did an elaborate pointing mime in our direction and the rabbit and the woman approached.

'Are you Oliver Sweeney?' the creature enquired, its whiskers twitching.

Oliver looked up with his scorched, tear-stained, lizard-skin face and both he and the rabbit recoiled simultaneously. A moment passed before Oliver was able to venture a hesitant affirmative.

'Thank God, I thought I might be too late,' the bunny said, beckoning to a man with a camera who was standing at the door. 'Your friend wasn't very clear about timing when I rang your office earlier.'

The photographer arrived, cocking his camera.

'Oliver, it gives me very great pleasure,' the rabbit said, producing a glittering gold envelope. 'As chairman of Sunnyland Farm Dairies, to inform you that you are the winner of our slogan competition and to present you with this ticket for a year's unlimited round-the-world travel.'

Oliver climbed uncertainly to his feet. The entrance of the outsize coney and its half-naked companion had drawn a deep semi-circle of spectators. Oliver's mouth was hanging open and his eyes were glazed. The rabbit grasped his hand and the swimsuit model put her arm (with some trepidation, it has to be said, given his appearance) around his shoulder. The photographer bobbed and weaved, his shutter snapping. A round of applause broke out. The rabbit pushed the top of its costume back to reveal the head of a balding, jovial man. Another glamour girl materialised and made Oliver hold up a placard featuring a stylised bunny wielding a butter knife above the legend: *Spreading The Word About His Dairy Treats!* The camera flashed and chattered. The clapping intensified.

Taking advantage of the distraction, I began to edge out through the throng. Fighting his way in the opposite direction was Fenton, a deck of Sizzlemaster vouchers in his fist. 'Those girls could do with a bit of colour on them, whaddya think,' he grinned as we drew level. My parents loomed and I adjusted my trajectory (I couldn't face my father), and was immediately forced to swerve again to avoid an angry, ink-smeared Grainne McCumhaill. I squeezed past a swaying Frosty-Wash. Agog at the sight of the bikinis, he was attempting a four-fingered wolf whistle but only succeeding in making himself retch. Suppressing a bad memory, I pushed on through the never-ending mesh of bodies until, at last, with a final wriggle, I was free. A quick recce: no sign of The Hawk and the nearest exit was clear. I started forward and then stopped. There, perched on the book table at the back of the hall, swinging her legs, was Rosie. Our eyes met. She smiled. I smiled back. She jumped down and came towards me, wagging a copy of *Twenty Poems*.

'You do know,' she said. 'There are only nineteen?'

In the background I heard Frosty-Wash go to work; the first shouts of bystander panic. I took Rosie by the hand.

'Let's get out of here,' I said.

EPILOGUE

So, there you have it. That's the way it was for me at the tail-end of the twentieth century's ninth decade, a time before the Internet and iPhones and email, and instantaneous mass media; when people still went to the bank to get their cash, and suitcases had to be carried rather than trundled noisily on wheels, in formation, four abreast. It was the year before the abandonment of the Cold War and the collapse of Europe's remaining communist regimes; the last months of complacency before the fall of the Berlin Wall revealed the true horror of the East German mullet. It was an era of headbands and shoulder pads and sports jackets with their sleeves rolled up, and – perhaps in itself an ironic indicator of the triumph of capitalism – *pinstripe* jeans.

What was it like to be young then? The same as it always is: exciting and confusing in equal measure. Although, we weren't *so* young. Signs that the years were elapsing were already apparent, even then. You know yourself, one day you realise you're holding your coat when you run (for a bus, say), that one or other of your nostrils is always blocked (try it now), that you've developed an interest in nightwear, that you've identified a favourite chair. Or that you've started reading books about the decisive battles of the Second World War. Another twenty years or so and you'll find yourself yearning for a life where everything is reduced to the barest essentials: Today is: Tuesday; The weather is: Rainy; The next meal is: Dinner.

When exactly do our lives turn from poetry into prose?

For me, it was the Dunseverick debacle. I may have skipped out the door pretty smartly with young Rosie McCann that snowy night but I couldn't outrun the consequences of my actions. There was hell to pay. Not to mention the money: six months' worth of grant-aid, rent, expenses, and printers' fees, as well as Pixie's wine and canapes tab and – thanks to Frosty-Wash – the (astonishing) cost of repairing the floor in the Great Hall. My father, bless him, took the immediate heat out of the situation with a large cheque, but only on the understanding that I work off every last penny in *Knicks 'n' Knacks*, an undertaking that consumed my Mondays and Saturdays for a whole year and provided more than enough time, believe me, to consider the error of my ways. Watching Fenton's smirking face float past the window each day on his way from parking his Mercedes was punishment in itself.

Needless to say, I was blacklisted by the Arts Council. According to Stanford Winks, The Hawk was incandescent when he ascertained the true extent of the deception, retreating to his top-floor eyrie and refusing to speak to anyone for an entire week. Winks himself was much more philosophical about the whole affair, and actually talked his boss out of pressing criminal charges. Obviously, what hurt The Hawk most was the sucker-punch to his poetic judgment, and I felt bad about that, but let's face it, the words were there in plain sight, and he liked what he saw. Speaking of which, the Council chiefs tried to hoover up and pulp the entire print-run of *Twenty Poems* but a few escaped: I saw a copy for sale on eBay just last week (it was going cheap, though, which suggests it may have been a fake).

My partner in crime, meanwhile, hopped on the next available plane to London before catching an onward flight to Tibet on the first leg of his world tour. He may have been well out of it, but his paranoia travelled with him; unsurprisingly really, given that in addition to the wrath of The Hawk he had Niblock to worry about, and The Mongoose – subsequently promoted to the rank of chief superintendent – was definitely not someone you would choose to have in your life. Occasionally I would receive a postcard from some far-flung location, each time signed with a different name: Kesh Clogherbog, Clabby Madden, Shrigley Macosquin. I missed him, and this was made worse, somehow, by the celebratory photo of his nuked and ink-smudged face on the side of the Sunnyland Farm milk carton every morning at breakfast. After trying his hand at a number of different professions in a variety of countries he eventually settled in New Zealand, where he runs a sheep ranch near a place called Whanganui. I wonder has he ever given a sheep the kiss of life?

Mad Dog, it gives me no great pleasure to report, was unable to keep his temper in check and went back to the slammer for an extended stay. He continued with his 'writing', but was unable to recreate the success of his debut. The last I heard, he was studying for a Phd in theology through the Open University. The text of *Suspicious Minds* was itself incorporated into the schools English syllabus some years ago, its profanities a source of much sniggering for students. Tristan Quigley, meanwhile, got off with a caution on the aiding and abetting charge but never really recovered from the humiliation of his public manhandling by Niblock's crew. He later left the theatre to set up his own broadcast production company, Metaphor Media, best known for the long-running soap opera *Where's The Vicar's Trousers?*

Who else? Dylan Delaney was picked up by Faber & Faber. It turns out there *was* a scout at the launch that night. He now holds the Humbert P. Frotter Quality Plastic Extrusions Chair of Creative Writing at Hershey Academy, an exclusive, all-female college in Screamersville, Virginia. Enough said. The artists? Following an ideological schism (Mick's neo-brutalist radicalism versus Devine's crypto-nihilist hedonism), the Collective imploded and they all went their separate ways. But not before a final, apocalyptic 'happening' at which Marty Pollocks cut off part of his own ear and glued it to a canvas entitled *Homage to Vincent*, and Devine and Mumbles were married by a 'priest' in a lobster suit.

Monroe and Trench, I'm glad to say, are still together and living in a whitewashed cottage in the Antrim Glens –

not far from where I am now, in fact – where they preside over a thriving vegetarian cookery school. Both of them were paid off during one of the education sector purges ('rationalisations') of the 1990s, and though bitter at first, they soon came to see it as a lucky break. Monroe has since published a series of books on a variety of topics, including one on how to make your own wine from unlikely household ingredients, which is widely considered to be the best of its genre.

And William Fisher? I never saw him again. After a month or so of unpaid rent the landlord dumped the contents of his flat on the pavement (I retrieved most of the books and, for old times' sake, his wig tree) and re-advertised. Strangely, once they had stopped, I found myself still listening for the daily vocal exercises from above: they had been comforting in a shipping forecast kind of way. Setting aside the possibility that The Hawk murdered him and stashed the body, I can only assume the actor struck out for one of the bigger, busier crucibles of dramatic endeavour, London say, or New York, somewhere he could start afresh, perhaps under a new name. That would explain why he never shows up in any credits. I still watch out for him though, especially in period dramas where there's plenty of beard action, hoping to detect even a hint of that tell-tale twitch.

There's something I forgot to say about back then, something it's taken me a long time to work out (I'm still not sure I've fully grasped it), and it has to do with the -ologies and -isms we latch onto when we're young and impatient to assume the world. Gradually, I came to understand that *everyone* in Northern Ireland had their own dogmas and doctrines, some of them more extreme than others. At times, even the 'niceness' of people in those days seemed more like the adoption of a position, unconscious or otherwise, against the horror in our midst. My own belief system, Poetry, was just another creed among many. It was a choice born of privilege, no doubt – by which I mean just being middle class – and one that insulated me from certain truths, as well as leading to dubious moral decisions that were ultimately my undoing, but (and this is important) no one else was hurt as a result. Not really. No one ended up dead. And maybe it was always going to take something like the episode with Dunseverick to wake me up, to prise me out of the Faraday cage in which I was sheltering. I once heard it suggested that disillusionment is a necessary prerequisite for a realistic happiness. I didn't think much of it at the time but I see some wisdom in it now.

Perhaps old Larkin was right after all. *What will survive of us is love.* As I've been sitting here, pretending to work through one of the files that take up most of the back seat, the afternoon has dwindled and a wind has started to buffet the car. The tiny lights of the Rathlin ferry are moving across the sound towards the island where (they say) Robert the Bruce, shivering in his dank cave, drew inspiration from the indefatigable spider. The sea is almost black, the scurrying white cataracts on its surface almost luminous. I start the engine, activate the heater. A sudden spatter of cold rain hits the window. I picture the scene back at home: the steamy warmth of the kitchen, my children coming in from school, dumping bags of damp sports gear, making for the fridge. And Rosie, at the table, reading or decoding a crossword, her face as she turns to me smiling, her eyes as they were all those years ago, as they'll always be: a blaze of blue-green.

Acknowledgements

Thanks are due to Eve Patten, Hugo Hamilton, Mary Rose Doorley, Julie McDonald, Gerald Dawe, my parents Maureen and John, and my brother Nolan for reading early drafts; to Moira Forsyth at Sandstone Press for responding so swiftly and warmly; to George Lucas for his help, and to Euan Thorneycroft at AM Heath for his advice and encouragement. And, of course, eternal gratitude to my children Milo and Esme for occasionally allowing me to use the computer.

I'd also like to thank my friend Patrick Ramsey who shared in so many adventures of the mid-1980s, some much stranger than the ones in this book.

The author is grateful for permission to reprint lines from the following:

'Smithfield Market' from *The Irish For No* (1987) by Ciaran Carson, by kind permission of the author and The Gallery Press, Ireland

'i like my body when it is with your' © E.E. Cummings, from *Complete Poems 1904-1962* (New York: Liveright, 1991) by kind permission of W.W. Norton, New York

Other works

'Un Hemisphere Dans Une Chevelure' by Charles Baudelaire

Proverbs of Hell by William Blake

'1914' by Rupert Brooke

'Leisure' by W.H. Davies

Ulysses by James Joyce

'The Passionate Shepherd' by Christopher Marlowe

Books I and IV of *Paradise Lost* by John Milton

'Ode to the West Wind' and 'Hymn To Intellectual Beauty' by Percy Bysshe Shelley